Praise

"When We Collide is a dark and gritty page turning read with dynamic emotions. The powerful force of her words brought forth both fear and love at the same time in me, making this author one of my favorites to read. She does it every time." ~*Taryn, My Secret Romance*

"As a lover of words I understand that they are extremely powerful. When chosen correctly, they convey so much. The ability to build suspense in such a way that it effects the reader physically is an art. Pulled and Take This Regret both set the bar pretty high, When We Collide not only met my expectations, but exceeded them and left me wanting more. AL Jackson is truly at the top of her game and has secured a place in my list of favorite authors."
~*Teresa, Teresa's Reading Corner*

"I have to say, she has once again hit it out of the ballpark for me. This was a raw and emotional read... To take a phrase from the book, 'It stole my breath.'" ~*Jackie Lane, Jax's Book Magic*

"There is an old saying that goes 'Love heals all wounds,' and I have always believed that to be true. A.L. Jackson has proven once again that love does indeed heal all wounds, both physical and emotional when the love that is given is pure and true." ~Janna, *My Secret Romance*

When We

Collide

A.L. Jackson

A.L. Jackson
www.aljacksonauthor.com
First A.L. Jackson trade paperback edition, November 2012

The characters and events in this book are fictitious. Names, characters, places, and
plots are a product of the author's imagination. Any similarity to real persons, living
or dead, is coincidental and not intended by the author.

ISBN-13: 978-1-938404-84-9

Cover Image and Design by Regina Wamba

www.aljacksonauthor.com

Dedication

Because it shouldn't hurt to be touched.

Acknowledgements

Chad, I wish you could know how thankful I am to call you my husband. Thank you for always supporting me in everything I do. I love you endlessly.

Devyn, you make the office so much fun, and I can't tell you how thankful I am you're here to share in all of this with me. I love you.

To my boys, Eli and Braydon. I love you both so much. Thank you for being so patient with me while my nose is buried in the computer, for laughing it off when it takes you calling "Mom" five times before I realize someone is talking to me, and for being the amazing, loving, kind boys you are.

Mom, I love you. Thank you for believing in me. And to the rest of my family. Your support means so much to me.

To Katie, because I wouldn't want to do this with anyone else. I love you so much. Thank you for going on this wild ride with me.

Ginger! Thank you for all the feedback, for the exclamation marks, and the *noooo*'s. Every single one of them made me smile. I love you tons, my friend.

To my amazing critique partners, pre-readers, and blogger friends. Thank you for the insight. Without you, *When We Collide* would not be what it is today. You know who you are!

To my Sapphire Star Publishing family. I feel blessed to have you all in my life.

And a big thank you to Roser Portella Florit for providing the gorgeous cover art for *When We Collide*.

Chapter One

Laughter floated over the vacant playground, an echo, a call. William pushed forward, drawn into the dusky haze. Wind whipped at his feet, stirred up the fallen leaves on the dead winter floor. Each step of his boots was leaden with a burden that simmered somewhere in the periphery of his understanding.

"Bet you can't find me." The innocent voice was distant as it fell upon William's ears, filled with mirth at the game the child played.

Those words rushed as fear through William's veins.

William's footsteps pounded in his ears as he followed the trail of the soft voice that lingered on the wind, past the empty swings and sandbox and into the forest at the back of the lot. Among the knotty, sinewy trees, their boughs twisted and twined, William paused to listen.

A branch snapped off to his right — another peal of laughter as the child dashed giggling from behind one tree to another more than a hundred yards away.

"Wait," William called, stretching his hand out in the child's direction. Please.

For a moment, the small boy peeked out from behind a large tree trunk and stared back at William with huge brown eyes.

William's heart lurched with the boy's face — a picture of himself — suddenly consumed with the need to protect and shelter.

The child giggled again, his feet too agile as he took off, his dark blond hair like a flare striking in the moonlight, before he disappeared deeper into the darkness.

Panting, William chased the boy, begging him to stop while he stumbled over exposed roots and overgrown earth that seemed almost alive as it worked to hold him back.

The child's laughter drifted along the breeze, brushed across William's face, beckoned him to a place he did not know.

William struggled to find him, to close the distance, but the gap only grew. The laughter shifted and faded. The boy's sudden fear hit William like a knife to the chest. Somewhere in the deepest recesses, far beyond William's reach, he heard the child scream.

I shot straight up in bed, gasping and disoriented. Faint slivers of silver light spiked through the room, stealing in through the slats of the window shutters. Gripping my head between my hands, I fought to right myself, to slow my thundering heart, and to stop the tremors rolling through my body.

Shit.

I shook my head and roughed a hand over my face.

My gaze darted around the massive room. In the dim light, my eyes adjusted. I focused in on the nightstand next to my bed. My black leather wallet and heavy silver watch sat next to

2

the clock that glowed four forty-seven. I glimpsed the entrance to the en suite bathroom off to my right and the short chest of drawers with the tall mirror across the far end of the room.

Everything familiar — everything I understood.

I released a weighty breath and drew in a cleansing one, my bare chest palpitating with one last tremor.

It was just a dream, I told myself as I ran a hand through my hair.

Just the same, fucked up nightmare that had been haunting me for months. Always the same, chasing myself as a boy through the darkened forest, waking when I screamed.

Glancing to the left, I looked to where Kristina slept soundly on her stomach, facing the opposite direction. The duvet was pulled up to just beneath her narrow waist, her blond hair cascading down her pillow and dipping onto the mattress. The pale skin of her arms and back seemed a severe contrast to the black sheets she lay on. Her body rose and fell with each even breath, unaffected and unaware of my distress.

It was hardly a surprise, not that I desired her comfort anyway.

We were little more than strangers sleeping in the same bed for the last six years. Marriage had never been mentioned. Neither of us pretended that was what this relationship was about.

I'd been in love once. It was that stupid kind of love that had kept me awake at night, wanting more. But *she'd* never really even been mine. I'd been young enough — foolish enough — to hope what we felt for each other could overcome her past, but not naïve enough to really believe it would ever work out.

Knowing that didn't mean losing her hadn't torn me apart. Even if she didn't choose me, I'd been desperate to save her from that path. But some things had been so deeply embedded in her that I doubted she'd really ever had a chance of breaking free of them. It was so ingrained she believed it was the only way to live.

I rolled onto my other side and squeezed my eyes shut as I attempted to force the memory of her face from my mind, but it was just as vivid as the day she'd forced me out of her life.

She'd touched me deeper than anyone ever had — deeper than I'd believed anyone could.

Pressing my face into my pillow, I allowed a glimmer of her presence to invade. That smile...so innocent and sweet. How she'd look at me with those warm brown eyes. The way her timid, trusting hands felt as they lightly skimmed over my skin. Even the memory stole my breath.

Sometimes I wished I could erase the mark she'd left on me, that I could finally be free of this ache. Another part of me held onto it because it was the only thing she'd left me with. The only thing I had to prove that what we'd shared had been real.

I'd wanted everything with her, but most of all, I wanted her to be happy. Safe.

I rolled onto my back and stared at the shadows playing across the ceiling, before I glanced again at Kristina. How different I'd pictured my life. Instead of lying here virtually alone next to Kristina, I should have been wrapped up in *her,* her auburn hair tickling my chin as she stirred in her sleep and nuzzled her face in my chest. I should have awoken to the welcome in her eyes, to someone who cared about me as much as I cared about her.

I'd accepted a long time ago that life I wanted would never be, but the isolation of the night always seemed to bring it all back, and it'd only gotten worse since I started having the nightmares six months ago.

Sitting up, I rubbed the back of my neck and tried to chase away the tension that had gathered in the muscles there, to shake off the anxiety that clung like decay. Climbing from bed, I was careful not to disturb Kristina. I knew from experience I had no chance of falling back to sleep now. In the bathroom, I flipped on the light switch and squinted in the brightness, seeing the strain from the recurring dream evidenced on my face in the mirror.

Sighing, I turned the faucet full blast and splashed cold water on my face.

This was getting really old.

Kristina stood in the opulent kitchen, stirring a cup of coffee while thumbing through a stack of paperwork on the counter. She wore her typical slacks, blouse, and heels, the perfect accessories for her perfect body, not one strand of her shiny, sleek hair in disarray.

She barely glanced in my direction when I entered through the archway.

"Meet me after work at *Nicoll's*?" she said. Her attention remained on the papers in front of her. Even though it was phrased that way, I knew it wasn't really a question.

My acquiescence was expected.

All of my success was in her hands, and she never let me forget it. As if she was giving me something I actually wanted. It made me want to laugh in her face. Did she really have no clue how I kept everything afloat?

"I'll be there," I muttered, going for my fourth cup of coffee of the morning, hoping beyond hope this would be the one that would finally counter the fatigue weighing down my mind and body.

Kristina's gaze fell on me, this time her eyes studying. "You look like shit, William." Her heels clicked against the slate tiles as she took the three steps needed to bring her to my side. Reaching out a hand, she turned me toward her, straightened the collar of my white button up, adjusted my tie, and stroked back the errant pieces of messy dark blond hair that had been purposefully cut that way. "What's going on with you lately?"

I shrugged, making a conscious effort to keep myself from flinching at her touch. "I'm fine. I just haven't been sleeping well."

She pursed her lips, one side drawn up higher than the other, before she turned away. Her brief moment of concern vanished just as quickly as it had surfaced.

Grabbing my briefcase, I headed for the garage. I backed my black luxury SUV out onto the narrow, winding road overlooking Los Angeles. Smog squatted heavily on the horizon, the early morning light a misty gray. The traffic-clogged freeway was no surprise. My car came to a standstill almost the moment I merged on I-10 on the way to my office downtown.

Feeling the effects of the fatigue, I slumped in the seat and rested against the headrest. My eyes dropped closed.

When all I saw were those same brown eyes from my dream staring back at me, my eyelids flew open.

What the hell is wrong with me? I pressed the heels of my hands into my eyes. I'd always prided myself on my self-control, my tenacity, my ability to get the job done. Now I felt as if my sanity was hanging by a quickly unraveling string.

Where this unease was coming from, I wasn't really sure. I guessed the dreams were just an extension of my dissatisfaction with life—a relationship I didn't want to be in and a job that was so stressful I could barely think straight at the end of the day. I'd lost myself somewhere along the way, and maybe my subconscious was telling me it was time I found that person again, because I sure as hell wasn't happy with who I'd become.

In the beginning, I'd embraced the escape I found in L.A., but it would never be home. It was only that—an escape.

My whole life growing up, I'd dreamed of getting out of Mississippi, until I left for college and slowly realized that small town was the only place I wanted to be. My older brother, Blake, had always teased me of being a momma's boy, an accusation that had caused us more than a few fistfights out in our backyard when we were kids. Growing up, I'd always strived to be tough, just like Blake, who was the star football player, the guy all the girls wanted. But I'd been the tall, gangly one—the scrawny little brother who'd end up with a fat, bloody lip after Blake put me back in my place when I tried to stand up to him. Proving Blake's point, I'd always run straight to our mom, who would tend to my bloody lip with an ice pack and a gentle hand through my hair.

Funny how times changed.

Now Blake had two little girls and a devoted wife, a quiet spirit and a soft voice, and I was no longer the awkward little boy. In the world I worked in, I slit throats before someone else could slit mine. I never thought twice about a quick stab to the back to get me one step closer to wherever Kristina wanted me to go.

Mom called us a *power couple* with no small amount of distaste, unable to hide her displeasure with the callused person I'd become.

Apparently something inside me didn't like who I'd become either.

Forty minutes later, I pulled into the underground garage. I parked in the slot plated with my name, drew in a deep breath, and fixed my face with an expression to match the persona that each day seemed to become harder and harder to slip into.

The doorman stood aside with a succinct nod. "Good morning, Mr. Marsch."

I dipped my head brusquely in a clipped show of power and strode to the elevator.

08๕)

Nicholl's was dimly lit and banked with men in designer suits. They were overshadowed by executive women with handbags that probably cost more than my first car. The restaurant catered to the affluent. Not the famous, but the educated who had clawed their way to the top, others who'd been born into it and inherited the seat, and, no doubt, a few who had slept their way in.

Kristina sat at a round, high table in a corner of the lounge, chatting with the two men facing her. She raised her hand in greeting when saw me from across the room, an artificial smile on her face.

I made my way over, and forced myself to kiss her on her proffered jaw.

"William, so good of you to make it." Her irritation was barely constrained.

I was five minutes late.

"Sorry," I apologized as I smoothed my tie against my chest and tucked myself onto the empty barstool beside her.

She didn't seem to get I was late because cleaning up her *Daddy's* messes was a never-ending job. How I'd ever fallen into the trap of working with the two of them, I'd never know.

She introduced me to our potential clients, her easy banter putting them at ease. From the way they looked at her, I could see she'd already cinched this account. Even though I'd pull out my laptop and show them how we'd make their investment grow, and Kristina would set out to convince them of the reasons why joining her father's firm would benefit them, it would all be completely unnecessary.

Kristina had caught me when I'd been an intern during my last year of college. I'd allowed her to draw something out in me then that I'd never known I possessed, something I wished now she'd never uncovered. Older by five years, she was already preparing to take her place at the top of her father's company and promised to take me along with her. In the beginning, it seemed like a great arrangement. It served as a perfect distraction from my past, a place where I could pretend I was someone I was not. And I doubted there were many men who'd object to sleeping with a woman that looked like Kristina night after night, but that kind of superficial attraction could only last for so long.

Several drinks later, the two men were signing on the dotted line.

No surprise.

Kristina was pleased and squeezed my thigh under the table. We parted from the men with the typical pleasantries of assured success. Following her home, I parked in the spot next to her red Porsche. She was all coy smiles and sex when she stepped from her car. A slow sense of dread settled in the pit of my stomach.

I really had begun to hate this life.

CRSO

Kristina slept curled up on her side, once again facing away from me. Her blond hair gleamed in the moonlight that streamed in through the window. Mimicking her pose, I allowed my eyes to trace over her bare skin, down her back where it sloped and met with her hip—and tried to *feel* something—something other than disdain.

A bitter taste soured in my mouth when I realized there was *nothing*.

Exhausted, I sank further into the mattress, further into my pillow, and drifted.

Laughter was his call, lost somewhere deep in the forest. The wind came fierce, blew across William's face, stung as he lumbered through the desolate play yard.

William tripped into the jumbled wood.

A flash of blond hair.

"Bet you can't find me." The boy giggled and ran.

Fear surged and twisted in William's gut, pushed him forward.

"Wait," William called, stretching his hand out in the child's direction. Please.

He peeked out from behind a tree, the boy with William's face.

The child was on the move again, hiding, laughing, stirring the unknown anxiety into a frenzy that beat like a drum against William's chest.

Please, wait.

The laughter dimmed and waned. The boy's sudden fear hit William like a knife to the chest. Somewhere in the deepest recesses, far beyond his reach, William heard him scream.

I jerked awake. Gulping for air, I clutched my head and tried to press the dream from my thoughts, but it dug its fingers deep, bored beneath my skin as the seeds of fear I'd felt for months firmly took root.

Chapter Two

Maggie ~ Present Day

Lightning flashed outside the living room window. It lit up the sleeping street and silhouetted the long, barren branches of towering trees. I stood in the quiet of the darkened room and flattened my palm on the cool glass pane.

So many years had passed, but I would never forget.

I would never forget his touch. The way he made me feel or what he made me see. Would never forget the gentle kindness in his eyes.

Another spark of lightning blanketed the night sky, and if I focused hard enough, I could almost see him standing in the middle of the vacant street. Tufts of his dark blond hair were whipped up by the wind, framing the intensity of his startling brown eyes. He was staring directly back at me.

William had been the only one who had ever cared enough to really see me.

Pressing my hand harder on the window, I wished to somehow draw him near, yet I knew I would never be brave enough to face him if he were to return.

Startled, I jumped when the back door rattled as it was unlocked, and I slowly stepped away from the only one I wanted. And like I'd had to do so long before, I let him go.

Chapter Three

William ~ Present Day

Straining to focus, I tried to make sense of the mess of numbers that seemed to swirl across the page. The harder I tried, the more jumbled they became. Three hours sleep, Kristina's bullshit, dealing with the financial disaster her father had created for this company, and I was about to snap. I was so tired of it all.

Tossing my pen onto the spreadsheet, I rocked back in my leather chair and massaged my temples as if it could silence last night's dream that was still screaming in my ears.

"Damn it," I groaned, rubbing my eyes and trying to shake myself out of it. "This is ridiculous."

"What's ridiculous?"

My skin crawled with the grating created by Kristina's voice coming from my office doorway. I blew the air from my lungs in an attempt to gather myself enough to deal with her.

She stepped forward and the door latched behind her with a soft click.

"All of this." My hand flung out in a flippant wave in an overt show of frustration.

Just everything.

Kristina took in the disaster upon my desk. My laptop was angled off to the side and papers were strewn in unorganized piles around it. She narrowed her eyes back at me.

"What is wrong with you, William?" Dissatisfaction dripped through her every word. "Dad needed this days ago. You have *got* to pull yourself together."

I wasn't exactly sure what they expected, because I could only move numbers around so much. But it was senseless to point it out. Making Mr. Crane's questionable business practices legal was what I was paid to do. Besides, six months ago, I *would* have had it done days ago. In the beginning, it hadn't been that bad, just some mixed up numbers that didn't quite match, but the longer I stayed and the deeper I dug, the more I uncovered.

Suppressing my resentment, I glanced to my left and out the window to the view of the skyscraper next door. Idly, I wondered if anyone there felt as trapped as I did here.

I turned my attention back to Kristina and wished I didn't feel the surge of animosity that came with it, my tone tight with restraint. "I'll get it done as soon as I can."

∝⼊⽅∾

So absorbed in trying to make the numbers match, I jumped when my cell phone vibrated and buzzed on the desk. Two hours had passed and I hadn't even realized it.

Grabbing the phone, I cringed when I saw the name that lit up on the screen.

Damn it.

I gave myself a couple seconds before answering, needing the time to curb the wave of guilt I felt every time I talked with one of them, and then brought the receiver to my ear.

"William Marsch." My standard greeting, all part of the façade, as if I weren't already aware of who was calling. It spoke volumes of the asshole I'd allowed myself to become.

Despite my every effort to keep my family at arm's length, they tried just as hard to keep me a part of them. Whenever I talked with my older brother, Blake was upbeat and asked me how I was, because he actually cared. He typically ignored the fact that I had essentially left them all behind.

But not today.

For a few painful moments, he was silent. There were just faint whispers and rustling in the background. When he finally spoke, his voice was strained. "Hey, Will...uh...it's Blake."

A fear so similar to the one I had felt last night when I'd awoken from the dream erupted in my chest. I was already anticipating Blake's words before he spoke them.

"Listen...I have some bad news."

In a blur, the faces of my family rushed through my mind, people I loved but barely knew any more, those I'd pretended to forget. My chest squeezed as each face passed, and I struggled to draw in a breath. Moving to lean on my elbows, I pressed my thumb and forefinger against my eyes and held the phone tighter to my ear.

Please...just not Mom. I chanted the silent prayer before Blake continued to speak.

"Aunt Lara...her...the cancer is back." Blake cleared the roughness from his throat. "It's bad this time, Will. It's spread too much. They can't do anything else but make her comfortable. It came on so fast." Blake choked over the explanation, and I tried to stop the spinning in my head. "They put her in home hospice and moved her to Mom's so she can be close to the family. She only has a few weeks at the most."

The news penetrated to my core. My Aunt Lara was going to die.

"God...Blake."

Even if I tried, this was not something I could push away. Not another thing I could bundle up and set aside and convince myself that it didn't matter.

There was a time when my Aunt Lara and I had been close. How many hot summer afternoons as a young boy had I snuck in her back door, sat at her kitchen table with a red popsicle in my hand, grinning while she asked me the little details about my day? Or the many Friday nights I spent in her den, on the floor buried under a blanket, watching movies over popcorn and soda. She'd never married, had never had children of her own, and she'd always considered Blake and me *her* boys. Yet another relationship I'd left behind.

"We need you here, Will. Mom needs you."

I hadn't been back to Mississippi in more than six years.

Aunt Lara had called me once and hadn't hesitated to unleash her disappointment on me. She told me she wouldn't stand aside and allow me to hurt her youngest sister by shunning my mother—my entire family—anymore. She'd accused me of thinking I was too good for them all and asked what any of them had ever done for me to think I could treat them that way.

What none of them understood was I couldn't go back. I couldn't stand to see *her*, couldn't stand to witness the life she had chosen. None of my family knew what had occurred that summer, the summer when my heart had come alive and then been crushed in what had felt like the same breath.

The only thing I could do was leave, turn my back and act as if it had never happened.

I'd buried it all in a place just under the surface where the memories of *her* touch ran rampant in my fantasies, freed only in the lonely moments of the night. She'd become a dream. I knew stepping foot back in Mississippi was going to make her real again.

But even if it did, I refused to ignore my family when they needed me.

"Yeah…" I slanted a hand through my hair and glanced at my desk, not sure how I was going to handle going back, but knowing I didn't have a choice. I swallowed, then forced myself to speak, committing myself back to the place I'd run from so long ago. "I'll be there."

Blake's surprise was evident in his loss for words. Finally he rushed, "Good. That's good. We're all…" He paused and his voice lowered. "Everyone here misses you, Will."

I tamped down some emotion, hating that I'd caused my family to believe I didn't want to be a part of their lives.

"Let me get some work stuff rearranged, and I'll give you a call sometime tomorrow to let you know when I'll be out."

Blake's heavy breath was almost palpable through the phone. "Okay. Just hurry."

⌘

Tugging shirts from their hangers, I tossed them with little thought into the suitcase lying open across the bed.

Kristina stood behind me, leaning against the bedroom doorframe with her arms crossed over her chest. "I can't believe you're doing this, William. Do you have any idea what we have riding on this account? How much money we stand to lose if you're not here?"

I cast Kristina a sidelong glance as I stalked back into the closet. She stood there fuming across the room. She'd been riding my ass since the second I told her I was leaving. I grabbed a few pairs of pants from the closet, pausing at its entrance on the way out. "My aunt is *dying*," I said, drawing out the word. "What do you expect me to do?"

"I expect you to honor your obligations."

I bit back a scornful snort.

Honor? Working for Kristina's father was the least honorable thing I'd ever done.

Taking four long strides to the bed, I turned my back on Kristina and flung the rest of my things into the suitcase, cramming the clothing in and struggling to hold it closed while I zipped it. I stood up straight and spoke toward the wall. I offered her an explanation I thought any normal person would understand. "My family needs me."

I felt the shift, the tilt of her head, could almost see her sneer. "Since when do you care anything about what they need?"

I balled my hands as guilt tensed the muscles in my back. Is this what the last years of my life had shown? Complete disregard for my family? Shaking it off, I grabbed the suitcase and dragged it from the bed and onto its wheels, realizing it was pointless to correct her. She had no clue about my past, how close I'd been to my family, or how close I'd come to living a life so different than this one.

I crossed the room to her, stopping a foot away. Her expression was hard, her eyes blue fire, all pretenses gone — cold — just like I knew her to be.

My anger dissipated when I took her in. I almost felt sorry for her. She allowed all this trivial shit to rule her world. It was the same shit I'd allowed her to center around mine. "When's it going to be enough, Kristina?"

Inching closer, I inclined my head to be sure I held her attention.

"Will you ever be satisfied? Because I refuse to live like this any longer." Somehow I knew I'd reached a turning point. I just didn't know which way I was going to go.

"What's that supposed to mean?" Her stony resolve wavered, her eyes flickering with a moment's uncertainty, before she set it firmly back in place. Of course she knew what I meant — the excess, when drive becomes greed.

I scrubbed a hand over my weary face, forcing the air from my lungs and dropping the subject, because I already knew there was no chance of changing her — no chance of changing the way I felt about her. "I'm going home, Kristina...call Neil, have him take over the account."

I pushed past her and headed toward the garage.

"When are you coming back?" Panic flooded her voice. For the first time since I'd known her, Kristina was on the verge of losing her carefully crafted control.

I paused but didn't look her way. "I really don't know."

CRSO

My hands were sweating as I gripped the steering wheel as I left L.A. I'd decided to drive, rationalizing the two-day trip to Mississippi would buy me some time. Time to decide what to do about the mess with Kristina. Time to delay my arrival back to the place I'd sworn to never return.

A shock of panic raised my temperature by what felt like thirty degrees when I thought of going back. I laughed humorlessly. Nothing like living the life of a coward. But was that what I really was? A coward?

I'd fought for *her*, would've given anything for her. I had to leave because there was no way I would have sat idle and watched her being torn down. I would have done…something. Chances were I would've ended up losing it like I'd done that night.

Her smile flashed across my vision, the softest eyes, the sweetest mouth. *"William,"* she whispered at my ear as she wove her fingers through my hair.

Chills shot across my skin and raised the hairs at the nape of my neck, spreading down my back.

God.

Old regret throbbed somewhere deep within my chest. Maybe I should have stayed. But what would it have ever changed?

Chapter Four

Maggie ~ Present Day

His callused hand burned against my skin. He was asleep behind me with his palm set possessively on my thigh. Hot breaths crawled along my skin and wrapped around my neck like an invisible noose, stealing the air as I struggled to suck it into my lungs.

My body felt like dead weight as I lay beside the last man I'd ever have chosen to give myself to.

Had I been marked for this life before I was born? Fated before time to suffer at the hands of the ones who were supposed to care for me? Or was it the choices I had made that led me here? Did one fatal mistake send me on a collision course, or was this simply a consequence of a lifetime of naivety and fear?

I retreated further into myself, seeking shelter in the shadows of my mind. There were few things there of comfort. But the small amount of comfort that remained shined bright.

William's face, laughing and kind. *"Maggie,"* he had murmured as he rolled to tug me on top of him. I giggled and relaxed into the firm body below me. William chuckled from deep in his chest and held me even closer as he buried his face in my hair.

Leaning back, I trailed my fingertips down the side of his face. He smiled as I traced them along the lines of his lips. My skin tingled, and I was unable to make sense of how any person could make me feel this way.

"You're so beautiful...do you know that?" he had said.

My heart thrummed wildly with joy, and I ached to feel more of his touch.

William had been perfect, a gift.

He'd changed me, deeply and in every way. When he found me, I was scared and insecure, and while those things still remained, they never looked the same. Every part of me had William written on it, the way I thought and what I saw.

What I desired and where my dreams laid.

No, I could never have him. I'd made too many mistakes. I had stayed on the same path that he had tried to save me from.

But I had never stopped wanting him.

Loving him.

He'd fought for *me*.

And I'd let him go without putting up my own fight.

Looking back now, I could finally see the glaring point William had been desperate to show me all along.

I regretted it more than I could ever say, more than I could ever openly admit.

I'd do anything to go back to the day when I'd let him slip through my fingers. Despite everything that happened, I had to believe now William would have accepted me.

Troy stirred behind me, grumbling deep within in his sleep. His hand traveled to my stomach and his hold tightened.

Nauseous heat filled my body and tightened my throat. I tried to swallow.

I'd do *anything* to go back.

But it was too late.

Chapter Five

William ~ Present Day

After two days of driving, I finally crossed the Mississippi State line at dusk. Traffic was light as I exited the highway and headed south, speeding down the open country road. Tall trees whipped by in a blur of green, gave way to open fields where houses were set back off the road with their porch lights shining, and then drove back into heavy forest—the countryside so alien from what I'd grown accustomed to over the last few years.

Yet still so very familiar.

My nerves ramped up what felt like a hundred notches when I turned onto Main Street and followed the single-lane road through town. It was exactly the same as I remembered. Angled parking spaces lined the storefronts of the one- and two-story businesses. Some had gone out of business and had been replaced by new owners, a few were vacant, and many were the same. I passed by the high school where I'd graduated and the county hospital where I was born.

I struggled to hold back the thousand memories that flooded me when I came upon the playground. It was the playground where my mom had pushed me on the swings when I was a small boy, where I'd played soccer in middle school, where *she* had left me six years before.

I slowed and inched by the vacant lot. Swings swayed in the gentle wind, the trees rustling as the night sucked the last of the light from the sky.

Like I'd known it would, it felt just like yesterday. Like I could reach out and touch her, wipe away her tears that had fallen when she'd broken both our hearts, kiss her one last time.

I rubbed a hand over my face to break up the memories.

Coming here had been a really bad idea.

Two minutes later, I turned onto the narrow street I'd grown up on, and I found myself fighting with conflicting emotions to both stay and run when I was engulfed in a swell of homesickness. Barren elms and full evergreens grew tall along the sidewalk bordering the road, the trees shading the mostly two-story houses, the yards boasting flowerbeds and trimmed lawns.

Something fluttered in my conscience when I slowly eased into my parents' driveway, a suggestion of nostalgia and regret. Gravel crunched beneath my tires, and I pulled up behind a huge monster of a truck that I could only assume belonged to my brother. My parents' house was much like the others, a modest white two-story with a stone path extending from the sidewalk to the five steps leading up to the front porch.

I felt like the prodigal son when my mother suddenly burst through the screened door and out onto the front porch.

She froze when she saw me, one hand covering her mouth and tears glistening in her green eyes, as if she couldn't believe I had actually come.

My mom, Glenda, was in her early fifties, a little wide through the hips, but thin everywhere else. Her brown hair had grayed a bit since the last time I'd seen her, and worry had lined her face.

Blake walked out behind her. A wary smile was forced on his face, and his posture was tense as he shoved his hands in the pockets of his worn work jeans. He and I favored each other, brown eyes and dark blond hair like our father's. He was a couple of inches shorter than me, though, stockier, his muscles thick from years of playing high school football and then his move into construction work as soon as he graduated.

For a moment I just sat there, staring out the driver's side window up at the family that had been waiting for me.

I finally allowed myself to admit how much I'd really missed them. *Six years* since I'd seen my brother. Three years since my mom had been out to California, begging me to come home. Two years since I'd even spoken with my dad. I hadn't even come out for Blake's wedding because I couldn't risk the chance of seeing *her*.

God, I was such an asshole.

Taking in a deep breath, I shut off the ignition and stepped from the car, not exactly sure what to do or what to say. Shame bit at my skin, and I shifted on my feet.

In a flurry of motion, Mom rushed down the steps. Before I could comprehend it, she threw her arms around my rigid frame. It took a couple of seconds for her welcome to sink in, for me to react and wrap my arms around her.

She was shaking and crying as she clung to me. She kept mumbling, "You came...you came."

I had no words. My throat was thick, my emotions tight. I just hugged her. She was wearing the same floral perfume she'd worn ever since I could remember, and I was struck with memories of how incredibly good she had always been to me.

I stood there wishing I would have at least been brave enough to give her a reason, that sometime over the years I would have explained that it had nothing to do with her or Dad or Blake.

She would have understood.

She finally pulled away and wiped beneath her eyes before she reached out a shaky hand to touch my cheek.

"I'm so glad you're here." Her eyes were serious, filled with disappointment and brimming with relief.

I resisted the urge to look away.

Instead I nodded and choked over the words, "I'm glad I'm here, too." At least it was partially true.

She smiled and turned to head back into the house. "Come on then."

I wasn't so foolish to believe that would be the last I'd hear about my absence, but for now, it would have to be enough.

Inside, my Aunt Lara lay dying, and this trip wasn't about me.

I went around to gather my things from the back of the SUV. Blake appeared at my side, his wary smile from before now welcoming.

"Here. Let me give you a hand with that."

I paused to look at my brother, six years gone, now a man, a father.

Blake had never been one for grudges. Our battles had been fought with fists and curses, the fight almost always forgotten by the next morning. *Spats*, my mother had called them. I wished it could be that simple now.

"Thanks, man," I said, tugging the large suitcase from the back of the SUV.

"Not a problem." Blake leaned into the cargo area and dug out the smaller suitcase and laptop case.

I followed Blake up the same steps I had taken a million times.

I glanced over my shoulder and up the road toward the playground that remained just out of sight, wondering if *she* still snuck to that secluded spot and if the memories of what had taken place there affected her as much as they did me. Did she feel drawn there, the way I did now? Or maybe I'd just always been drawn to her.

Shaking myself from the thoughts, I turned back to follow my brother inside. My feet faltered halfway through the front door. My guilt amplified when I set my eyes on the people in the living room.

I knew them only from pictures, Emma and Olivia, Blake's two little black-haired, round-faced girls. They were on the floor on their bellies, Emma coloring, Olivia scribbling. Their mother, Grace, sat on the edge of the couch, watching over them. Her mouth twisted up into an obligatory, faked smile when she looked up at me. I had known Grace for years, had grown up with her, graduated in the same high school class.

Her expression told me how little she thought of me now.

I don't think I'd ever known a more awkward moment than when my brother had to introduce me to my two- and four-year-old nieces who I had never met.

"Hey, Olivia, Emma. Come here. I want you to meet someone. This is your Uncle Will, my brother."

The oldest regarded me with cautious curiosity and the youngest with outright fear.

Apparently expensive gifts sent on birthdays and Christmases didn't make me any less of a stranger.

I rushed a hand through my hair and averted my eyes, never feeling more like an outsider than I did now. I'd missed so much, what felt like a lifetime. How could I have been such a fool to allow my past to chase me from my family?

"Your father is already asleep," Mom said from where she stood in the middle of the living room, looking just as unsure about me being there as I felt. "He's still working the early shift. Why don't you get settled and then you can go in and see your Aunt Lara?"

Nodding, I started up the stairs to my old room. Blake's footfalls echoed on the wooden staircase behind me. I nudged the door open. The hinges squeaked from disuse. Flicking on the overhead light, I stood aside and allowed Blake to enter ahead of me.

He dumped my things on the floor and cast a cautious glance around my room. "Everything's pretty much the same in here. Mom couldn't bring herself to change anything."

If it weren't for the lack of dust, I would have wondered if anyone had stepped foot in it since I'd left. The same worn blue and green plaid bedspread was draped over the full-sized bed, posters of cars tacked to the walls, the shelves cluttered by academic trophies.

Blake suddenly laughed. His eyes glinted with the same old amusement that had always come at my expense.

"God, you were such the little nerd." Blake grinned in my direction, and I smiled in spite of myself at the memory. "It was so easy to piss you off. You'd come after me with fists swinging. For some reason, I thought it was my job to toughen you up. Figured if I kicked your ass enough, I'd make a man out of my little brother. Guess I taught you well. Remember that time you kicked the shit out of Troy Clemons?" Looking at the ground, he shook his head as if he still couldn't believe it. "Shit. You nearly killed that guy. Nobody was going to mess with you after that."

My jaw ticked involuntarily and my fists curled, an instinctual physical reaction evoked at the mention of Troy's name.

Maybe I should've killed him.

God knew I wanted to.

Blake cut his narrowed eyes my way. "Of course, it didn't matter much. Wasn't long after that you disappeared."

I looked to the ground when Blake's disappointment covered me like a shroud.

"What happened, Will?" Blake took a step back to lean against the bedroom wall with his arms crossed over his chest. "One minute everything was just fine and the next we never see you again."

I struggled to find a valid explanation, but there wasn't one to give.

Dragging a hand through my hair, I released an ashamed breath.

"I just..." I glanced up at my brother and wished I could say something to erase the last six years. I'd been wrong to take the path I had—maybe just as wrong as she had been. Finally I said, "I'm sorry," because I had no excuse for the choice I'd made.

From across the room, Blake lifted his head and exhaled toward the ceiling. The sound hung in the air, filled with questions and dissatisfaction and a sense of letting go. He looked back at me and jerked his chin in my direction. "How long are you staying?"

I glanced around the room in discomfort, then looked back at him. "I'm not really sure. A while..." I shrugged. "I guess."

Frowning, Blake studied me, his expression one I knew well, one of the protective big brother.

No. Some things never changed.

"You and Kristina having trouble?"

I resisted the urge to laugh.

"Something like that," I said, scratching at the side of my jaw to mask my unease. *Having trouble* didn't begin to describe it.

Blake nodded as if he understood and rubbed his hand over his chin. "Well, if you decide to stick around here for a while, Grace and I have a little guesthouse out back. We lost our renters a couple of months ago. It's not much"—he gestured around my old room—"but anything's gotta be better than this. It's yours if you want it."

"I...uh..." I didn't know what to say or how to respond. Six years I'd been gone, without a word, without an explanation, yet my brother welcomed me back as if I had never committed the offense.

Blake grinned. "Don't sweat it, man. Just let me know what you want to do." He clapped me once on the back as he walked by, only to pause and turn around in the doorway with his hand on the knob. All evidence of the smile had been wiped from his face. "Just promise me you won't take off like that this time." Something passed across Blake's face, an emotion I wished I couldn't read. "I mean it, Will. I won't let you do that to Mom again."

Guilt rushed up my spine and settled in the back of my neck. I looked away and palmed the tense muscles, unable to face Blake and what I'd done. It'd been a bitch to ignore it in California. Here it was almost unbearable. "I won't."

Blake said nothing more, just turned away and pulled the door shut behind him.

I released a heavy breath through my mouth and rushed an incessant hand over the back of my head, feeling like a bastard standing in my own room.

CR&O

Twenty minutes later, I crept out the door and into the dim hallway, the only light emanating from downstairs.

Mom had just taken the last step onto the second-floor landing when I emerged from my room. She paused and offered a guarded smile, as if the satisfaction of my arrival had waned and worry had set in, a wall of unease and unfamiliarity that the years of absence had built between mother and son.

"Hi," she said. Her gaze swept over me. Her eyes were red but tender, and they softened further when she looked back up to my face.

"Hey," I whispered and stepped forward, noticing the distinct silence that had set in the air. It was a calm, almost disturbing quiet. "I was just coming to find you."

She smiled at the words. It appeared as if the action hurt.

"Blake and the girls left for the night, so I came up to check on Lara." She glanced in the direction of Blake's old room then back at me, her face suddenly swamped in sadness. "Did you...want to see her?"

My gut twisted, and I instinctively looked in the direction where my aunt lay dying. A dense haze of dread clouded my mind as I thought of facing what waited behind that door. I looked back at Mom, swallowing hard. "Yeah. I'd like that."

She nodded. "I need to warn you, she's sedated. She's not awake much, but when she is, she isn't making a whole lot of sense." Pausing at the closed door, Mom turned back to look at me, her mouth trembling. "She's getting near the end."

I reached for my mother's hand and squeezed it. I wished I could give her some form of comfort while knowing I could offer her none. She pressed her eyes closed in return, a rush of tears suddenly falling down her face, then opened the door and stepped back to allow me to pass.

All the breath left me when I saw Aunt Lara lying in the hospital bed. The head was inclined to keep her propped up, her hair thin and patchy. I'd always remembered her strong. Now she was bone thin. Her face was sunken, her cheekbones prominent, her skin brittle and gray. A single machine sat next to her bed, attached to an IV administering narcotics to make her comfortable.

I forced myself across the room and sank down onto one of the two chairs at the side of the bed. I took her cold hand in mine. Her mouth hung open while she slept. Each breath seemed to be a struggle as she forced the air in and out of her lungs.

Had I forgotten how much I loved her?

Dropping my head and eyes, I ran my thumb over the back of her hand, hoping she could feel me and that she somehow would know I was there. I whispered, "I'm so sorry, Aunt Lara."

Her grip was weak, but I felt the change in pressure when she tried to clasp mine. When I looked up, her eyes were fluttering, unintelligible sounds voiced from her moving lips.

Quickly, I shifted forward and touched the back of my other hand to her forehead.

"William." It was raspy, but clear. Her eyes came into focus when they locked with mine.

I smiled down at her, ran a hand down her stringy hair, and wished I could take back the last six years. "Hi, Aunt Lara."

"I knew you'd come." Her lips quivered as she attempted to smile, gurgling audible in her throat as she fought to suck in air.

"I'm—"

"Don't." She coughed, her eyelids fluttering as if she were being pulled under again, barely hanging onto consciousness. "I know you're...sss...sorry. You're here...now...is all that matters." Her hand tightened in mine as her lucidity faded, the hint of a smile touching the edge of her mouth. Her breaths came heavy once again and her jaw went slack, her mind dragged back into oblivion.

I looked up at the white, stained, popcorn ceiling, fighting the quaking that jackhammered against my ribs.

This was harder than I'd ever believed.

I sat with her for the longest time, longer than I probably knew. I finally stood and brushed my lips across her forehead.

When I stepped back out into the hall, Mom was still there, waiting in a cloak of anxiety, passing time by studying the pictures lining the wall that detailed mine and Blake's childhood.

"How is she?" she asked when I latched the door shut behind me.

"Resting now. She woke up for a couple of minutes. She knew I was there."

I watched her reaction, the small dose of joy mixed with what I now recognized as suffocating grief. I'd felt it myself, the helplessness, the impending loss. I could only imagine how much greater it was for my mother.

"I'm going to sit with her for a while...make sure she's comfortable for the night. Can you get yourself settled?" She drew her brows tight, almost as if she were bracing herself for my answer. "You are...staying?"

I knew what she was asking. Not whether I was staying the night. She was well aware my things were in my room.

She was asking for a commitment, for a promise that I wouldn't suddenly disappear from her life, the way I had done six years before.

My head was tilted down and my hands were stuffed in my pockets while I looked at my mother beneath the hedge of hair hanging over my eyes. It was the best I could do to expose myself and hide all at the same time. "Yeah. I'm staying."

⟨⟩

I collapsed facedown onto my old bed in a heap of exhaustion, my body weary from the long hours of travel, my mind and soul broken and filled with loss.

I'd wasted so much time.

The sheets were cool against my skin. I pressed my palm flat on the mattress where *she* had lain the first time I made love to her. I could almost remember how soft her hair had been as I wound it between my fingers. Could feel the sting of her fingertips digging into my back. Could see the love and trust overflowing in her eyes as she stared back up at me.

Suffocated by her lingering presence, I pulled the covers tight over my body, buried myself in the pile of sheets and blankets to protect myself from the cold seeping in through the cracks of the old, drafty house. Gusts of wind knocked at the windows and clattered the panes. Forcing my eyes closed, I struggled to shut off my head full of memories. Just for one night, I needed to rest. I'd face everything else tomorrow.

The fatigue that had chased me for months hit me in waves, and I sank deeper, fell further.

Drifted.

Desperation pushed William forward.

Howling wind cut through the trees, beat against his chest as he plodded through the deserted playground. Squalls swept low as they rushed over his body, opposing every arduous step. Swings flapped and rocked, metal scraping metal, shrill and high.

Laughter came from what sounded like every direction. Confusion ignited his fear.

In the middle of the grounds, William fell to a standstill. Ramming his hands against his ears, he squeezed his eyes closed and screamed for it to stop. The sound was devoured by the driving wind. With his hands urgent against his ears, William spun in a circle while his world spun faster. The child's laughter coiled in ribbons around his body. Wept against his skin.

The boy screamed, begged, and cried into the night.

William dropped to his knees.

I flailed in the small bed, my legs twisted in the blankets. The room spun as I lurched to sitting in my fight for consciousness.

No. This was supposed to stop when I got back home. It *had* to stop.

I wheezed as I sucked desperately for any air I could find. The wailing was still just as clear. The sound slipped through the thin walls, ripped and agonized.

Not the child.

I shoved my panic aside and stilled to listen to the torment coming from the next room.

"Shit," I whispered as I untangled myself from the blankets and climbed from bed, quiet as I crept out the door.

A lamp shone bright from Blake's old room, slicing into the darkness of the hall.

From the doorway, I watched my mother falling apart over my aunt's lifeless body. My father held her from behind,

36

promising against her ear it would be all right, that Lara was at peace, while my mother clutched her sister's hand and begged her not to leave.

I turned away and pressed my back against the wall. I slid down onto the cold hardwood floor and buried my face in my hands. Wetness seeped from my eyes.

Fifty-seven years old.

Life was hardly fair.

Chapter Six

William ~ Present Day

On Friday afternoon, I hung back near the far wall of my parents' living room. I had one hand shoved deep in the pants pocket of my black suit while I tugged at the charcoal-gray tie that felt much too tight around my neck with the other. Even though it was the middle of February, the Mississippi days stayed mild, almost warm, and the temperature had escalated to a near smothering level in the crowded room.

Sinking deeper into the recesses, I did my best to hide along the outskirts of the mass of people packed wall-to-wall. They were gathered for Aunt Lara's reception.

It'd been three days since she'd passed. Two hours since we'd laid her in the ground.

I pushed a breath from my lungs and roamed my eyes over the people conversing in muted whispers. I was not immune to the sadness weighing down the room. Mine only added to it, though I found myself wishing I were alone, in a quiet place with my thoughts, with my memories of her.

In a town this size, most everyone had known Lara, and it seemed all had come to pay their respects.

Most would eventually make their way over to me to welcome me home and tell me they were sorry for my loss. Almost all of those wishes seemed genuine, though a few clearly believed I was only there out of obligation. I could read the questions evident on their faces, the wonder at my disappearance, the disappointment in my abandonment, and the surprise that I had returned. I knew what I appeared, shallow and pretentious, and I doubted hiding in the shadows was doing anything to change their opinion of me.

But even if being here was excruciating, obligation was not the case.

One of the worst parts of the whole thing was every time the door opened, I couldn't stop my attention from being drawn in that direction, couldn't stave off the surge of apprehension that surfaced when I thought of seeing *her* again. I hated even more the twinge of letdown I felt when she didn't come.

Over the last three days, I'd realized I needed the very thing I'd run from for all these years.

Just to catch a glimpse of her. To know she was okay.

God knew I didn't dare ask about her.

I looked down at my feet when the screen door slammed closed once more behind an elderly couple who lived across the street.

Why was I torturing myself this way?

The only person who possibly looked more uncomfortable than me was my father. Peter Marsch stood tall and burly, his dark suit ill-fitted and tight. He could never be considered a social man, but there was no doubt he loved his family and was devoted to his wife. I watched as he leaned against the wall. His only concern was my mother, keen to her every move. Ready whenever she needed him.

I sighed and shifted in discomfort.

I'd forgotten that about my father. How he'd always been our protector, our provider. I could see Blake had inherited that strong streak of protectiveness. If I paid close enough attention, I could feel it simmering deep within myself, as well.

Overwhelmed by it all, I slipped behind the crowd and quietly mounted the stairs to steal a moment for myself. In the solace of my room, I discarded my coat and tie, undid the top two buttons of my stiff white dress shirt, and rolled up the sleeves. I breathed out in relief when I sank onto the edge of the bed.

All I needed was a minute to clear my head. I was just so damned tired. So mixed up. I had no idea what I was going to do, where I was going to go, or how long I would stay.

Standing from the bed, I scrubbed my palms over my face and sucked in a deep breath to pull myself back together.

When I stepped from my room, I was assaulted by the smells of a southern kitchen—comforting and warm—and the hushed voices that rose and married from below, my family and the people I had once considered friends. I slowed as I approached the photos displayed on the wall in the hallway, pausing to linger and study the collage of my past and the many family pictures where I'd been absent. There was just too much of it I had missed. I could fight it, but somehow I knew it was here I would always belong.

"Excuse me, sir. Is there a potty up here? I gotta go real bad and somebody's in the one down there."

The same timid voice that had haunted my nights for months hit me from behind, but may as well have been a kick directly to the stomach. It knocked the air from me, turned me inside out as awareness flowed through my consciousness.

I was frozen, facing the wall, trying to talk myself down, trying to wake myself up.

But I wasn't asleep.

Slowly I turned around.

The child stood bouncing at the top of the stairs, holding onto the wooden railing with one hand while he had the other covering the spot where his legs were crossed and pressed together. Dark blond hair fell to the nape of the little boy's neck, brushing just above his bright brown eyes. Those eyes were wide and almost fearful when they locked with my shocked gaze.

The little boy from my dreams.

Through the daze, I lifted my hand and pointed toward the door sitting halfway open beside my room. With a look of relief, the boy rushed past me and into the bathroom, flipping on the light switch before he slammed the door shut.

I stood there, staring at the closed door as realization tumbled through me.

Gripped and gutted me.

For a moment I was empty—numb—before feeling came swooping back down in a fusion of anger.

My hands curled into painful fists as my vision clouded, my mind reeling as it tried to reject what was unfolding in front of me.

The toilet flushed and water ran. I braced myself when I heard the slide of the lock and the turn of the knob.

Peering out through a crack in the door, the boy averted his eyes to his feet when he saw me still standing there. He squeezed out and headed back for the stairs with his attention trained on the ground in front of him, peeking once behind him.

I took two steps forward so I could see over the low parapet wall, watching the child go, knowing exactly where he would end up. My eyes raced ahead of him, searching through the crowd.

It didn't matter that I was prepared, that I already knew who I'd find.

It destroyed me all the same.

I struggled against the crushing weight on my chest as I watched *her* press a dish into my mother's hands. Her entire body shook and she forced a smile across her distressed face. She was fidgeting, her gaze darting in nervous tics around the room. Distinct relief took over her face when the boy suddenly snuggled up to her side. She cast another cautious glance around the room, wringing her hands as she nodded away at whatever my mother was saying. Gesturing toward the door, she appeared to apologize, then she ducked her head and hurried with the child toward the front door.

The screen door clanged shut behind them.

Anger burned beneath my skin, and I was moving before I could stop myself, my feet pounding as I ran down the stairs. At the landing, I slowed to weave through the guests huddled in groups, muttering tight apologies as I pushed and squeezed my way through.

I jerked the door open and flew out of the house and across the porch. I took the steps two at a time and ran down the stone path toward the street.

It was to the left that I saw her making her way down the sidewalk, holding the child who was obviously too large for her to carry. Her head was hung low, as if she could hide herself. Her long black skirt swished around her legs, and her black dress flats clacked on the concrete as she bustled away, her pace just shy of a jog.

Auburn hair fell in long waves down her back, pinned beneath the boy's arms where he held her tight around her neck. Bewildered brown eyes stared back at me, the child regarding me with confusion over his mother's shoulder.

I knew she felt me following. I could feel her tension, the swells of apprehension that grew, then broke and rippled across my flesh. Quickening my pace, I matched her, step for step. Her running only fueled the anger that threatened to spin me out of control. When she increased her speed, I did the same. A hundred feet ahead, she suddenly darted across the street, stopping to wrench the sliding door open to an old blue mini-van parked on the other side. She maneuvered the child around to set him inside and slammed the door shut.

She fumbled with the driver-side door handle. Her hands visibly shook as she struggled to jerk it open.

I was right behind her. I grabbed her upper arm to stop her from climbing inside when she swung the door open.

"You're not going anywhere until you explain *this* to me." My words dropped out in a low hiss.

Led by the motion of my hand, she spun around in a submissive cower, her free arm drawn to shield her face. To deflect the blow.

Her reaction stung as it cut a path from my palm and up my arm, spreading out over my consciousness.

I slowly drew my hand back.

"Maggie," I whispered, the name unspoken for so many years.

A small cry pressed from her mouth, and she shrank further against the inside of the door.

I lowered my head, searching for her face beneath the feeble attempt she'd made at protecting herself.

"God...Maggie..." I tried to keep my voice soft, but couldn't conceal how much it hurt she'd reacted to me that way or how much I hated those who'd bred it. My pulse thudded with a swell of protectiveness. Still, after so much time, all I wanted was to protect her.

She flinched when I reached for her again, her expression nearing terrified when I tugged her arm away from her face.

"You know I'd *never* touch you like that." Never. It didn't matter what she'd done or how angry I was.

Though she straightened, her body still sagged, her spirit beaten and broken.

"I know," she finally said, so low I could barely hear. She sniffled and hung her head in what appeared humiliation, holding herself across her middle as she raised her face just enough to meet with mine. Eyes, the warmest of brown, met with my intense gaze. They were steeped in a pain that seemed to verge on fear and still held in them every single thing that I had run from.

And her face.

She was so beautiful—still. Maybe more so. But she was so different than the young girl I remembered. All traces of innocence had been erased. In its place was a woman who had borne too much. I saw it. Knew it.

Need tensed my muscles.

Shit.

I had to look away to reclaim the reason I had chased her out here in the first place. I took a step back to put some space between us. Closing my eyes, I tried to keep my voice steady. It came out a plea.

"Tell me that's not my son."

Maggie whimpered. With the sound, I looked to see her slump over herself, pressing her hand over her mouth before she visibly steeled herself. I watched as she fought for an impassive expression, and she rigidly looked me in the eye.

She shook her head. "No, William, he's not."

I suppressed the urge to scream, to call her the liar I knew she was, contained the impulse to put my fist through the closest inanimate object.

Her attention flitted between the house and me, acute anxiety firing in each jerky movement. I glanced behind me to the few people who idled on my parents' porch. None of them even seemed to notice we were there. I turned back to level my eyes at the girl who once again had shaken my world.

"After everything, Maggie, you're going to stand there and lie to me?" I wanted the words to reflect my anger. Instead my voice cracked. "Tell me the truth. You owe me that."

She squeezed her eyes shut and tears escaped from the corners and slid down her face. She twisted her hands in the hem of her black sweater.

I pushed aside the familiar desire to comfort her. I had to take another step back when she laid the full force of her brown eyes on me again.

"Please...William, you have to believe me," she begged. "He's not—"

My eyes blurred, burning with the betrayal. "How could you do this to me, Maggie?"

How? How was any of it possible? The presence of the child hidden away in the van next to me was nearly insufferable. A new weight that had been added to my shoulders.

The innate need to protect her hit me again. Doubled.

She jumped when a screen door slammed shut at the house beside us, the sudden fear that had worried her face twisting into shame.

"I have to go," she said, tripping over herself as she turned to climb into the driver's seat. She was shaking so uncontrollably she didn't seem to have proper function of her limbs.

"Damn it, Maggie. You can't just..." I reached for her again. I had to stop her, make her talk to me.

She slapped my hand away, her expression desperate as she retreated into herself.

"You have to let it go. Please." Her eyes were pleading, filled with a silent communication she knew only I could understand.

I stepped back in disbelief, shocked she would actually suggest that I could, and she took the opportunity to shut the door in my face.

Stuttering, the old engine sprang to life.

I stood in the middle of the street, watching her go, clueless what I was supposed to do now.

As misled as I'd always believed her to be, I would never have imagined she could have betrayed me this way.

She'd been good — to a fault.

I knew first-hand how far that goodness would go, how far she'd go to deceive herself into believing something was right when it was so obviously wrong.

Chapter Seven

William ~ Present Day

There'd be no sleep tonight, I was sure. There were only memories and anger and betrayal that I didn't know how to deal with. So many questions consumed me, ate at me, twisted me up with dread. My mind raced while my heart felt as if it might shut down. Through the walls, I heard my mother weeping quietly in her room. Deep strains of my father's voice murmured comfort, though I couldn't make out what he said. The day had taken its toll, had left her spent. Thank God she knew nothing about what had transpired this afternoon, but that in itself added to my questions. How had no one else noticed? How had no one else seen?

But my family didn't know that over the summer six years ago my life was rocked—permanently changed. They didn't know that one night had me inexplicably drawn to a girl I didn't even know. I'd stood up for her without understanding why and then spent the next three months falling for her. They had no idea that one day I'd finally had enough, that I'd fought for her and, like a fool, had believed she was mine.

William ~ May, Six Years Earlier

I plodded up the back steps of my parents' house, a duffle bag slung over my shoulder. Fatigue slowed my feet, but I was excited to be home, so much so I had driven almost straight through. I hadn't seen my family since Christmas break.

Turning the key to the lock, I tiptoed into the kitchen of the darkened house, careful not to wake the rest of my family since it was close to three in the morning. A small light burned over the stove and another cast a faint glow from the base of the staircase when I walked through the archway and into the living room. A blanket lay twisted and discarded in a pile on the couch and a coffee cup with a tea bag sat half empty on the coffee table.

I felt a smile pull at the side of my mouth. I'd bet a million bucks my mother had waited up for me as long as she could before she'd given up and gone to bed.

Quieting my footsteps, I lumbered up the stairs. My parents' bedroom door was cracked open an inch, and I paused to peek inside. My mom and dad slept curled and wrapped together, my father's typical hard exterior erased in the deep abyss of sleep.

My smile from downstairs grew.

I quietly moved on from their room into my own. My bed had been turned down, waiting in welcome. Peeling my clothes off down to my boxers, I dropped them to the floor, then gave into the fatigue that had chased me for miles as I fell onto my childhood bed, thinking how great it was to finally be home.

CR&O

What the hell? I blinked, trying to orient myself to the surroundings, unable to do so before I was pummeled in the face a second time. With a pillow.

Ugh.

He was so gonna pay when I wasn't so damned tired. But for now, I was desperate for some more sleep. Burying my face in the safety of my pillow, I groaned and turned my back on the would-be attacker.

"Go away."

Blake just laughed, loud and without remorse, and hit me again. "Wakey wakey, little brother."

I rolled to my back, dragging the pillow with me to shield my face, mumbling into the dense fabric. "What time is it?"

"Nine."

I groaned again. "No way, man. I need some more sleep. I didn't get in until almost three last night."

Blake ripped the pillow from my grip. I was blinded by a sudden burst of sunlight I'd hoped not to be faced with for at least another couple of hours. I squinted up at my brother who stood above me with a ridiculous grin plastered on his face, then pressed my fists to my eyes.

"Come on, Blake." I'd beg if I had to.

"Mom's making breakfast. Quit being such a baby and get your ass downstairs," Blake said as he tossed both pillows to the foot of my bed. "Everybody's waiting for you."

Sounds from the kitchen directly below filtered into my room, the running of water and the clatter of dishes. The distinct smell of bacon frying jarred my senses.

I sat up, running a hand through the tangled mess on my head. "Okay…okay, I'm up."

Clapping a hand on my shoulder, the grin on Blake's face softened to a smile. "Welcome home, Will."

I glanced up at my older brother and smiled. "Thanks."

Blake just nodded once and headed out the door.

Heaving out a weighty breath, I pushed the tiredness aside. My mom would have been up with the first hint of morning, and I knew it had probably taken every ounce of willpower she had to wait until nine before she sent Blake up to wake me.

I pulled on a pair of pajama bottoms and a plain black tee and started downstairs. A sudden sense of belonging struck me with the voices coming from the kitchen.

It'd been no secret I planned on moving away from Mississippi permanently once I graduated from UCLA. I'd always wanted the big city and a fast life. I was going to be the one who escaped this small town, the one with a huge house and a bank account to match. But the older I got, the more I had begun to question those intentions. I had begun to miss my life here, and each day, those goals seemed to become less and less important. Really, I couldn't imagine not having *this*.

I paused at the archway of the kitchen to take them in. At the table, my dad was buried in the pages of the morning paper while he ate breakfast, and Blake sat beside him, shoveling food in his mouth while he talked to our mother. She stood at the stove, facing away, pouring pancake batter into a hot skillet while chatting with my brother from behind.

It was Aunt Lara who noticed me first. She was leaning with her back against the kitchen counter, sipping coffee from the giant mug I had made for her for Christmas years before, back when I was just a kid. A smile slid over her face when she saw me, lit all the way up to her eyes.

"Well, look who's finally up," she said with a bit of a tease. "We thought you were going to sleep away the entire day." Her expression was soft, her brown eyes glinting in humor, though that humor could never cover the way she adored me and Blake.

I offered a sleepy, "Mornin'," to the room.

Dad and Blake looked up from their places at the table.

Mom released an ecstatic, "Oh," as she turned and clapped her hands over her mouth. For a couple of beats she bounced on her toes as if gaining momentum, then rushed across the room and threw her arms around my neck. "I'm so glad you're home."

I hugged her close, muttering into her neck. "Missed you, Mom."

She squeezed me tighter. "You can't imagine how much I've missed you." She leaned back so she could see my face and then suddenly grinned and squeezed my chin. "Look at my baby boy...all grown up."

I laughed and rolled my eyes. "Mom, it's only been five months since you saw me last. I doubt I've really changed all that much."

Waving me off, she laughed quietly as she stood aside so Aunt Lara could step in to take her turn. She giggled when she wrapped me up in a suffocating hug.

"Don't mind your mother, Will. Glenda is sure getting emotional in her old age." She shot my mom a playful glare. "And she could hardly stand it that she missed your twenty-first birthday."

"Oh hush, Lara." Mom laughed, pointing an accusatory finger in her sister's direction. "Don't pretend like you didn't sit over here with me on his birthday crying that our little Will was all grown up."

Embarrassed by the spectacle they were making over me, I dropped my gaze to the ground and shook my head, chuckling under my breath. They always made a big fuss every time I came back for a visit. I used to hate it, but now, not so much.

Still laughing, Aunt Laura shifted to my side to wrap her arm around my waist. She smiled up in my direction. She always played the tough one, but I knew she was as soft as they came.

A gruff voice cut into their banter. "All right you two...leave the poor boy alone before you go and run him off again."

"Hey, Dad," I said as I wiggled out of Aunt Lara's hold and crossed the room. He stood as I approached.

He extended his hand, a wry smile lifting only one side of his face. We shook hands and he patted me twice on the shoulder. "Glad you're home, son."

I nodded and took the seat beside him. "Thanks...glad to be here."

Conversation filled the room as the five of us shared breakfast. A million questions were thrown my way about the last semester, complete with the expected good-natured badgering I'd come to expect.

Yes, I'd passed all of my finals, and my grades were good. No, I hadn't met anyone worth telling them about. Nope, I still had no clue what I was going to do with my Bachelors in Accounting when I graduated next year.

Blake filled me in on everything that had happened while I was away, told me work was great, and he'd been saving to buy his own place. Said he had a new girl. When he told me who, I teased him that I'd known her my whole life, and maybe I should have had the first shot with her. Blake didn't hesitate to smack me on the back of the head, ushering in a round of our usual jest.

We laughed and joked, and, once again, I found myself thinking how great it was to be home.

CR80

"Come on, man, hurry up," Blake yelled up from the bottom of the stairs, impatience seeded in each word. "I told Grace we'd be there to pick her up five minutes ago."

"I'll be down in a second," I shouted over my shoulder in the direction of the door as I pulled a clean tee over my head. I was still dripping from my shower. Why I'd let Blake goad me into this, I had no idea. All I wanted was a couple of days to unwind from the trip, to sit and vege, but Blake was already carting me off to a party the first night I was home. Blake had guilted me into going by telling me to consider it a welcome home party because all of my old friends would be there. He'd then pushed me toward the stairs, warning me we were leaving in fifteen minutes, shower or not.

"Don't make me come up there and drag your ass down here."

I didn't even respond. I just shoved my feet into a pair of Converse and ran a hand through my wet hair, wishing I was crawling into bed instead.

It'd been established years ago I would do just about anything for my brother.

At the door, we called out a goodbye, and Mom popped her head out of the kitchen archway. "You two have fun...and be safe."

I couldn't remember a time I'd left the house that she hadn't issued the same warning.

I climbed into Blake's truck, my feet dragging. The cab smacked with the odor of dirt and sweat and hard work. The old, beat-up truck roared when he turned the engine over.

Grace's house was only about five minutes away in a neighborhood almost identical to ours. She waited on her parents' porch with an excited smile on her face. Blake let the truck idle as he hopped out and ran up to her, swung her around and hugged her close, kissed her hard. I had to turn away from how intimate their interaction seemed and stare down at my fingers, but I couldn't stop the smile from taking hold, glad my brother seemed so happy.

Climbing in on Blake's side, Grace settled in the small space between us. I moved as far away as I could and pressed myself up against the door to give her room.

She grinned at me as she put on her seatbelt.

"Hey, Will. It's great to see you." She spoke in a casual way, as if we'd been close friends all our lives, even though we hadn't talked since graduation. I liked that about her, remembered how genuinely kind she'd always seemed.

I smiled. "Good to see you, too. How've you been?"

For two beats, she turned her attention to where her hand was clasped with Blake's on her lap, then looked up at me with a shy, satisfied smile. "Really good."

Blake drove to the outskirts of town and down a stretch of what felt like an abandoned two-lane road lined with towering evergreens. Streaks of bright orange light fanned in rays to the heavens as the sun began its descent westward, giving way to pinks and blues. The horizon blazed for one last moment before the sun completely sank out of view. An easy silence fell over us as we traveled, Grace's head resting on Blake's shoulder, my mind carried away by thoughts of just how easy this was. How simple this life could be. How right being here felt.

Blake slowed and took a sharp right onto a barely visible dirt road. The truck bounced along the path that had been carved out by the slow turn of tires, the headlights illuminating the grasses that grew tall straight down the middle and slapped against the truck's front fender. Spindly trees grew along both sides of the road, full and green with the approaching summer. Ahead the trees broke and opened up to a field. Flames from a bonfire rose high at the center.

We'd come here for years, no question the generations before us had too, our own secluded spot hidden away from parents and authority. It wasn't lost on me that all of us in the truck had outgrown the need to hide, but this was what we'd always done, and I doubted any of us found the need to change that now.

Blake pulled his truck up close to the line of trees on the left and threw it in park.

A small group had gathered around the rising fire, sitting on old fallen tree trunks that had been dragged in from the forest bed years before.

Tugging the door open, I jumped from the truck, surprised by the rush of anticipation I felt with seeing my old friends, with the thought of spending the night hanging out with my brother.

I was suddenly glad Blake had talked me into this.

I helped Blake haul the cooler of ice and beer from the back of his truck. We laughed as Blake reminisced about one of the many times we'd been here and the trouble we'd caused. We set the cooler beside one of the old oak trunks that lay decaying around the fire. Names and dates had been carved into the wood, covering almost all of its exposed body. Grabbing a beer, I leaned against the taller end of the log and traced a finger over the spot where I'd whittled my initials when I was a freshman in high school. I shook my head, chuckling at the ridiculous things we had done when we were kids.

Tonight's crowd was small, just a few of my old friends and some of the guys Blake hung out with now. Most of them sat with a girl resting between their knees, smiles on their faces. Laughter was in no short supply as the evening was spent telling stories of their past, as if we were spending one last night clinging to our youth.

Grinning from across the fire, Blake held his beer up in my direction. Grace sat on his lap and he had his free arm wrapped around her shoulder and across her chest. She held onto it with both hands, as if an anchor. I smiled and tipped my can back in Blake's direction, a silent cheer.

I couldn't help but think this felt good.

Really good.

Several cars came and the party grew just as the level of voices did. People gathered around the fire, some standing behind the logs talking, others sitting crossed-legged in front of the logs right in front of the fire, while a few had collected in small groups along the outskirts.

I looked behind me when headlights broke apart the darkness and a loud truck rumbled into the clearing. It parked sideways at the base of the road, the small area nearly at capacity. Kurt stepped out from the behind the wheel, an old teammate of Blake's from football. His brother Troy, who was just a year younger than Kurt, climbed out from the passenger side.

Groaning, I turned my face to the star-filled sky and drained my beer.

Troy was the biggest asshole I knew. He'd always been cocky, thought better of himself than he was, and treated everyone around him like shit. The guy had taken it upon himself to make my elementary school years miserable, taunting my friends and me every chance he got. Then one day it'd stopped and I'd never heard another word from him. It hadn't occurred to me at the time, but I'd put money down now that Blake had intervened. It'd just shifted Troy's attention, though, his mockery turned to other easy prey. He was like a classic afternoon-special—the bully kid with the belligerent, alcoholic father. Most everyone seemed to tolerate him because of it, but the guy won no soft spots with me.

Kurt and Troy shouted hellos at the crowd as the tailgate of their truck moaned and clanked as it dropped open. Troy's voice was loud and obnoxious when he approached, exactly as I remembered it to be, as if he were begging to be seen. They appeared at the far end of the crowd, dragging a cooler toward the fire.

I glanced toward the commotion they caused.

It was then I saw her. I had a vague sense of familiarity, as if I should know her, though I couldn't place where she fit into the web of this little town. She shuffled behind Troy as he pulled her along by the hand. Long waves of auburn hair hid her face, her attention on the ground as she stumbled over thick patches of grass and broken branches. She was petite, not extremely thin, but somehow appeared...delicate...as if something were just waiting to break. Or maybe she was already broken.

I frowned at the unbidden thought and popped the cap to another can of beer, forcing myself to look away. But it was no use. In just those few seconds of contemplation, I had felt a pang of *something*, felt something I'd never felt before stirring deep inside of me. I couldn't resist the urge to seek her out. My eyes followed Troy as he wove them through the groups of people and stopped to shake guys' hands who sat around the fire. I watched the girl avert her gaze when he did.

She appeared as if she wanted to hide, only offering shy hellos and subdued smiles when she was spoken to. At those times, I would catch glimpses of soft, round cheeks, the skin a rosy pink, lips so dark they were almost red, and once in a while, when I got really lucky, I saw the briefest flashes of warm chocolate eyes.

Stupid, I rebuked myself. There were fifteen other girls here I could sidle up to, flirt with, maybe take for a walk into the seclusion of the dense forest capped with the shelter of night. I'd enjoy myself for the hour, just as I always did, and I'd be sure she enjoyed herself too.

And here I was, eyeing the girl who was here with the one guy in the world I couldn't stand.

Attempting to force the foolish notion aside, I turned my attention to an old friend sitting beside me and tried to listen to him recount the story of a bar fight he'd seen the weekend before, but my ear was captured by the sound of a gentle voice, no more than a whisper, a soft blanket of warmth.

I was helpless to do anything but give in, and I tipped my beer to my mouth and stole a sideways glance in her direction. She sat on the ground close to the fire. Her knees were pulled to her chest, her movements slow and rhythmic as she rocked herself and talked quietly with the girl next to her.

Troy sat on the log behind her with his legs possessively stretched out on either side of her.

I had to look away from the two of them to deflect the jab of envy that sliced into my chest. I went for my third beer, wondering what the hell had gotten into me.

Time wore on and everyone seemed to become lulled by fire. Voices lowered, the atmosphere tempered, and spirits mellowed. The fire popped and cracked, spewed sparks into the air as the logs burned, crumbled to coal, glowed red embers.

From across the fire, Blake and Grace were wrapped up in each other again, lingering kisses and whispered words, as if everyone there had evaporated and they were the only two who remained.

A pang of jealousy flared.

The shake of my head was almost imperceptible as I chugged the last of my beer, thinking maybe—maybe I was ready for it.

With that realization, I involuntarily looked at her, drawn for the first time in my life. Of course I'd been attracted to girls before, but this was different. Stronger. Something I didn't entirely understand.

Like the rest, she was mesmerized, silent as she stared unseeing into the fire. Flames licked up toward the sky, casting glinting shadows against her eyes. They lit and danced—a slow dance that burned with the intensity and sadness of someone many years older than the girl I guessed she must be.

Stupid, I thought again. But I couldn't help but think she was the most beautiful girl I'd ever seen.

Her eyes flicked up from under her hair, and she caught me staring. She dropped her gaze and hugged her knees closer, although she couldn't hide the shy smile ridging the edge of her mouth and the redness that tinted her cheeks before she sucked her bottom lip between her teeth and ducked her head.

Oh God, I hadn't even gotten a good look at her face, and all I could think about was what it'd feel like to kiss her.

What the hell was she doing with an asshole like Troy? The guy was a complete fake. I'd seen over the years how he'd tried to chum up with my brother and his friends, acting the cool guy, but he was always the first to start a fight. He was trouble. How could she not see through his bullshit?

Exhaling, I forced myself to stop staring at her. Instead, I closed my eyes and let the fire warm my face while I gave in and relished in the prickle of nerves I felt across my skin every time she shifted.

A barking laugh cut into the peace, as offensive as it was vile.

My eyes flew open.

I didn't know what he'd said, but I could only imagine it was disgusting as Troy mumbled something to the guy next to him as he wound his hand in the thick locks of the girl's hair and yanked her back.

She cried out, then quickly suppressed the sound as she cringed and blinked, reaching back to rub the spot on her head. I watched her attempt to scoot forward, but Troy only tugged her back, laughed again as he placed his slimy mouth on her cheek.

She pinched her eyes shut.

"Troy...stop it...please," she whisper-pled. Her shoulders fell, and she hugged her knees closer. I got the distinct feeling she was trying to hide again.

I'd never felt this way before, the frisson of protectiveness that swept like wildfire through my veins and dripped from my pores.

"What? Are you deaf *and* dumb?" I spat the words, unable to hold them back. Not sure I wanted to.

Troy jerked his head up, looked at me, his eyes narrowed as if he couldn't believe I was talking to him.

"The girl asked you to stop." It came out a sneer, rippled over the crowd, and coalesced as a silent, collective gasp as everyone turned their attention to me. Silence stretched on as I stared Troy down and Troy sized me up. I could feel the girl begging me with her eyes. Could almost hear her silently pleading with me to let it go. Could almost taste how much she thought she wasn't worth it.

I refused to look away.

Clenching my jaw and fists, I struggled to control the shaking, to cover up my nerves that were all over the place that I really had no clue what to do with.

Troy glared at me with cold, light-brown eyes. A jeering smile suddenly split his face, a taunting laugh erupting from his throat. "You really wanna fuck with me, Marsch?"

I was on my feet before I knew they were below me, happy to *fuck* with Troy if that's the way he wanted it, but Blake was between us before I could take two steps. Blake slammed his palm against my chest, holding me back while he angled his body to face Troy, who had jumped up and was standing three feet away.

Blake pointed at him. "Don't even think about it, Troy. We don't need any of your shit tonight."

Troy leaned to the side, leering at me. "Come on, Marsch. What?" He jutted out his chin. "You still need your big brother to protect you?"

Raging against the restraint of Blake's hand, I was desperate to feel Troy under my fist, to unleash the rage that had come out of nowhere, but Blake struggled against me. "Come on, Will, knock it off."

I tripped over my feet as I floundered backward and landed hard on my back, the air knocked from my lungs.

"Why don't you go back to California where you belong, you whiny little bitch?" Troy laughed and spit in my direction, the wad landing in the ash next to my face.

I roared and struggled to get back on my feet.

Blake caught me just as I stood, fisting his hands in my shirt. "He's not worth it, Will."

No, Troy wasn't worth it, but she was.

I wrestled against Blake and tried to break free.

Blake tightened his hold and jostled me across the field, shoving me against the side of his truck. His voice was low and full of force as I came into contact with the smooth metal.

"Calm the fuck down, man." When I thrashed against him, Blake slammed me back again. "I'm serious, Will. Cool it. Are you trying to get yourself killed?"

Troy was still throwing insults from near the fire, the girl at his side begging him to stop.

I made another attempt to break free when Troy yelled at her to shut up.

"Are you really just going to stand there and let him treat her like that?" I flailed a hand in their direction.

"It's not any of our business."

Narrowing my eyes at Blake, I shook my head in disgust. "How can you say that?"

Blake reached over to wrench open the passenger door, didn't meet my eye. "Just get in the truck, Will."

I looked back and forth between Troy and Blake, unable to believe my older brother, felt something rip open when Troy dragged the crying girl toward the truck they'd arrived in.

I cried out in pain and fury when I twisted and rammed my fist into the side of Blake's truck, having nowhere else to inflict my anger.

This was complete bullshit.

Begrudgingly, I flopped into the cab of Blake's truck, laid my head back on the headrest, and closed my stinging eyes. The door slammed shut beside me.

A couple of seconds later, Grace climbed in through the driver's door, Blake right behind her. I didn't open my eyes, just stared at the blackness behind my lids.

The twenty minute ride back into town was taken in silence, the only interruption when Blake whispered, "I love you so much, Grace," into the darkness.

"I know," she answered, so quiet I could barely hear her, though I could tell she was crying.

Grace squeezed my knee when we stopped in front of her house to drop her off. I couldn't find it in myself to acknowledge her. I just continued to pretend I was asleep, to pretend as if this night had never happened.

For a few moments, the cab was silent and still when Blake and Grace exited the truck, the only sound my labored breaths filling the space. I tried to control them when the door cranked open and the cab rocked a bit as Blake plopped down onto his seat. The movement felt heavy with strain.

Blake emitted a loud sigh and shifted the truck into gear. I felt his hesitation, could almost see him opening and closing his mouth, before he finally spoke.

"I'm gonna ask her to marry me." His words trumpeted with awe and a flood of devotion, peppered with a hint of apprehension and fear.

I cracked an eye open, unable to ignore my brother any longer. "Yeah?" My voice sounded rough, and I cleared my throat. "That's...really good. I'm happy for you. Grace is a great girl."

Blake smiled a bit and rubbed a hand over his face. "Listen...I'm sorry about earlier." He ran his tongue across his bottom lip, shook his head before he cut his eye in my direction. It was dim in the cab, but I saw the sadness there. "Just don't go getting yourself mixed up in that situation."

I frowned, focused ahead on the headlights splaying light across the black pavement. "That wasn't right, Blake, and you know it."

"Hell no, it wasn't right."

I jerked to face him. "Then why did you stop me?"

Blake scoffed. "Because I didn't want to stand there and watch my little brother get his ass torn to shreds...that or get into an all-out brawl with Troy and Kurt. Is that what you wanted?" He palmed and squeezed the steering wheel, his tone softening. "And because it won't change anything, Will. That girl...she's every kind of messed up. She doesn't need you making things any worse for her."

The constriction Blake's assertion caused in my chest told me I was already in too deep.

"Who is she? She looked...familiar." I tried to play it casual, tried to hide the desperation in my voice, to pretend as if she were any other girl who I would have stuck up for.

"Maggie Krieger." Blake raised a brow as he delivered the blow.

Of course.

I dropped my face into my hands. I should have known. But really, she'd just been a little girl the last time I'd seen her, maybe ten years old at the most. She was young enough that through school we hadn't run in the same circles, but that didn't mean I was too old not to have heard the gossip that was prevalent in this town.

Blake pressed on, shrugged, though it didn't seem in indifference. "Troy probably treats her ten times better than her daddy ever did. I'd bet good money she'll get herself knocked up by the end of summer just to get out of that house."

Blake parked in the drive, and I stumbled out and trudged inside and upstairs, muttering a halfhearted goodnight to Blake before I fell into bed. Curling around my pillow, I focused on ridding my mind of whatever insane, convoluted feelings I must have conjured up about her. I told myself again and again that I'd never even spoken with her, that I didn't know her, and that I definitely didn't *want* her.

Yet every time I closed my eyes, all I saw was that shy smile mixed with the intense fire that had roared in the depths of her eyes, and I knew beyond anything else, Maggie wanted more.

William ~ Present Day

I stared up at the ceiling from my childhood bed, watched the shadows from the tree outside my window spread out across it, my throat tight with the memories. Somehow Blake and I had both known we were at a crossroads that night, and life decisions were about to be made. Blake had been wise and loved a girl who'd loved him back. I lay thinking now how I should have just looked away like everyone else had done that night. I should have turned my cheek and my heart away from the hook I'd allowed her to sink deep into my soul. But I'd been a fool, had chased her when I'd known I could never really have her, when I knew it was both wrong and so incredibly right.

I closed my eyes, saw the face of Maggie's little boy, thought of the dreams, questioned my sanity. I believed nothing in superstitions or fate or any of that other bullshit. But whether it meant something or meant nothing at all, it didn't change the fact I was here and I had a son. One look and I'd known. The other thing I was certain of was that Maggie would deny any claim I made.

And I had no idea what to do about it.

God.

The bed creaked when I rolled to my side.

Confusion and emotions I didn't know how to deal with plowed through my senses, left me weak and drained and unbearably restless.

I couldn't just leave the child there, but I didn't think I could take him away from his mother, either. I wouldn't pretend to know the boy, but his bond with his mother had been clear. I also didn't think I could ever openly expose what we'd done, hurt her that way.

Something inside wouldn't allow me to believe she'd put her child in danger, but did I really know her at all? I never would have believed she could be capable of keeping something like this from me.

And then there was this little nagging voice that kept asserting my instincts might be wrong and the boy might not be mine. It whispered I'd just overreacted and made assumptions that should never be made. I mean, I'd been careful *every* time, but then I had to admit I'd been warned before nothing was one-hundred percent.

I groaned and flopped onto my other side.

The worst part of it all was that gnawing in the pit of my stomach. It was the same familiar ache I'd tried to bury and stamp out beneath years of work and faked satisfaction, a need that glowed bright, unearthed and exposed.

I loved Maggie now as much as I did the day she walked out of my life.

Chapter Eight

Maggie ~ Present Day

I sucked in a shuddering breath and tried to hold the fractured pieces together. Regret splintered through my heart and cut me in two.

How could I have been such a fool to have believed he wouldn't be there? That one day, even if it weren't today, he wouldn't have eventually returned? But I had spent my entire life being a fool.

So many years had been spent fantasizing about him at night that I'd never imagined it'd be possible that he'd manifest in the day.

Sinking to my bedroom floor, I hugged my knees to my chest and hoped for the same numbness that fell over me when the fists came to pervade me now.

But William had always made me feel alive, and there was nothing I could do to shield myself from that light now.

I *felt* everything.

His anger, my shame, the love for him I'd kept stored up and buried so deep inside—a flicker of his before it had been chased away by his disgust. It all culminated in a searing, scorching burn.

I had known better, but my mom had been so insistent earlier this afternoon.

Every weekday after I dropped Jonathan off at kindergarten, I would slip in the back door of the ratty old house I'd grown up in, pushing aside the memories of that place. My mom needed me, and the echo of my father that lingered in its walls was not enough to keep me away. Usually I'd climb the stairs to find my mom curled up in bed. I would feed her, bathe her—love her—even though there was a huge part of me that hated my mother. It was the same part that hated myself.

Today, though, she had been downstairs where she was hunched over the kitchen counter. Her hair was dingy and straight, and almost an inch of gray roots had grown into the dull color I had washed into it three months before. With unsteady hands, she'd handed me the casserole she made and asked me to take it over to the Marsch's. Her eyes were glassy as she told me to tell them how sorry she was for their loss.

"Lara's always thought of us...taken care of us," she'd said when I tried to refuse and offer up an excuse why it was a terrible idea for me to go over there.

I hadn't been able to come up with one my mom found acceptable. I couldn't exactly tell her the real reason, could I?

"I still can't believe Lara is gone," Mom had said with a disoriented sadness, shaking her head. The movement was exaggerated by the tremors that plagued her body. "And Glenda, losing her sister so young. Both of 'em have never been anything but kind to us."

I'd understood. For once, my mom was giving and not taking.

Reluctantly, I had accepted the dish, but I was unable to stop the acute anxiety that came with the thought of going over there. For years, I'd avoided the Marsches the best I could in a town this small. I try not to make eye contact with any of them when we crossed paths.

I'd been the reason they'd lost him. I knew all the rumors. I had heard the disparaging words about the notorious William Marsch who'd shunned his family once he'd graduated from college. The town talked about his mother's heartbreak and Blake's anger that he had somehow thought himself too good for them and too good for this town.

But I knew better. I knew what'd happened the night he left.

And I knew it was my fault.

He'd never come back in six years, and I hadn't expected him to now, either. It was stupid, really, to think he wouldn't come back for his aunt's funeral.

I'd had to sit in my van for an hour to even build up the nerve. By then it was already time to pick up Jonathan from kindergarten. I'd buckled him in while I told him we just had to make a quick stop, my voice strained as I imagined walking through the Marsches' door.

I'd kissed Jonathan on the forehead to give myself some courage and to gain that sense of being whole I felt whenever I was near my son. He was the one thing that kept me sane.

I'd just step in and come right back out, I'd told myself, give my mother's condolences, as well as my own.

Then I'd run.

But when I helped Jonathan from the car and took his hand to cross the street, he whispered up to me that he had to go to the bathroom. He always held it until the last minute. Feeling a hint of panic, I squeezed his hand and asked him if he couldn't hold it.

With a baby-faced grimace, he'd shaken his head and almost begged, "No, Mommy...I gotta go right now."

Pointing to the house up ahead of us on the right, I said, "That's where we're going. I'm sure they have a bathroom you can use...but you have to hurry, okay?"

He nodded and ran ahead, taking the sidewalk and steps as fast as his little feet would carry him, and he had followed a couple inside.

It wasn't until I was halfway up the walk that I noticed the expensive black car parked in the Marsches' driveway, partially hidden from view by the huge truck parked behind it.

It had California plates.

My knees had gone weak.

There was nothing I could do, nowhere I could run, and I'd had to face the ultimate consequence for all of my sins — looking at the hate on the face of the only man I'd ever loved and knowing that hate was directed at me.

He'd thought I was scared of him, I knew. That reflex to protect myself had come unbidden with the touch of an angry hand. But never for a minute would I believe William would strike me, even though part of me had wished he would instead of looking at me the way he did.

Then maybe the numbness would come and I wouldn't have to feel *this*.

I hadn't lied, though.

Jonathan shouldn't be his.

Wiping my face with the back of my hand, I pulled myself together enough to stand. I swayed with dizziness with the sudden motion, but Jonathan would soon wake up from his afternoon nap, and I didn't want him to find me like this.

I found my feet. My legs wobbled under me, and I fumbled out of my room and down the hall. The little house we lived in wasn't much, but it was a hundred times better than what I'd grown up in, and I took good care of it because it was Jonathan's home.

Late afternoon light seeped through the floral drapes on the living room window. The house was wrapped in shadows, cold and much too quiet. I crossed the room and flicked on the overhead lights in the kitchen. I blinked against the harsh light, and I was hit with another wave of nausea.

It seemed in the light too many things became clear. Every mistake I'd ever made. The fact that as much as I might like to, I could never take them back.

And unmistakable fear.

Above everything else, it was the most glaring. I had no idea what would happen now. Would William pack his things and go, disappearing into the night like he had before? Would he stay and seek me out, and if he did, what questions would he ask? And how would I ever answer when I didn't know myself? Or would the anger that had clenched his hands into fists prevail, would he whisper accusations into the minds of his family and of this town. Would he try to take from me the only thing that mattered?

No. I shook my head. Not the William I knew.

Fear throbbed inside me when I was struck with the memory of his face from earlier. I had to admit, I really didn't know that William I'd left standing in the middle of the road two hours before. He'd changed, I could tell. Those brown eyes no longer swam with the warmth I remembered. They were hard. Hurt.

The best thing for us all would be for him to go, and I prayed he would. I just wished the thought of him leaving didn't hurt so much.

ೞഇ

"Hey, Jonnie Boy." Troy bent down to rumple Jonathan's hair where the child played with his cars on the kitchen floor. Jonathan looked up at him with an uneasy smile. I bit back a cringe. I hated that Troy called him that, hated more that my son didn't know how to act around his *dad*.

Troy dropped his lunch box on the counter as he kicked his work boots from his feet. "Smells good in here. What's for dinner?"

"Pork chops." I stirred milk into the pot of potatoes I'd boiled for mashing.

"Mmm..." Troy leaned in, pecked me on the cheek, and ran a hand through the hair hanging down my back. It always amazed me that he could waltz in here and act as if we were the all-American family, he the perfect husband and I the perfect wife.

Inclining his head, he studied the side of my face, his brow drawing up as if he were concerned for my well-being. "You been cryin'?" he asked.

I had the urge to laugh, though there was nothing funny about the absurdity of his question. Apparently he found it in himself to care if I was crying if he wasn't the one who'd caused it.

I held it in, buried it with everything else.

It wasn't hard to fake the sad smile and sniffle. "Yeah...today was Lara Collins' funeral. I stopped by to drop off

72

something Mom made for the family." I shrugged as if it really didn't matter all that much. "I don't know...guess it just made me sad to see all those people grieving."

Frowning, Troy uttered a tight, "Hmm," before he turned away and left the room without another word. It was no secret he didn't think much of the Marsches. William had been the only person I had ever seen stand up to Troy, the only person who'd ever stood up for me.

I felt the place I kept hidden away for William expand.

Troy had never forgotten it—and neither had I.

I looked down at my son playing on the floor, and smiled at the sweet child when he looked up. I extended my hand. "Come on, baby. It's time for dinner."

He scrambled to his feet. "'Kay, Mommy."

With his clothes changed and his face and hands washed, Troy walked back into the kitchen. His light blond hair looked almost brown from running dampened hands through it. He plunked down into his chair with an exaggerated sigh.

"I'm starving."

I set a plate in front of him, another in front of Jonathan, and sat down with my own. These were the hardest times for me. It was so difficult to pretend that I wanted to be here. Even more difficult to hide from my son how much I hated the man he knew as *daddy*.

Troy rambled on about his day at the shop, talking about the classic car that'd been brought in for restoration, and he asked Jonathan about school. Jonathan offered few words. He only answered Troy when he was asked a direct question. His voice was always hesitant and insecure when he did. He'd barely make eye contact when he glanced up to meet Troy's face.

I wondered if Troy ever noticed his *pride and joy* was terrified of him.

No.

Troy had never once touched Jonathan. If he did, he wouldn't live to see the next day. I'd die before I allowed anyone to harm my son.

The guilt that excuse caused was piercing, and I had to turn away from Jonathan and stare down at my plate. As if being exposed to this life didn't affect him? Harm him?

But I didn't have much of a choice, did I?

The scars hidden beneath my long-sleeved sweater stung in memory. Troy had left me with a permanent reminder that he would never let us go.

With a sense of hopelessness, I looked back up at my son. He sat on his knees so he could reach the table. His face was downcast, and he pushed food around with his fork.

"Eat, Jonathan." Troy pointed at Jonathan's plate with his fork.

Jonathan grimaced and whined, "But my tummy hurts."

Every night, it was the same. My heart fell.

"I said to eat your dinner, Jonnie." Troy's voice hardened. "I don't work all damned day so you can waste your food every night."

I watched Jonathan spear a piece of meat with his fork and force it into his mouth. He chewed then swallowed hard as if it caused him pain.

My eyes dropped closed. I knew the source of that pain. I felt it all the time.

"He said his stomach hurts." I mumbled the words toward my plate in a mix of disgust and apprehension. I only ever spoke out if it was for my son. I did whatever I had to for the attention to remain on me.

I didn't look up, but I felt Troy sit back and glare at me. "I didn't ask you."

An oppressive silence fell over the room. Jonathan took the opportunity to slither from his chair and disappear into the living room. His footsteps were light as they echoed down the short hall, and then his bedroom door clicked closed.

It was as if there was a certain tenor in Troy's tone that was Jonathan's cue. He'd learned it long ago, when Troy would instruct him to go to his room when his voice was vise-grip tight, and now Jonathan would go before he'd ever been told. Troy never let Jonathan see him hit me. I didn't know why, but I was thankful for it.

I remained still as I waited, my insides steeled. Troy didn't even bother to stand when he struck the right side of my face with the back of his hand. It wasn't very hard, just enough to rattle me, body and soul, enough to stoke the hatred that grew every day.

I refused to look his way, refused to acknowledge the monster who shoved his chair back from the table and braced his hands on the top as he leaned across and snarled close to the side of my face. "Don't you dare talk to me that way in front of my son." Grabbing a handful of my hair, he tugged me back and forced me to look at him. "Do you understand me?"

Still I remained silent. It was for the best. He pushed me away by the wad of hair he had curled in his hand. With a painful snap, my neck twisted to the side and a thick lock of hair ripped free when Troy jerked his hand back.

I wanted to cry out, but I bit it back. I wouldn't give him the satisfaction. Instead, I cradled my head in my hands and waited. His footsteps were heavy as he tore across the floor and slammed the back door shut behind him. The engine of his truck rumbled as he turned it over, and the wheels dug into the dirt when the truck was thrown in reverse. Gravel spit up and pinged against its sides as he backed out of the drive. My body stayed rigid until the sound of the engine faded when he turned left at the end of the street.

When it did, I crumbled, spilled from the chair and onto the floor.

To think there had been a day when I'd sought escape from my father through this man. Thought him the lesser of two evils. Maybe this was my punishment for being so selfish and seeking refuge in a person I'd known I would never love. But I *could* have, had he really loved me — would have even if he'd just treated me right.

Memories of William sprang into my mind, the tender way he used to look at me, the tender touch. I was lying to myself. I could never have loved Troy, or anyone else for that matter, the way I loved him.

I lay on my side with my knees hugged to my chest, the cold, hard floor biting into my hip, hating my life, hating myself.

I'd tried. For Jonathan, I'd tried. But in the end, I'd stayed with Troy to save us both.

I'd never understand how I'd gotten from my father's house to Troy's, when I'd promised myself so many times as a girl that I'd never end up like my mother. Like second-nature, I'd made an almost seamless transition from one vicious hand to another without even realizing it. The only blip of happiness in a life full of pain had been William.

With the little will I had left, I pushed myself up to my knees, picked myself up and dusted myself off the way I always managed to do. My life was lived for my son, and right now, I knew he'd be scared and worried about me.

Stumbling my way back to the bathroom nestled inside my bedroom, I wet a washcloth beneath warm water, wiped my eyes and the small amount of blood that had dried at the corner of my mouth, then tiptoed out into the hall, pausing outside Jonathan's door.

Muffled whimpers echoed from inside. They broke me just a little bit more.

Quietly, I pushed his door open and walked to where my son lay huddled in a ball on his floor. He was so much like me—exactly how I didn't want him to be. I pried him apart and took him into my arms. "It's okay, baby, it's okay," I whispered against his head when he wrapped himself around me.

I walked out to the living room and settled us in the worn rocker recliner. He snuggled against me, his thumb in his mouth as he exhaled a ragged breath against my neck. At times like these, he regressed into a child so much younger than he was.

God...somebody save us.

I had to get him away from here before he was ruined. Before he had no chance. All I wanted was for my son to grow up to be strong and good and kind. I ran my fingers through the locks of his dark blond hair, the love I felt for him overwhelming.

William had been my light in a lifetime of darkness, a glimpse at hope. I'd thought I'd lost it forever when I let him go. That darkness had been suffocating when I'd found out I was pregnant. Never would I have chosen to give another person a life like this.

Yeah, I knew what people thought, the rumor I'd done it on purpose, but I'd never felt less of a person than when Troy had taken me against my will. Every vile thing my daddy'd ever done to me didn't compare to that moment—the malicious grin that had marked Troy's face as I'd fought him and he'd held me down and dripped his body into mine.

But as scared as I'd been for the child growing inside me, it hadn't stopped me from loving him. It didn't matter who his father was.

When Jonathan was born, though, I'd been blinded by that same light, and for a fleeting second, I'd *known*. I'd pushed it aside and told myself no. I was sure I knew the moment he'd been conceived—the moment one of the worst of my short, miserable life.

But Jonathan had grown and many times had taken my breath away when he'd look at me just a certain way. The faint dimple to the right of his mouth above his lip that was barely visible with his small, sweet smile. The depth of his eyes that seemed to see more than they should. The hair that was neither blond nor brown, but a color all its own.

He'd easily pass as Troy's son, and most of the time, I believed he was.

But then there were the times when I saw more—when I saw what I was sure William had believed he'd seen earlier today—his blood dancing through Jonathan's veins.

I drew my son closer and whispered into the softness of his hair. "I love you, Jonathan."

"Love you, Mommy," he said, his fist locked in my shirt. His heart thrummed against mine. His sadness blanketed across my chest, soaking into my skin. I'd bear it all if I could.

Maggie ~ May, Six Years Earlier

I was crying, couldn't stop. "Troy, please."

His hand constricted tighter around my wrist as he hauled me behind him. My feet dragged through the dirt as I tried to keep up. Over my shoulder, I dared to look back toward him.

William.

I remembered him, Blake's younger brother.

All I wanted to do was break free from Troy's grasp and run to him. What I would do when I got there, I wasn't sure. Apologize? Thank him?

He'd watched me all night. I'd had this sense of awareness as his eyes traced my face. I was ashamed it'd felt so good. But the way he'd looked at me, it was different than anyone ever had. It had caused butterflies to tumble in my stomach and my heart to pound. No one had ever made me feel that way before. Even if it'd just been for a couple of hours, I felt...special. I'd reveled in it, basked in this feeling I'd never experienced before. Pretended I actually was.

It was foolish, because I was anything but special.

My mind and heart reeled as I struggled to keep up with Troy.

Troy had a reputation for his temper, but this was the first I'd seen of it in the two months we'd been dating. My mom had warned me to stay away from him. She'd said he was too old and too fast, but my mom was the last person I was going to take relationship advice from. Five times he'd asked me out before I said yes. Each time I refused, mostly because he really was *too* old, even if I wouldn't admit it to my mom. Six years older seemed like a lot to me, especially when I'd just turned eighteen. I'd been so upset that afternoon when I finally agreed. Crying—always crying.

Troy had pulled up alongside where I was walking down the sidewalk, coaxed me into his truck with an understanding smile on his face, and had just driven. He'd laughed and joked, doing his best to make me feel better. He'd grinned and nudged me with his elbow until he finally got me to return his smile.

In the couple of months I'd been seeing him since then, he had become an easy escape, getting me away from my house when it was the last place I wanted to be. I couldn't say I liked him, but he'd been nothing but nice. And nice was always better than Hell.

Something had shifted in him, though, over the last few weeks. A frustration simmered somewhere below his forced smile. I'd felt it, but had done my best to ignore it.

Tonight, it'd finally broken through.

But he'd promised he was different, so I begged again and tugged against his hold. "Troy...just...wait."

"Get in the fucking truck." Troy shoved me toward the passenger door. My foot caught on a branch, and I lurched forward. Shooting my hands out, I caught myself just before my face slammed into the side window.

Holding myself up, I suppressed the terror building in my gut—churning fear and anger—a feeling I was so familiar with, but this was the first time I'd associated the feeling with Troy.

From behind, he pressed my body flat into the metal with his, breathing into my ear. "I'd better not catch you looking at Marsch again." He dug his fingers into my sides. The pain made me gasp and then hold my breath. "Do you hear me?" he said as he tugged me back against him.

I nodded as I squeezed my eyes closed. Another round of tears raced down my face.

He jerked me back to open the door. It was excruciating not to look in William's direction as I climbed into the cab and Troy forced me onto his lap, locking his arm around my waist— impossible when Kurt gunned the accelerator and flipped a U-turn and the headlights illuminated Blake's truck. The driver's door was open and the cab was lit. William's eyes were closed, and his head was tilted up where it laid on the headrest, though I could see the torment raging in his posture and the anger twisting his face. Anger for me.

I was rocked by a torrent of intense longing. If only once I could have that—someone who really cared about the way I was treated.

I lowered my gaze, feeling sick as I listened to Kurt and Troy mock the one person who'd ever been concerned enough to defend me.

As we entered town and Kurt slowed, Troy loosened his hold. He hugged me and nuzzled my neck with his nose and mouth. He gathered my hair to the side and kissed me behind my ear. "Don't be mad, baby," he whispered, "I just love you so much…I can't stand somebody else looking at you."

I swallowed hard. It was the first time Troy said he loved me. But it didn't feel anything like love.

He walked me to the door. It had been a very a long time since I could remember being thankful I was home.

Shaking, I slid my key into the lock and snuck inside. The house was quiet, and I tiptoed upstairs to the room I shared with my little sister, Amber. Changing into my pajamas, I crawled under the covers of my twin bed. I prayed for silence, for peace, and for the room to be defended from intrusion, because I was sure there was no way I would survive my father sneaking into my room tonight.

Tears filled my eyes, and I bit my lip to keep from crying.

I was so stupid to think Troy was any different than my dad. Men were all the same. Mom had taught me that from the time I was a little girl.

Maggie ~ Present Day
I swatted at the tears running down my face.

My mom had been wrong.

William was different. His hands had been gentle and his words had been kind. I'd taken what he'd given me, something pure and good, and allowed my fear to destroy it.

Shifting my dozing child, I gathered him up and carried him to his room where I pulled back his covers and laid him in his bed. A burdened breath escaped his lungs, and he rolled to his side.

So precious and already so damaged.

I sighed as I tucked him in and made sure he'd be warm before I wandered back out into the living room, parted the drapes, and stared out into the night.

It'd be hours before Troy would return. I'd be long asleep, and he would slide into bed next to me and act as if the night had never happened.

And I'd hate him a little bit more.

Before he came, though, while I lay there alone, I'd dream of William. I'd pretend I was a different person from a different place, pretend I'd been strong enough for him.

Those dreams were usually an escape, but tonight I knew they were going to hurt. He was so near. I felt as if I could reach out and touch him.

I imagined him waiting for me at our spot, tucked behind the trunk of the fallen oak at the back of the playground where we'd always met, although I no longer saw the William I had pictured for the last six years. Instead he stood with his hands deep in the pockets of a dark suit, his face haunted by the choices I'd made. That face was striking, matured and strong, his brown eyes a raging storm.

A beautiful man I no longer knew.

Chapter Nine

William ~ Present Day

I followed Blake out the back door and into the frigid air. A cold front had blown in overnight, chasing out the normally mild Mississippi February and freezing everything in its path. I ducked my head to shield myself from the cold lash of wind that whipped at my face. Perfect weather for the sour mood I was in.

The cardboard box I carried felt as if it weighed fifty pounds rather than ten, and I shifted it to my side and took the back porch steps to the driveway.

Grim lines formed on Blake's face when he took the box from me. He placed it in the bed of his truck and slammed the tailgate shut. "Guess that's all," he said as he exhaled heavily and stared at the things piled in the bed of his truck.

Glancing back, I caught our mother watching us from the kitchen window, her hands overlapped and pressed against her chest as if she were trying to hold her heart in. Our eyes met, and my mouth formed into a thin, sympathetic smile. Everything was so hard on her, but this had been the worst. Packing up Lara's things, sifting through the memories, keeping the few things she couldn't bear to part with, and setting the rest aside.

A few moments later, the back screen door slammed shut behind her. The heavy winter coat she wore appeared as if it would swallow her whole.

"I'll ride with you." Mom lifted her face to me, mustering half a smile as she descended the stairs. She brushed an appreciative hand across Blake's arm as she passed before she went to stand at the passenger side door of my SUV.

Blake didn't question it. He just agreed with a bob of his head and climbed into his truck.

I drew a lump of cold air in through my nose, felt it burn down my throat and expand in my lungs. She'd heard me last night, I was sure. I'd seen it in the way she had regarded me all morning and into the afternoon. Worry had been held in the appraisal of her eyes as she'd steal surreptitious glances from wherever she sat and packed a box, worry in the way she watched me going in and out of her house to load Blake's truck.

Sliding into my seat, I started the car and fiddled with the thermostat to turn the heat to high. I shifted the car into reverse and looked over my shoulder to back out of the driveway. This time she didn't try to hide the intent gaze. She was studying.

My stomach twisted, tied up all the way to the top of my throat.

It'd been six days since I'd seen Maggie. Six days since I'd seen the child. Each one had been excruciating. A war had ravaged inside of me, a battle between heart and mind. My heart claimed the child, claimed the girl, while my head screamed at me to run, screamed neither of them were my concern.

Forcing myself into believing Maggie wasn't my concern had been the only way I'd survived in California. I couldn't allow myself to believe there was anything else I could do.

But seeing her had shattered that belief.

I'd spent the week holed up in the confines of my room, unable to eat, unable to sleep.

Last night I had reached the boiling point.

I'd fought with Kristina. I'd been so tired, verging on deranged from the days spent in my room pacing— contemplating—that I should have known better than to have accepted her call. I should have waited until I'd cleared my mind and decided what I was going to do. But I'd grown so frustrated with the demanding messages and the snide little remarks she used to try to control me, and I'd snapped when my phone lit up with her name again. She'd demanded I be back in California in two days, threatening to fire me if I wasn't. Anger had burned, spewed as hatred from my mouth. Six years of pent up discontent and resentment were unleashed into the phone. I told her even if I went back to California, it wouldn't be to her. I was done.

Hours later, cut free from the life I'd bound myself to for the last six years and drained from the days I'd spent in dread, I finally succumbed to the exhaustion of my body.

And I'd dreamed. Saw the boy for the first time through new eyes. When I'd awoken, I wept for a child I didn't know.

I trained my attention out the windshield, felt my mother's probing stare.

"What happened to you, Will?" It spilled as fear from her mouth, abject intuition.

I found myself wanting to confide in her. Tell her I thought I might be losing my mind. Tell her I was terrified I wasn't and have to admit the dreams were real. I just didn't know how.

So much time had been spent deceiving myself, believing my own lies, it was easy for me to shrug and play it off the way I always had. Locking my face in the same, persuasive expression I used whenever I wanted to get my way, I glanced across at her. "Nothing's wrong, Mom...I just...had a weird dream. It was nothing."

Hurt knit up her brow. "Don't lie to me." She turned away and faced forward. "Do you really think I can't tell that there's something going on with my *own* son? That I ever believed you all of a sudden just *didn't* care about us anymore?" I felt her gaze fall on me again. "What are you hiding from?"

I braked for one of the few lights in town, hands gripping the wheel. My mother had always known me so well. Our separation hadn't changed that. I doubted any amount of time would. On a heavy sigh, I sank back in my seat and rolled my head to look over at her, hoping she'd find in my expression she was right—I'd never stopped caring about them. At the same time, I prayed she could see it on my face that I wasn't yet ready to tell her why.

Her face softened and sympathy filled her eyes as she slowly nodded, the silence a declaration as understanding passed between us.

She fidgeted and looked down, adjusting her purse on her lap into almost the same position it had been. She seemed to struggle to find the right words. "Last night...earlier," she clarified as if to give me reassurance that she wasn't pressuring me for answers, but was at least asking for *something*, "I overhead you on the phone...with...Kristina."

I rubbed my forehead, turned away for a beat before I accelerated through the light when it turned green.

As if the entire neighborhood hadn't heard our screaming match.

Sighing, I turned left into the parking lot of the donation center. I eased my car into an open space, put it in park, and turned to face my mother.

"It's over with Kristina. I told her last night I wasn't going back." I paused before I gathered enough courage to continue. "I'm staying here…in Mississippi." I swallowed over the fear my decision elicited. It was a decision that had been cemented in those bleak hours I'd spent being tormented last night. In them, I'd accepted leaving was no longer an option, but I had no clue what staying would mean.

"Is that what you really want?" she asked, her eyes wide, as if she were more concerned with the answer on my face than with my actual words.

Biting at the inside of my lower lip, I nodded.

"It is." Confirming it was easier than I'd expected.

"Good," she said. The sudden disdain in her voice caught me by surprise. "I hated her, you know, keeping you from where you belonged…hated that you chose it." She opened the door, ranting mostly to herself as she stepped out, "I *never* taught my boys to run from their troubles."

CRLSO

That night, we all filed into the pizza parlor, thankful to get out of the cold. Mom grinned at me as she pulled out a chair and sat down, patting my leg. I shifted further down the table to make room for her and my dad.

"Who else is as hungry as I am?" she asked as she unfolded her reading glasses and situated them low on her nose.

Donating Lara's things had proven therapeutic for her, as if a small burden had been lifted because she'd accomplished something that had been so important to her sister. Ever since I could remember, Aunt Lara had volunteered at the center. The temporary shelter and second-hand store had been something she'd forever held close to her heart. She'd dragged me along on more than one occasion, even though as a child I'd protested, thinking she was wasting my time when I could have been riding my bike and hanging out with my friends. She'd said she wanted me to learn to be compassionate and one day I'd understand.

Maybe it had been a waste of my time. Any compassion that had been instilled in me over those long summer days had only made me bitter, because still, I didn't understand why some people made the choices they did.

Blake rearranged the chairs around the table and dragged a highchair over for Olivia. Every few seconds, he'd cast glances toward the entrance of the pizza parlor to see if his family had arrived.

The place hadn't changed in all the years I'd been gone. This had been our regular high school hangout. All my friends and I would come here for pizza before we ended up piling in trucks and cars to head out to our secluded field or to whatever party was happening. Red-backed booths still lined the walls, and the tables sitting in the middle were surrounded by the same generic red-cushioned chairs I associated with just about every crappy restaurant I'd ever stepped foot in. Lance still shouted "order up" every time he slid a pizza through the kitchen window, and I couldn't help but be surprised that I recognized only one of the two waitresses who were working that night.

The front door chimed and Grace entered. She held Olivia in one arm and Emma's hand with the other.

"Oh good, the girls are here," Mom said as she glanced up at the door over her menu.

They were all bundled up in jackets and knit hats, their cheeks rosy-red from winter's bite. Grace snaked her way through the restaurant and over to the table, her smile only for Blake as they approached. He was already standing, waiting as if unwilling to waste even a second of this life with them, kissed her and hugged his girls, said he'd missed them.

I snubbed the shame that worked to wind itself around my heart every time I saw Blake's kids. If I was going to be around, it was about time I got over it.

While Blake and Grace fought with Olivia's flailing feet to get her buckled into the highchair, Emma attempted to crawl onto the empty chair to my right. Lying on her belly, she grunted and struggled to lift her knee to the cushion to push herself up.

"Need help?" I asked, fumbling awkwardly as I reached out to help her, extending my hand for her to use as leverage. I was almost surprised she accepted it. Emma popped up on both her knees, and I pushed her chair in until her stomach touched the table, smiling at the cute little girl who smiled shyly up at me.

"Thank you," she said.

"You're welcome."

"Thanks, Will," Blake said over the howling of his youngest as he snapped her belt in place. "This one gives us fits every time we try to put her into a highchair."

I had to restrain the threat of disconcerted laughter when Olivia screeched her dissatisfaction and raked her hand across the table in front of her, sending the coloring page and crayons Blake had set down in front of her scattering across the floor. Blake seemed unfazed when he picked them up and set them in front of her, kneeling to get in her line of vision. "If you do it again, Olivia, you're not going to be allowed to have them back."

Peeking over at my mother and father, I gathered this was common as they continued to look over the menu. Mom glanced up every couple of seconds to discuss with Grace what kind of pizza they wanted to order.

Emma leaned with her forearms against the table so she could see around me, shouting her preferences above the loud cries of her sister. "I want cheese, Gramma!"

Mom smiled and reached around me to touch her hand. "Anything you want, sweetheart. How about you, Will? What are you in the mood for?"

I glanced at Emma with a knowing smile, then back to Mom. "Cheese is good with me."

I felt as if I'd been thrown into a chaotic new world. It was disorienting, being in the midst of such easy affection, how much patience was extended without giving it a second thought. Had I been eating with Kristina, not that she'd ever have stooped low enough to come to a place like this, she would have been complaining about just how rude some people were.

We ordered, and once the pizza was served, the table settled into quiet conversation. I tried not to let it bother me that Grace had not said one thing to me since I'd been back. She was still questioning my reasons for being there, and I couldn't blame her.

At the tug of my sleeve, I looked to my right.

"Look it, Uncle William." Holding up her coloring sheet, Emma showed me what she'd drawn, pointing with her chubby little finger as she traced the rainbow connecting her house to her gramma and grampa's house. She was grinning, animated, no question excited to be holding my attention. She looked up at me for approval, and for the first time since I'd come home, I didn't feel like a complete outsider.

I smiled down at my niece, thinking *this* was where I'd start, begin again, a second chance at knowing my family. "This is really beau…"

I stilled, contending with the overwhelming desire I had to look up from the drawing when I felt the shift in my world. A rush of freezing cold air singed my cheeks when the door was opened, mixed with the undeniable flame of her presence. The shocking intensity of her eyes pinned me in place as the bell chimed again when the door closed.

My mind clouded, and again, I cursed this little town. This was why I'd left in the first place, unable to face it, but unable to look away as I gave in and stole a glimpse at the three who'd walked through the door. Maggie's eyes locked with mine for the briefest second, but it might as well have been an eternity.

During that time, my anger was suspended. I couldn't remember that I'd been betrayed or that she'd lied.

All I could think of was how much I'd missed her—wanted her.

It flooded me in desire and warmth, the memory of how perfect this girl had felt in my arms. How I'd been her sanctuary and she'd been my everything.

She dropped her gaze and broke the spell, the moment passing just as quickly as it had come, sending reality crashing down over me. With it came the smoldering resentment that had stolen the last six years of my life.

Troy led her by the hand. She kept her head down and her hair fell around her face—hiding. It was the same fucking unbearable scene I'd had to witness time and time again through that summer. The rage it derived, the stabbing pain it'd caused as I had to sit and pretend that her heart didn't belong to me.

Only now it was worse.

A child clung to her leg, timid and scared. Hiding.

I dug my fingers into the table, held myself back while fury exploded, completely leveling the walls I'd constructed to keep her out.

He was exactly like his mother.

Except *he* was mine.

The little voice that had me lying to myself all week was gone — the one that had tried to convince me there was no possible way that child could be mine. It was silenced in those wide brown eyes that seemed to be drawn my way by an unknown recognition. The boy stumbled along behind his mother who trained her attention on the ground. Over his shoulder, the child strained to maintain eye contact with me as he was steered across the floor.

I almost expected him to call out to me, to giggle and run.

And I'd chase him, helpless to do anything else, because I recognized him too.

Led to a booth toward the front of the restaurant, the boy climbed in first, moving far enough inside to be cut from my view. Maggie scooted in next to him. Troy slid into the opposite side, facing away, concealed by the high-backed booth, apparently unaware of my presence.

Thank God.

I wasn't sure I could control myself if Troy were in my line of sight for the entire night. I doubted Troy could control himself, either.

I could feel her spirit pulsing against me, wrapping and coiling around my being while she tried to withdraw from me at the same time. I knew then Maggie couldn't escape me any more than I could escape her.

She hazarded me another fleeting glance, another plea. *Let it go.* I saw it as another lie. I minutely shook my head. It felt like an apology.

There was no chance I'd simply *let it go.* All I'd ever wanted to do was protect her, and she'd never let me.

Protecting her was no longer a choice. Whatever I had to do, I would.

I realized my mother was whispering. Her voice was low and directed at Blake. "…Always has been a nice girl…Did you see she stopped by Lara's reception…Jonathan is such a sweet little boy…"

Blake nodded as he ate. "Yeah, I noticed her when she was heading out."

I wanted to scream as my attention darted between them, shake them, demand to know if they saw even a hint of what I'd recognized. My father fed Olivia small pieces of his pizza, paying little attention to the conversation happening around him.

It was obvious none of them had any clue.

Grace continued with her distinct aversion to my presence, ducking her head to deflect my eye when I tried to search her face, her movements jerky when she suddenly pushed away from the table to set Olivia free. She somehow both grumbled and cooed at her child about the mess she had made, wiped a dampened napkin over Olivia's face that was smeared with pizza sauce.

Every one of them was unaware of what the child across the room meant, how he was tied to them, bound by an unseen connection.

I swept my gaze back to Maggie's table. God, part of me wanted to hate her. Blame her.

Tentatively she raised her head as if she felt everything I did. She looked at me beneath her veil of hair and risked meeting my eyes. Exposed herself and all of her vulnerability, the agony in her face, the shame.

I lost myself there, ended up back where we'd begun.

It didn't matter if I wanted to hate her. I could only hate the choices she'd made. Maybe the choices I'd made as well.

Never once in all those years had I thought maybe, just maybe, I could have changed her decision. That I could have made a difference. I couldn't help but question it now. Had I stayed, would things have been different?

Troy leaned across the table and stole her attention, and she turned away from me. Gave in to him. The same way she always had.

I closed my eyes. Would it be different now? Could she see this wasn't the life she wanted to live? Did she understand she deserved *more*? That her son deserved *more*?

"We should at least stop by and say hi," my mother said. She grabbed the bill from the center of the table and gathered her things to stand. "You remember Maggie, don't you, Will?"

I fumbled through the thoughts in my mind to find an acceptable answer, when Blake suddenly laughed as he sucked the last of his soda through his straw. Ice clanked when he dropped the cup back to the table. "I don't think William and Troy get along much, Ma."

Grace straightened with Olivia in her arms and turned to smack Blake against the shoulder, her eyes narrowed in warning.

"What?" Blake asked in mock defense, throwing a grin in my direction.

After that first night at the bonfire almost six years ago, I'd spent the entire summer watching Maggie and Troy together. I'd sat idle for *three* months while my love for her had grown and my rage toward Troy had built. At the end of the summer, it had all erupted in a hate I couldn't have controlled even if I'd wanted to.

Blake had been proud of me, I knew, again standing up for what we both knew was right, even after he had warned me not to get involved. But Blake had had no clue just how involved I'd gotten over those months.

He had no idea how important that night had been to me or what Maggie and I had shared after. He had no idea I would have gladly died for her. To Blake it had been nothing more than me standing up for the same girl a second time because I believed it was the right thing to do.

When in reality, it had been the only thing I could do.

Mom looked at me, her expression piqued in question. She'd never known about the incident. I was sure she would have freaked out. She would have said she was scared for me, said she'd never raised me to completely lose myself that way.

"It was nothing," I said to reassure her, helping Emma from her chair and taking her hand. "We just had a little disagreement...that's all."

Blake's whole face lifted in a *you're full of shit* sort of way, but he dropped it and took Olivia from Grace's arms, whispering, "Let's get you home, sweetheart," against his daughter's head.

With Emma's warm hand in mine, I cast one last glance in Maggie's direction. She pretended to be absorbed in the menu. I turned my attention to the well-trodden floor.

I didn't dare look at the boy.

I forced myself to put one foot in front of the other. Near the front door, Emma tugged at my wrist and handed me the picture she'd drawn, shy once again. "This is for you, Uncle William."

My smile was almost a grimace as I accepted her gift.

"Thank you so much, sweetheart," I said as I looked down at my brother's sweet child and thought this is the way it is supposed to be. A child loved by her father. Loved by her mother. Safe and protected in their care.

A sudden need collided with my spirit, and I jerked to look back toward the booth. Troy looked up just when I did. At first he stared, working his jaw as if it took a minute for his mind to catch up with the fact that I was there.

Recognition dawned and a new challenge seemed to be drawn.

I was sure Troy had never known what had happened between Maggie and me, was sure Troy had no idea the child sitting next to her was *mine*. In my head, I saw myself walking up to the table and throwing it in Troy's face, taking Maggie and Jonathan by the hand, and leading them out the door. As if that would somehow be a magical solution. That this situation could ever be that easy.

I wasn't even sure Maggie felt the same. She was the one who'd pushed me away.

Yet, in some way, I had too. I had left her standing there, sobbing as she'd cried out my name. Given up on her. Maybe when she'd needed me most. Her words had ripped me apart, and I'd sworn then I was done. I'd promised myself I'd no longer allow her that control over me, the anguish I'd endured just to have a small token of her love.

I had turned my back on her and walked away.

"You ready?" Blake called as he opened the door, a burst of winter thrust its way inside.

Pulling on my hand, Emma grinned up at me and said, "C'mon, Uncle."

As painful as it was, I walked away from her again.

But I promised myself this time it wouldn't be for good.

On the sidewalk, Grace called for Emma and reached out to take her hand, and they raced across the parking lot to the warmth of their car.

I trailed behind, falling to a standstill when the small square window came into view. Pressed to the glass was the boy's face framed by the palms of his hands, his short breaths fogging up the window.

Jonathan.

My son.

I allowed myself the smallest smile. Huge brown eyes blinked back at me, pure and innocent. In my mind, I heard his footsteps echo in the forest.

Startled, I jumped at the hand on my arm, felt like a fool when I looked down at my mother's concerned face.

"Are you okay?" she asked as she followed my gaze to the window, blatantly worried when she looked back.

Nodding, I whispered, "Yeah, I'm fine."

I'd never told a greater lie. I was the farthest place from okay.

She frowned, hesitating when she pulled away. "All right then…I'm just…I'm going to tell the girls goodnight."

I stuttered out a sigh of relief when she turned and tread across the lot to Grace's black mini-van to say goodnight to the girls.

"Night, Will," Grace called from her door as she hiked herself up into her seat. It seemed forced, but it was the first thing she'd said to me since I returned.

"Night," I said, so low she probably could never have heard.

She started the engine. Headlights cut across the parking lot and then she drove away.

Mom and Dad headed toward my car, and I looked at Blake who stood by his truck, watching me intently, the levity from earlier somehow replaced, as if he sensed my despair.

"You okay, man?" The same troubled question asked by our mother, though this time I couldn't find an answer.

Instead, I approached him, each purposed footstep pounding in my ears. I fisted my hands deep into the pockets of my coat as if it would somehow give me courage. I began speaking before I even reached my brother, almost shouting as I advanced. "You know what you offered the other day...about the guesthouse?"

I'd made the decision to stay, now it was time to make good on it. I wasn't going anywhere.

Blake's face shifted to understanding. "Sure, I remember."

I stopped in front of him. "Does it still stand?"

Skeptical relief bubbled out from Blake's mouth. "You're really staying?"

"Yeah, I am."

Blake grinned. "Of course it still stands."

Chapter Ten

William ~ Present Day

I peered out the living room window and watched the gentle sway of barren trees give way to plundering squalls. Branches thrashed and raked against the eves. Moonlight spilled in from above, slanting across the deserted road, melded with billows of rising dust to create a thick, milky haze.

Chills crawled up my spine and raised the fine hairs at the back of my neck. I had to turn away. It reminded me too much of the scene that had been haunting my dreams for months. At moments like these, fear prevailed, an ominous cloud that had me questioning how it was possible to be connected like this to a child I didn't know, because the rational side of me knew it was *impossible*.

Exhaling aloud, I took two steps toward the middle of the dim room. My feet faltered when I realized I wasn't alone.

Mom stood on the first step of the staircase, twisted toward me, as if she'd been on her way up and had only just noticed me there. We'd gotten back from the pizza place a few hours earlier, and I'd thought she'd already gone to bed.

She hesitated, looked me in the eye. "We're all going to be okay. You know that, don't you?" she said, a merciful encouragement, far from ignorant that something was tearing me apart.

I shook my head as I allowed the waves of hopelessness to ripple across my face, showed my mother just a little bit more.

No.

I didn't know that we were all going to be all right. I knew the goal, but I had no idea how I was going to get there.

"God, William, what—" She stopped herself as if remembering our interaction from this afternoon, visibly backed away without moving an inch. "I'm here for you...whatever you need. Just...when you're ready." Then she spun and headed up the stairs.

"Night, Ma," I murmured just loud enough for her to hear. I hadn't called her that in years. It was an affection I'd reserved for those many times she'd come to my rescue as a child, when she'd soothed me and loved me and made me a better person. Right then, I almost remembered how it'd felt to be that boy.

She stilled, holding onto the railing. Her movements were measured when she turned around to face me. Her mouth twisted up in an affected smile. "Goodnight, Will."

I didn't move while I watched her mount the stairs.

Running a hand through my hair, I plodded over to the couch and lowered myself onto the cushions. I scratched at the weathered upholstery and thought of how I'd sat in this very spot when my life had been upended.

William ~ May, Six Years Earlier

The morning after the bonfire, I lay in my bed, rubbing my eyes with the back of my hands. It'd been no use. No matter how hard I'd tried to forget about her, she had consumed every second of the night. Every second I'd spent awake, my eyes squeezed closed as if I could force myself to sleep, she had been there. When I finally had found sleep, she'd hunted me there as well. I shouldn't have been surprised when I'd awoken to a picture of her face.

It wasn't so much the memories I couldn't escape, but what had been born from them. I had no idea what I was feeling, but what I did know was I'd never felt this way before.

Sure. I'd dated. Even liked a couple of the girls all right.

But never once had I felt an inkling of what had been kindled in me last night—a feeling I couldn't grasp—something that hurt and felt perfect at the same time.

Groaning, I shrugged out of my covers and sat up in bed.

This was so messed up.

Yawning and scratching at my bare chest, I wandered out of my room and into the hall. I stopped to peek in my brother's room. Blake was sprawled, face-down, across his bed. All of his blankets were pushed to the floor, one foot hanging off the side, his back rising and falling with each deep, slumbered breath.

I didn't know if I was actually growing up or the events of last night had changed me so drastically they'd left me without the urge to retaliate for yesterday morning, but I turned and let my brother be.

Hauling myself downstairs, I mumbled a weary, "Good Morning," to my mother as I shuffled into the kitchen.

"Morning?" She continued to whip whatever was inside the large, silver bowl she held braced against her middle. "It's passed one o'clock." She smirked in that all-knowing, motherly way. "Rough night?" she asked as she turned to pour the contents of the bowl into the waiting pan on the counter.

I made my way to the refrigerator and grabbed a carton of orange juice. "Something like that," I mumbled as I poured myself a large glass.

Rough. Yes. Should I feel ashamed it was kind of amazing too? Just that small passage of time when my spirit had sought to know hers. When this girl had tugged something loose inside of me. I shook myself from the thought. I really didn't know how I was supposed to feel.

When I looked up, Mom was watching me. I ducked my head and shifted my feet, feeling exposed. Her expression was soft. I felt like a twelve-year-old boy with his first crush, who didn't quite know what to do with the butterflies assailing his stomach. But I was a 21-year-old man, and it was so much more complicated than that.

I had never been one to fall for the whole *love at first sight* bit, and I never believed that one day I'd see a girl and know she was the one. I was reticent to allow my thoughts to veer in that direction now. I'd only seen her once, and I'd not even spoken with her. It was ridiculous to entertain that type of notion.

But what did I feel?

I tried to swallow some of the fullness in my throat, to rid myself of the lump of emotion that had been stuck there since last night.

Whatever I felt, I knew it was permanent.

CR⧓SO

On Tuesday, I sat on the couch while the television droned. To me, each station seemed the same as I clicked aimlessly through the channels. No matter how hard I tried to fight it and alternatively tried to ignore it, I couldn't force down the restlessness clipping through my nerves. Today, I resolved to stay in and stop being such a creep.

I glanced behind me when I heard the soft thud of feet coming downstairs. A laundry basket was balanced at my mother's side.

"You're going to have to get off that couch," she called as she disappeared into the small laundry room tucked away beneath the stairs, reappearing a few seconds later. "We have a housekeeper coming today."

"What...did you win the lottery and not tell me or something?" I quirked a sarcastic, teasing brow at my mom.

She rolled her eyes and gave me a good-natured swat on the knee as she passed.

"Don't you wish." She shuffled through the living room, picking up the shirt and shoes Blake had left discarded on the floor the night before. "Your Aunt Lara has been helping out a family in town and one of the girls is looking to make some money for the summer. Figured it'd give me a little break. Lord knows you boys don't pick up after yourselves around here." She shook Blake's wadded up shirt in my face. "What is it with you two, anyway?" She turned away, mumbling, "Poor Grace is going to have to break that boy if he gets lucky enough to get a ring on her finger."

I pushed to my feet and stretched. "Sorry, Mom. What do you want done before she gets here?"

Mom waved a hand around the room. "I just want to get all the little stuff picked up. She's not going to know where anything goes, and I don't want to overwhelm her the first day she's here."

Gathering the dishes I'd left to dry out on the coffee table, I wandered into the kitchen and rinsed them in the sink. I placed them in the dishwasher and switched it to start. I had to admit, it was pretty pathetic Mom had to ask me to pick up after myself. It was so easy to get lazy when I came home. I set about to help her, worked through the kitchen to put away anything that appeared out of place, and wiped down the mess Blake had spilled on the counter before he'd rushed out to meet Grace. What a slob, I thought just as the doorbell rang.

I paused to listen as my mother moved across the living room, unlatching the lock to open the door.

"Oh, hello, dear," I heard her say in welcome.

My heart faltered for a beat and then took off in a sprint when a shy, "Thanks for having me, Mrs. Marsch," was offered in return.

My footsteps were almost silent as I stole across the kitchen floor to the archway. I froze when I saw her.

Fidgeting, Maggie lifted her head just enough to meet my mother's face. Her posture was guarded in apprehension.

"Of course..." Mom's words were muffled, like water lapping at my ears. My focus was entirely on Maggie, this girl who had taken me hostage, body, mind, and spirit. "We're thrilled to have you. Come on inside."

In the last four days, I'd seen her much more than I should have, only because I'd watched, searched, waited. It had made me sick, nauseated—weak with a want and a worry I didn't understand.

She'd known I was watching, too. Welcomed it, even. The way her body seemed to recognize mine, the subtle quiver of expectant nerves that traveled between us whenever I got brave enough to brush passed her—once on the sidewalk and once more when I followed her into the grocery store. Maybe I was imagining it all, because in all those times, she'd never once looked up.

Until now.

Slowly she raised her eyes to find mine, as if drawn. Wide brown eyes stared back at me. They seemed to be caught in the same stupor I'd been lost in for the last four days.

My heart stuttered again, and I knew I wasn't imagining this connection. She felt it too.

In this small town, I probably shouldn't have been surprised she was here, standing in my living room. There were only a handful of families who would have sought the help of the shelter where Aunt Lara volunteered her time. But I couldn't help but think that this was some twist of fate, that she belonged here, and this was all supposed to be.

Mom's attention flashed to me, her eyes wide as if trying to convey a message, then she whipped her attention back to Maggie and gestured in my direction. "Maggie, do you know my son, William? He's home from college for the summer."

Maggie stared across the space at me. She slowly shook her head. "No," she whispered, though her face spoke a different answer.

For the first time, I was given the opportunity to really look at her. Her cheekbones were high and defined, though the slight fullness of her cheeks and her tiny nose somehow made her appear innocent. The slender slope of her neck seemed almost a contradiction to the sweetness of her face, the smooth, creamy skin exposed in the gentle swoop of her dark blue tee. But it was those sad, knowing eyes that threatened to steal my sanity.

God. She was beautiful.

Every inch of my body bristled in awareness, filled me with a need that was so much more than just latent desire. What was it about her? Yeah, she was gorgeous, undoubtedly someone who would have turned my head had I passed her on the street. But she gripped me deeper than that. Maybe it was who she was, the mystery surrounding this girl's life, the need I saw on her face. The innate need I felt to protect her. Yet I'd been captured by her before I even knew who she was.

Whatever it was that drew me to her, I knew I wanted it all.

Managing to gather my senses, I cleared my throat and spoke to her for the first time.

"Hi, Maggie. It's nice to meet you." My hand fluttered up in an awkward wave.

Dropping her gaze to the floor, she muttered a timid, "Hi," though she couldn't hide the faint smile that graced her lips.

My mother shattered our moment with a sudden urgency.

"Here...let's show you around." Ushering Maggie toward the stairs, my mom began in nonstop, nervous chatter as she followed close behind the girl.

I couldn't look away as the two ascended the stairs.

Maggie peeked at me over her shoulder, a flush of red coloring her cheeks, before she turned away.

I watched as they vanished at the landing, Mom's voice fading when they entered my parents' bedroom.

When I'd stared for too long at nothing, I finally retreated back into the kitchen to finish cleaning up. I tried not to focus on the echo of the footsteps above me, pretended the object of my every dream and every nightmare for the last four days hadn't manifested before my eyes. I pretended she wasn't here, moving through my home, moving through my heart.

Shaking my head at myself, I rinsed the rag under the kitchen faucet. I was a fool if I thought I was going to get her off of my mind.

Stupid.

Two hours later, I lay flat on my back on my bed. I used one arm as a headrest and with my free hand played toss with a small rubber ball. I could still hear her—feel her—as she slipped in and out of rooms, the whoosh and crack of blankets as they were shaken out, beds remade, the intermittent roar of the vacuum, though even that somehow seemed subdued. How typical, I thought, for this girl to have the ability to hide even in the noisy clatter of cleaning.

Earlier, Mom had snuck up on me in the kitchen, whispering that I should make myself scarce while Maggie was here. She said the girl was very shy and my presence would only make her nervous. Obviously, my mother had mistaken the tension in the room as fear. But I figured it was for the best, and I relegated myself to the confines of my room. I probably would have made a fool of myself and followed Maggie room to room had I been left to my own devices, anyway.

I just hadn't anticipated the kind of torture this would be—holing myself up in here when all I wanted was to be out there.

I blew the air from my lungs, tossed the ball up again, and missed it when a light tapping sounded at my door. I jerked to sitting. "Yeah?"

The door barely cracked open an inch, and Maggie peered through the gap.

I couldn't help the smile from tugging at the corner of my mouth, my voice a little rough when I wheezed out a relieved, "Hey." I couldn't see her face, couldn't read her expression, but I felt the hesitation in her presence. "You can come in," I said, shifting forward to sit at the edge of the bed.

Shuffling in, she held her head low, insecurity woven through every awkward movement she made. Those locks of auburn hair I couldn't get off my mind fell in a cascade around each side of her face. So soft, I'd bet. I fucking hated it that she used it as a wall.

"I'm sorry to bother you," she all but whispered as she trained her attention on the carpet and tugged at the hem of her shirt, "but this is the last room."

I looked around the bedroom I'd only inhabited for the last four days. I couldn't stand the idea of her cleaning up after me. "It's not really dirty. I've only been back for a few days."

"Oh..." Her eyes jittered around the room, never at me, the brief second of openness we'd shared earlier at the front door seemingly erased. She began to back away. "I'll...just..." She stammered and motioned behind her before she stopped and squeezed her eyes shut in a visible cringe. Then she spun away from me and took two hurried steps toward the door.

Shit.

I'd embarrassed her, made her feel unwanted in the very place I wanted her to be.

"Wait," I called just as she reached the door. She seemed to waver between running and staying, her hand trembling on the doorknob when she stalled in the doorway. "Please," I begged to her back, although I really didn't know what I was begging for. All I knew was I couldn't watch her go.

Uncertainty stretched tight between us, a twisted ribbon taut with longing, fear, and need. Every part of me knew she was forbidden, that her heart already belonged to whatever shit she'd been put through in her life, but I couldn't stop myself from wanting her to stay.

Even from behind, I saw her breaths came in an exaggerated rise and fall of her chest, as if she had to put everything she had into each one just to stay alive. The movement felt calculated when she finally turned. She reached a hand out to brace herself against the jamb.

"Thank you," was all she said, but I heard so much more. Saw it in the warmth of her eyes.

I pressed my lips together, trying to rein in the emotion that raced ahead of me.

"I'd do it again," I said, a promise from where I looked up at her from my bed. Standing up for her had been no mistake. I'd never felt stronger about anything in my life.

Maggie chewed at her bottom lip and dropped her gaze, before she raised it to meet mine. "I know you would."

From across the room, we stared at each other. Tenderness filled her expression, the sadness that normally aged her eyes softening and warming.

In the handful of times I'd seen her this week, I'd never witnessed her like this. Vulnerable, yes. But this was different. From behind the wall that she hid, I was able to see *her*, what I'd glimpsed from across the fire over the weekend.

Shy. Sweet. Good.

The fullness present in my chest for the last four days hummed and heightened, grew to fill places I didn't know existed.

Was it wrong that all I wanted to do was kiss her?

I smiled, and Maggie blushed.

Oh God. So cute.

I knew then, I'd give this girl anything she asked me for. I'd probably beg her to take it.

The next Tuesday, the doorbell rang fifteen minutes earlier than it had one week before. From the kitchen, I yelled, "I got it."

I rushed across the room, hoping to beat Mom to the door.

During the last week, I'd only seen her once — on Saturday night. Blake had talked me into going to one of his friend's parties. It hadn't taken much prodding, a night out with my brother and the chance of catching a glimpse of Maggie a win-win for me. Of course, I hadn't counted on the way I'd feel when she walked through the door with her hand in Troy's, trailing two steps behind him.

Seeing the two of them together had sparked a possessive anger just as strong as what I'd felt the weekend before, and from the expression on Troy's face, his anger hadn't dissipated any, either. I'd had to endure a night of Troy continually glaring at me, as if searching *me* for wrong, while Maggie never looked in my direction. Even though I sought it, waiting for the perfect moment to approach her, none had ever come. She was closed off, a silent adornment affixed to Troy's side. If possible, her unease had been greater than it was at the bonfire, her posture defeated and ashamed.

From across the room I'd cursed and berated myself for being so *stupid* to believe there was some kind of connection between Maggie and me. I was beginning to think I left every ounce of common sense I had back at college, because I wasn't sure if I'd had a rational thought since I crossed the Mississippi state line.

Until I caught her face through the front window as she'd followed Troy out. Soft eyes locked on mine as she walked passed, shame still present in the heaviness of her shoulders, but that same tenderness abounding in her gaze.

That tenderness had been directed at me.

Raking my hair back from my face, I pulled open my front door.

From behind the screen door, Maggie looked up. Surprise flitted across her features when she realized it was me, before a shy smile took its place. She chewed on the outside of her bottom lip and rocked onto the outside of her shoes.

She was nervous. And so unbelievably cute.

"Hey, Maggie. Come on in," I said as I stepped forward and opened the screen door, losing control of my thoughts when she glanced up at me from the side as she entered. She must have just showered. Her hair was damp, the smell of shampoo and soap and everything I wanted to sink my nose into powerful as she passed by.

She stopped just inside, her attention bouncing around the living room before she turned to face me.

I shifted, wanting to say so many things, but finally settled on a simple, "How are you?"

She smiled her shy smile and said, "I'm all right."

It felt as if we'd shared so much, even though the only time we'd ever spoken had been in my room last week. The casual words we spoke seemed to mean more, like they ran deeper than a nonchalant hello.

"Is your Mom expecting me?"

"Yeah." I closed the door. "She's upstairs. She didn't think you'd be here until noon."

Maggie blushed, this time she turned beet red. "Oh...I'm sorry. I was just—"

"It's okay," I cut her off. I didn't dare tell her she'd spared me the minutes waiting for her to arrive. "She'll be down in a minute. Can I get you something? A soda or some water?"

Maggie emitted an almost surprised laugh under her breath and shook her head. "No, but thank you, William. That's really nice."

I shrugged. "Not a big deal. Just let me know if you need anything, okay?"

That tenderness came flooding back. The feeling it gave me was fast becoming addictive.

"Okay," she said.

Inclining my head, I smiled, my fingers itching to reach out and run through her hair.

"Oh, Maggie, I didn't know that was you at the door," Mom said as she appeared at the top of the stairs. She plodded down and stood at the bottom, giving me a look that said it was time I excused myself.

Maggie fidgeted, a timid smile on her face as she looked between my mother and me.

"I'd better let you get to work," I finally conceded, making a move to cross to the stairs, pausing beside Mom. "It was nice to see you again, Maggie."

"It was nice to see you too." She extended a little wave, and I smiled again as I headed upstairs, counting the minutes until I knew she'd come to my room.

Mom wasn't joking when she said I'd turned into a slob. By the time I gathered all the dirty clothes from the floor and piled them in the hamper, threw away the wrappers I left crumpled around the room, and made my bed, the vacuum was whirring in Blake's room.

Anticipation stirred, expectation igniting through my body as I thought of her being just down the hall. So close. I hated the blaring voice that reminded me just how far from my grasp she really was. The way she'd acted on Saturday night had proven it. Still, I wanted her near.

That voice was forgotten when she knocked on my door. "Come in."

This time she wasn't so reserved when she opened it, but allowed herself to quietly appraise my room.

"You are either one of the cleanest guys I've ever met, or you just picked up your room before I got here so I didn't have to do it," she finally said with a slight tease winding through her tone. She glanced at me with the sweetest grin as she set a plastic bucket of cleaning supplies on the floor, then she stepped out to pull the vacuum in behind her.

I dropped my head, chuckling under my breath, before I dragged my hair out of my face and looked up at her from where I sat in the middle of my bed. "No, not the cleanest guy in the world."

"Thought so." There was still that timidity about her, a sadness that emanated in her movements and in her words, but something about her felt different today. It felt like maybe she wanted to show me the girl I'd already seen, the one she hid from everyone else.

I knew what the town said about her and about her family. How much of it was true and what had been fabricated to sate the gossips' thirst, I wasn't sure. Clearly, she was shy, self-conscious, and insecure. But Maggie was no cliché.

"Do you want me to get out of your way?" I asked as I scooted back further in my bed, having no intention of making good on my offer and praying she'd want me to stay as much as I wanted to.

"It's up to you. You're not bothering me." She knelt down to plug in the vacuum. "Just give me a couple of minutes and I'll be out of your hair."

She laughed when I returned her words. "Stay as long as you need. You're not bothering me."

"All right, then."

She flipped on the switch, the vacuum a dull roar as she pushed it back and forth in an overlapping pattern across my floor, every few seconds glancing up at me, that bottom lip between her teeth.

It was all too much, and not nearly enough, Maggie in my room, the energy in the air charged but relaxed. A heated calm. The motor hummed, and I leaned against my headboard and watched as she moved. I could feel it radiating from her, everything I felt, this invisible bond being forged between us.

She flipped off the switch.

I smiled, but the gentle playfulness it held earlier was gone. My head lolled against the headboard, and I stared at this girl I was desperate to understand. My voice rasped. "How old are you, Maggie?"

Frowning, she inclined her head, her eyes searching. "Eighteen. Why?"

A woman. Grown. She seemed so much older, but younger somehow. I couldn't place it. God, she had me mixed up.

"Just...I don't know. Are you going to go to school? Get out of this place?"

Maggie laughed, but the sound was completely devoid of humor. "No, William. Girls like me don't go to school."

"What do you mean, girls like you? Look at you" — I sat up — "you're smart...and...and you're..."

Beautiful and kind and deserved so much better than *this*.

She shook her head and leaned down to grab a dust rag and spray from the bucket. "You don't know anything about me."

Did she understand how much I wanted to?

She turned her back to me and began stacking the notebooks and papers piled randomly across the top of my dresser that sat against the wall, across from the end of my bed. I could see her reflection in the mirror. The sorrow was back, the sadness that made her look old. She sprayed the dresser top and wiped the rag over the surface, keeping her head bowed when she spoke. "I've always taken care of my mom and sister. I don't know how to do anything else."

The distance was too great, the girl too far, and I edged down to sit at the end of my bed. If I reached out, I'd be able to touch her.

I rested my elbows on my knees and tilted my head up so I could see her face through the mirror.

"But if you had the chance...the choice? Would you go?"

Maggie looked up at me. "Of course."

I'd been right that night. Maggie wanted more.

Pressure filled my chest, something that felt unbearable but good.

"Why Troy, Maggie?"

She stilled, her throat bobbing when she swallowed. It felt like an entire minute had passed before she answered. "I don't know...it just...happened."

"He's an asshole." I couldn't stop myself from spitting the words.

"People aren't all bad or all good, William. He's had a rough life."

"Does that make it okay for him to treat you the way he does?"

She squeezed her eyes shut. "No, of course not," wheezed from her mouth. "He hasn't always acted the way he's been acting lately. I just..."

Silence followed, filled up the room with words neither of us knew how to say. Maggie opened her eyes, stared at me through the mirror.

"Do you love him?"

Mom suddenly poked her head in my doorway.

"Are you okay in here?" Concern laced her voice, her attention darting between Maggie and me.

Sighing, I sat back. Mom always had perfect timing.

Maggie surprised me by answering first. "Yeah, we're just talking about school and stuff."

"Oh." Mom stepped back a fraction, seemed confused as she searched Maggie for discomfort. "Well, I'm just right down the hall if you need me."

"Thank you, Mrs. Marsh."

"You're welcome." Mom looked at me again, her lips a thin line, drawn up at the side. It was a warning. Then she nodded and walked down the hall.

Maggie turned around and forced a smile. "I think I'm finished in here."

"Maggie—" I leaned forward.

"It's okay, William. Really...I'm okay."

We both knew it was a lie.

"Listen," she said as she glanced behind her, "I have some more cleaning to do downstairs. Would you mind carrying the vacuum down for me?"

Maggie was waving a big, huge stop sign in my face. She didn't want to talk about it.

Sighing, I climbed to my feet. "Sure."

"Thank you." Her smile was soft.

She didn't seem to mind that I followed her room to room for the rest of the afternoon. She'd laugh as I joked and did anything I could to wipe that sadness from her face. We talked about nothing, everything light, never verging into the topics that weighed so heavily on my mind.

And for a few hours, Maggie was mine.

William ~ June, Six Years Earlier

Tuesday had become my favorite day. I awaited each with barely constrained anticipation. Those mornings, I found I couldn't sleep and would wake with the first call of the sun bleeding in through the narrow slit in my drapes. Then I'd pace the floor until she arrived.

Just like I was doing now.

The rest of the week was agonizing, caught in the paradigm of hoping I'd catch a glimpse of Maggie while I was out, all the while praying I wouldn't. Almost every time I did see her, she was with Troy. Her hand would be wrapped up in his as if it belonged there, even though it was so obvious to me that standing next to Troy was not where she wanted to be.

The worst part was she never so much as batted an eye in my direction when she was with him. Never even gave a hint of acknowledgment to my presence. I understood why, the stifling hostility that roiled between Troy and me. It was so thick there couldn't be a person in the room who wouldn't choke on it. It'd grown over the weeks, the bitterness that tightened his jaw and hardened his eyes.

I wondered if it was obvious to him just how much I wanted his girl.

It was only a matter of Troy walking through the door of wherever we were hanging out and Blake was suddenly ready to leave. I knew to Blake this animosity was not so much about the girl Troy towed alongside him, but the principle behind it. Reluctantly, I would follow my brother out from wherever we'd been, conceding to let the bad blood simmer.

Maggie had been back to the house three times since that first timid knock on my bedroom door. She began coming earlier and earlier each time, lingering a little bit longer before she left. After the conversation we shared in my room, I struggled to maintain safer subjects, giving her space. I learned little snippets of her life. She'd be happy to read all day long, but the thought of taking a math test made her sick to her stomach. I teased her when she revealed she loved Harry Potter, and then she blushed when she admitted she liked to sing. It was a whisper when she told me her little sister was the most important person in her world, saying she'd do absolutely anything for her.

Beneath those everyday words grew an affection I was certain was only noticeable to the two of us.

Giving her that space had become hard to do when I opened the door last Tuesday to find her eyes tear-stained and puffy. I waited until my mom went upstairs, and then I followed Maggie into the kitchen.

"Are you okay?" I'd pled to her back. "Is it Troy?"

She'd only shaken her head, turned and lifted her gaze to mine.

The expression on her face killed me.

"Maggie, please...tell me what's wrong."

"I can't," she'd said, but she hadn't hidden her face, had openly showed me the pain she held there.

I'd just stood there, wishing I could somehow wipe it away.

That place she discovered in me expanded again when the doorbell rang downstairs. I glanced at the clock on my bedside table. Fifteen minutes earlier than the week before. Taking a quick peek at myself in the mirror, I pushed my fingers through my hair while telling myself to get it under control before I bolted out the door.

When I stepped from my room, I paused to listen to the voices coming from downstairs.

"I'm so sorry, Maggie," I heard my mother say. "Lara just called to say she isn't feeling well, and I promised her I'd stand in for her down at the shelter."

"Oh...oh...I'm sorry. I didn't know...," Maggie seemed to ramble, the uncertainty making a resurgence. "I'll just—"

Mom began to speak at the same time. "You can come back or stay, it's up to you." Mom's voice dropped in a sort of ruefulness. "William's here, though. I'm not sure..."

With my gut in knots, I moved forward to watch the interaction over the wall, to see my mother have to look down because she couldn't bear to finish the sentence, to see the embarrassment rush to redden Maggie's cheeks, then to see the resolution take its place. "No. It's fine. I can stay."

Mom looked up. "Are you sure?"

Maggie crossed the threshold. "I'll be fine, Mrs. Marsch. Really."

I wasn't quite sure how to describe the way it made me feel that she chose to stay with me—that she felt safe with me. What I was sure of was it made me sick to think of why she had to contemplate it in the first place.

With my mother away, I ended up spending the entire afternoon trailing Maggie's every move, found myself working beside her while we continued on in nearly constant conversation. I couldn't pull myself away. All I wanted was to be near her, to swim in the attraction saturating the room as it slowly simmered between us. She kept smiling over at me, always shy, but somehow free.

It was almost painful not to reach out to touch her. Instead, I busied my hands and my mouth, helping her straighten the pillows on the back of the couch while I told her about the time Blake and I got busted stealing a street sign off Main when I was in junior high. The words were just to fill the space. In the undertones, there was a plea. Please, open up, talk to me.

I continued on when she shook her head and laughed. "The cop had his flashlight on us, yelling 'Stop,' while Blake was screaming 'Run,' I just stood there, frozen. Blake was so mad it was my fault we got caught."

"I can't believe you two. You were so bad." She grinned at me, those brown eyes warm and amused.

"Blake was constantly causing trouble in high school, and of course, I wanted to be right there beside him. I mean, it wasn't anything super bad, but I think he was grounded more than he wasn't."

Maggie's movements slowed and she squinted her eyes, as if in thought, absentmindedly fluffing a pillow before she tossed it to the couch to grab another. "He seems so different now." She turned to study my face. "You seem different."

I could feel the shift in the air. The attraction flared. Swallowing, I forced myself to keep talking. "Yeah." I thought about Blake in the truck after the bonfire, the way he'd spoken about Grace, how he wanted to marry her, the devotion that had gushed from his mouth. "I guess we're just growing up."

Maggie nodded, seemed lost in memories.

"Maggie," I said, my voice softening as I inhaled through the tension in the room. I'd been tiptoeing around topics, careful not to tread too deep, but I couldn't do it any longer. Continually wondering and worrying about her had begun to wear me down, and I knew Maggie wouldn't just come out and tell me. I had to ask. "You never answered me."

Her face pinched in awareness, but she asked, "What are you talking about?"

"Troy...do you love him?" I could barely get the words out. I thought I knew her well enough to know how she felt, but I was pretty sure I wouldn't know how to handle it if I were wrong.

"William..." She tilted her face down.

"Please, I need to know."

With the slant of her head, her expression was indiscernible, and she barely shook her head, but in it was her answer. No. Again, I didn't understand her or the choices she made.

"Then...why don't you just break up with him? I know" — my hand fisted as I emphasized the word — "you don't want to be with him, Maggie. Break up with him...please."

Maggie inclined her head so she could look over at me. "It's not that easy, William."

Old wounds filled her eyes.

Her family was the root of it all, I was sure, what brought on the sadness that haunted her eyes. What made her think someone like Troy was good enough for her. What made her believe breaking up with some loser wasn't that easy. How could I convince her otherwise if I didn't know the truth?

"Will you tell me about them...what your family's like? I mean...I've heard stuff..." I trailed off, feeling sick when I realized I'd pushed her too far.

She stilled, and her face paled. She turned ashen white. Her hands trembled and the pillow slipped to the ground.

"Maggie..."

She squeezed her eyes shut, then fled from the living room into the kitchen with her hand covering her mouth.

Stupid...careless. I cursed at myself as I sank down onto the couch. So foolish to broach a subject I knew she wouldn't want to talk about. But I was desperate to know her — to really know her. But then I had to admit I was probably ill-prepared for what I might learn.

I warred with the urge to go in the kitchen, to offer her comfort, to tell her she could tell me anything and I'd never think any less of her. I forced myself to sit still and wait for her to decide.

Three minutes later she returned, hesitant as she approached me. She stopped a foot away from where I sat and apologized to the floor. "I'm so sorry, I..." She glanced at the front door. "I should go."

I grabbed her wrist, not hard enough to restrain her, but firm enough so she knew I wanted her to stay. Just the slight contact was enough to knock the wind from me.

What had this girl done to me?

I stared up at her, pleading without words, hating the monster inside her that caused her to believe she was worth anything less than what she was, wishing she would see what I saw. Wished she wouldn't hide. I recovered my voice, though it was broken, choppy with emotion.

"Don't leave."

Her eyes dropped closed, I feared as another means of escape. Instead, she shocked me by twisting out of my grasp to weave her fingers through mine.

A moment was spent contemplating the connection, the surge of warmth that rushed straight to my heart and settled in the pit of my stomach, before I looked back at her face to find her staring down at me.

"Tell me you feel this, too." I wet my lips and tried to make sense of how I felt. "Because I can't stop thinking about you."

Slowly, she untwined our fingers, and Maggie took a step forward to stand between my knees, moving to hold my face between her hands. They were warm and trembled against my cheeks. Her touch was soft, as gentle as her eyes, just as gentle as the cautious hands I placed on her hips.

Everything thrummed and sped—my nerves, my heart, and my mind.

Locks of hair fell all around her face when she leaned in, and I reached up with the intention of brushing it back, but I couldn't stop myself from winding my fingers through the auburn waves just because I needed to *feel*.

Yes.

So soft.

Desire prickled over my skin.

I cupped the back of her head and slid the hand at her hip around her waist. I was so far out of my element, and I cautioned myself to move slow, knowing Maggie was nothing like any of the girls I'd dated in the past.

"William," she whispered. She hovered two inches from my face, wavering, rocking in indecision, before she pressed her lips to mine.

The close-mouthed kiss felt both innocent and obscene, something stolen, forbidden. It was the single most intimate moment I'd ever shared with anyone. We lingered, breathing into each other, our hands shaking and pulses thundering.

I wanted to weep from the loss of contact when she pulled away.

Visible panic welled up in her, that old sadness darkening her face when she touched her fingertips to her lips, the pain in her eyes when she took one fumbling step back.

"Maggie," I implored, reaching out. "Please don't do this."

She squeezed her eyes shut and fisted one hand at her side, as if she were struggling to find something to say, before she turned and ran.

William ~ Present Day, Later That Night

It was that moment six years ago when I realized it was too late and there was nothing I could do. I'd fallen for the first time in my life and I'd fallen hard. That fall had left me battered and scarred. Had left me with a child I didn't even know.

I lay on my stomach across the length of the couch, hugging a pillow with my face buried deep.

The wind gusted and shook the window pane.

It suddenly occurred to me that I'd become just as good at hiding as she was.

Chapter Eleven

Maggie ~ Present Day

I stared out the passenger window of Troy's truck after we left the pizza place. Buildings whizzed by as a blur of obtuse shapes and flashing neon lights. I ignored the churning anger emanating from Troy, the tendons on the back of his hands flexing and tensing as he gripped the steering wheel. I pretended I had no reason to believe anything was wrong. Troy had never given what happened between him and William that summer any acknowledgement.

In his wounded pride, he had glossed over the incident as if it'd never occurred. It was one of the few times life had ever cut me a break. I knew Troy had his suspicions. The contention between him and William had always revolved around me, but for once, Troy's ego had been my safeguard, keeping watch over the one secret I'd protect with my life. Troy was dying to vocalize it, I knew, to curse William's name and his sudden reappearance, but saying it aloud would only be a testament to the one person who had ever dared to put Troy back in his place.

It seemed both a miracle and a punishment that I hadn't run into William the entire week. The time had been spent wondering whether he'd stayed or gone, both longing to see him and contending with an all-consuming fear of what would happen if I did. I couldn't really make sense of the feeling, how I was so torn between an intense desire to catch even a single glimpse of his face and the ardent prayer he had gone.

I listened to the gossip whenever I went out and engaged in conversations I normally would have avoided. No one had so much as breathed his name.

As preoccupied as I had been with watching for him, it was no surprise that I spotted William's car the second Troy pulled into the parking lot at the pizza place. Maybe I should have come up with an excuse to keep Troy out of that restaurant. Then he wouldn't be seething beside me and I wouldn't be so damned sick to my stomach. But in the moment, the need to see William outweighed any rational thought.

I glanced over at Troy as he jammed the gear of his truck into park under the detached carport outside our house.

"Goddamn it," he swore at nothing at all, then he jumped from the truck. Slamming the door shut behind him, he stormed up to the house, jerked the back screen door open, and disappeared inside.

It'd been worth it.

I'd been so scared of seeing William again. I was terrified over what he would say and what he would do, and I hadn't expected the relief I felt when I'd seen him there with his family where he belonged, taking up the space my choices had driven him from so long ago.

And I was sure I'd do just about anything for that instant when William and I had been caught up and lost to each other, when, with just a look, he'd taken me back to how we'd once been.

I sat fixated on the empty space between the carport and house that Troy had just occupied, the winter air seemingly inflamed by his anger. The tire swing pitched and rocked from where it hung beneath the massive tree that took up most of our small backyard, the tree's branches pummeled by a sudden gust of harsh wind that followed in Troy's wake. Sadness swelled within my chest. I'd bore witness to that type of anger my entire life. Still I couldn't grasp from where it could come.

Troy had been left just as damaged by his childhood as I had been. Sometimes I saw it beneath the hatred in his eyes — remorse. But the icy bitterness was too thick for regret to ever break through. He'd forever hold us captive in this miserable life.

"Mommy...isss cold," Jonathan complained, breaking the silence from the backseat of the truck.

I shook myself from my thoughts and turned to smile at him, reaching out to brush his cool cheek with the back of my hand. "I'm sorry, baby. Let's get you inside."

CR≈80

I tugged the blankets up to Jonathan's chin. He snuggled down into the covers and grinned up at me, and I gently swept the hair back from his forehead.

"Tell me your favorite part of today," I murmured into the dimly lit room. On the floor on my knees, I leaned against the edge of his bed. I wound a lock of my son's silky hair through my fingers, felt the wistful smile playing at my lips. I loved these quiet moments, when the two of us would shut the door behind us and lock out the rest of the world, when I rested and remembered the things I did have to be thankful for. These times felt like mine and Jonathan's special secret as we spoke in hushed voices and honest words. It was a sanctuary never invaded. Not even by Troy.

Jonathan twisted his brow up, concentrating, as if his answer were the most important thing in the world. His eyes lit. "I liked eating pizza."

I chuckled and my smile spread. I tickled his sides. "You do love pizza, don't you?"

A subdued laugh broke free from his mouth, and he nodded his head vigorously as he rolled onto his side to protect himself from my playful attack. "Yes, Momma...is' my favorite," he whispered as he giggled and squirmed beneath my gentle fingers.

My love surged, tingled all the way from my fingertips brushing his sides and traveled to my toes.

Gasping for breath, Jonathan stopped to gulp for air then fell into another fit of repressed laughter when I tickled him again. We might as well have been elementary school children at a sleepover, buried beneath a blanket with a flashlight, trying to stay as quiet as possible so we wouldn't be caught staying up long after we'd been told to go to bed.

"Mommy," he wheezed, clutching my hands when he finally had enough. He sat up, his little hands still gripping mine. His head was cocked to the side with an adorable grin drawing up only one side of his mouth, his hair sticking up everywhere in a tousled mess.

I laughed and smoothed it down.

"All done?" I asked. I straightened his twisted covers so he could get situated back in bed.

He climbed in. The smile never faded from his face, even when he yawned. "Yep."

Yes.

I adored these times.

I kissed his forehead and whispered, "Goodnight," against his baby soft skin.

"Night, Mommy," he said, sinking down and cuddling into the warmth of his blankets. I began to stand when Jonathan grabbed my hand. "Wait, Mommy," he said, almost frantic, "we forgot your part."

Oh.

I sank back to my knees. I wondered if my expression was the same as his had been when he'd asked the same question, because to me, my favorite parts of the day *had* been the most important things in the world. I sighed and drew my lips together in thought. Was it wrong to share this with my son?

"I had two favorite parts," I finally said as I fiddled with a loose thread at the corner of his blanket. "*This*," I murmured, softly nudging his chin with my knuckle. He wiggled in unabashed pleasure, expecting my invariable answer. "And..." I weighed what to say, settled on sharing the snippet of joy I felt. "I saw a friend today. That made me happy."

I swallowed the lump that formed in my throat and glanced away.

Friend.

I fought the moisture threatening my eyes.

"He used to be, anyway."

God. Maybe this was the worst thing I could do, rambling to my son about the man who'd confronted me a week before, demanding to know if Jonathan was his. But I'd held it in for too long and it felt too good to let it out. Just once to give voice to William, a declaration that what we'd shared had been real.

Jonathan frowned in a searching way. "The friend…that's…mad at you?" he asked.

I grimaced and ran my fingers through his hair, not surprised by the conclusion he'd drawn. I knew I was crossing a line by speaking this aloud, but I at least owed Jonathan this. I saw the fear that had widened his eyes when I sped away from William before. Jonathan had strained in his seat to get a better look at the man who stood staring at us as we left him behind. Then tonight Jonathan had seemed unable to look away from him when we walked into the restaurant. It had only increased. It was as if a tether of awareness had linked them when Jonathan stared out the window at William who stood unmoving in the parking lot. It was almost unbearable to witness the way William had looked at Jonathan. I wanted to hide my son away from the protective longing that lined William's face, because I'd seen it before when William shined his light into my life six years before. William was not going to give up.

"Yes…Mommy did something that made him very sad a long time ago."

"How come?" Sadness slowly seeped into Jonathan's features, as if he couldn't comprehend I had done something to harm another person and this news had chipped a little away at the complete faith he had in me. As difficult as it was admitting my faults to my son, I knew it was a given opportunity to instill something in him that I'd always lacked. I wasn't going to waste it.

"Because I was too scared to do what I knew was right…too scared to fight for what I wanted." I lowered myself to look him fully in the eye. "I wasn't brave enough." And how I wished I'd been. Shifting, I took his small face in my hands and stressed the words. "But you're brave, Jonathan. You can do *anything* you want...you just have to decide...decide how you want to be treated."

Jonathan seemed confused, as if he didn't understand — or maybe he just disagreed.

His attention went to the door and to the one who lurked behind it just outside this little haven. "Is your friend...bad?" he whispered low, cowering as he made the obvious comparison.

A skitter of emotions flashed through my body, guilt and sorrow and overpowering bitterness.

"No, baby, he isn't bad."

Unable to hold myself together any longer, I leaned in and brushed my lips across his forehead. "You should get some rest, sweetheart."

"'Kay, Mommy." He rolled over and tugged the covers over his shoulder.

Everything felt heavy as I forced myself to stand. Up until then, neither of us had ever voiced our fears out loud. We acknowledged it in the tears we shed together. Soothed it in the way we clung to each other when we wiped those tears away.

I hadn't been prepared to hear my son call his father bad.

I found myself with my back pressed against Jonathan's bedroom wall, biting my fist to keep from weeping aloud as I watched my son sleep in the shadows of his room. He tossed fitfully, as if the darkness had sucked him under and held him hostage in this nightmare that was our life. He whimpered from somewhere in the blackness of his mind.

Trembling, I forced myself from the room and into the equally darkened hall. I drew in a sharp, shocked breath when I noticed Troy hovering as a quivering ball of aggression on the brink, just inside the living room.

I shook as he approached. His steps were menacing, purposed as he slowly stalked toward me. Splaying one hand across my chest, he pushed me back against the wall. His breaths were ragged as he loomed over me.

His mouth descended on mine. Forceful. Hot. Angry.

It took everything not to cry out. This was how he would take his frustration out on me. He'd mark me, claim me—assert I was his without ever saying a word.

Pulling me into our room, he pushed me onto the bed. He never seemed to mind that I lay limp while he consumed me, and I couldn't help but think that was the way he wanted it.

Only once had I fought him, and, in the end, I'd lost everything. Now I didn't even try. I focused on the distorted spot on the wall, one I wasn't sure was really there.

His hands became impatient in the normally controlled violence. His voice was harsh and out of place. "Maggie, look at me."

I pinned my cheek to the bed and squeezed my eyes shut, seeking refuge in my mind.

"I said look at me." His fingers were at my jaw, and his nails dug into my skin as he forced me to turn to him. His brown eyes were wild yet sharp and defined. "Do you see me? I'm never going to let you go, Maggie. Never."

As if I didn't already understand that. He'd made it perfectly clear what he would do if I ever tried to leave again.

He shuddered, rolled from me, sated, his anger quenched.

He just passed the anger on to me.

I faced away from him, and Troy draped his arm around my waist and pulled me against his chest.

Nuzzling his nose in my hair, he kissed my neck and mumbled, "I love you so much, baby," close to my ear. I cringed as I was overcome by memories and regret.

One of the hardest things to stomach was he actually believed he did.

He drew me tighter before his breaths evened out, and he fell asleep.

I let the tears come, listened to the wind beat at the walls of this house, the words silent on my lips. "No, you don't."

Maggie ~ June, Six Years Earlier

I held my breath when I felt him. My senses keened with William's presence, prickling in awareness as I felt his eyes burning into me from behind.

Though the way he watched me now was different. This time it was with a sadness I hated was there.

Moving through his house, I kept my face downturned as I worked. My mind was so twisted up in confusion that I didn't know up from down or inside from out. I didn't know myself.

He'd brought something out in me I hadn't known existed, and I didn't know what to do with it. I wished I were brave enough to look at him. I wished I could find even an ounce of the courage I'd found in myself last week.

Kissing William was the bravest thing I'd ever done.

It was also the most honest.

In the house I grew up in, I'd learned to hide. The quieter I was, the less attention I received. My mom tried to show us love in the moments she wasn't fighting for her own life, but every effort was overshadowed by my father. Even her attempts at affection had become unwelcome, because they only drew more attention to me. So I never asked for anything and only took what I was given—which was usually the last thing I wanted.

But with William I'd *taken*, giving into something I'd wanted since I met him—to feel his skin under my hands. I'd longed to touch him, even just a gentle brush of skin. I wanted to know if it'd feel anything like the way I imagined it would.

I doubted William understood what he'd come to mean to me over the last few weeks. How important he'd become. I doubted he knew how much I looked forward to the moment when I'd see him again. I couldn't wait until he smiled at me with those soft brown eyes and made me laugh.

He had made me feel not only special, but almost normal, as well.

Then he'd asked about my parents. He said he'd *heard*. It had shocked me from that fantasy, reminding me of just how far from *normal* I was.

So ashamed, I ran into his kitchen and wished I could disappear from his house forever, whisked away to some unknown spot where I'd never have to face him again. I'd intended on fleeing out the back door, but then thought I at least owed him an apology.

No one had ever treated me as if I were a person.

To my father, I was a puppet, a plaything reserved for his sadistic mind. To my mother, I was the one who picked up the pieces, helped her to bed when she couldn't stand, lied for her the way I'd been taught to do since I was just a little girl. To the town, I was a rumor, at best, a charity case.

But William never looked at me as if I were any of those things.

He looked at me as if he actually saw *me*.

Then he had touched me, and the same warmth I felt brimming in his eyes had overflowed, wrapped me up and made me whole.

When I opened my eyes to find him staring up at me and he breathed our connection aloud, I'd had to show him and make him understand.

It'd taken all of about fifteen seconds for fear to take hold.

I'd fought it. I wanted so badly to stay — to smile and just be *normal*.

But I'd run.

Coming back today had been hard. Every bit of will I had was put into lifting my finger to ring the doorbell.

Now he watched me with an unease I wished I could erase. I'd do anything to take us back to how we'd been before, when he'd treated me like a friend and not some weak, damaged girl he had to tiptoe around.

Something broke apart inside when he finally escaped upstairs, the blunt click of his door shutting me out.

"You're such a fool, Maggie," I muttered to myself. Wanting something more with someone I knew I could never really have, and then screwing it up when he offered me a little taste of it.

William was so far out of my league.

The teenaged girl in me knew he was gorgeous. He was tall and lean, though I'd seen the strength when he'd stood up for me. His muscles had bristled and flexed beneath his skin. His face was equally as strong, though his cheeks still held a bit of roundness, a fading trace of youth that gave him a boyish, subtle charm. But in his gentle eyes, I saw something much deeper than all of that. William was kind and beautiful and smart and deserved someone a thousand times better than me — deserved someone who could actually look him in the eye.

I shuffled toward the kitchen. Mrs. Marsch sat at the table. Bills and invoices were spread out around her.

"I'm finished, Mrs. Marsch," I called quietly from the safety of the archway, feeling too timid to make my way in without being invited.

With a smile, William's mother looked up and beckoned me in with a wave. "Oh, thank you, Maggie. You don't know how great it's been having you here to help out." She turned her attention back to writing a check while she continued to speak. "With my filling in for Lara over at the thrift store, I can't seem to get anything done around here...and you know how messy my boys are."

I approached her and stopped a couple of feet away, feeling more self-conscious than normal after what had happened with William the week before. I wondered if she'd be disgusted if she knew I kissed her son. "I'm glad to help...and I really appreciate the job," I added.

A warmth so similar to the one I felt with William spread over me when Mrs. Marsch brought her attention back to me, and her head tilted to the side. "Are you feeling okay today, Maggie?" she asked as she handed me a check.

Under her watch, I somehow didn't feel like a rumor or a charity case.

I forced myself to smile and meet her eye. "I'm fine...thank you. I'm just a little tired is all."

Mrs. Marsch's mouth turned up in understanding. "Well, you know you can let me know if you ever need anything, don't you?"

I bit my lip and dropped my gaze to the floor, and I mumbled, "Yes, Ma'am."

A modest, friendly laugh tinkled from her mouth. "Please, call me Glenda."

Nodding slightly, I said, "Thank you...Glenda."

"Anytime."

Walking back out into the main room, I glanced up in the direction of William's room. I hated that I felt like this, hated I wanted something so badly, hated I was too scared to do anything about it.

On a heavy breath, I turned away. My feet were sluggish as I headed to the front door. Relief and uncertainty flooded me when I felt him emerge from behind. For a moment, I stilled with my hand on the knob before I gathered myself enough to look over my shoulder. He stood at the top of the stairs. His expression was pained as he searched my face.

Maybe I was a fool, but right then, I didn't care if I was. I'd never exposed myself to anyone. I had lived my life entire life in secrecy, and for once, I wanted to share myself with someone.

I wanted William to know.

Twisting the knob, I stepped out into the afternoon sun and rested the door partially open. I took the chance he would understand.

Humidity clung as a thin mist on my skin as I made my way up the sidewalk. Wrapping my arms around my middle, I hugged myself, watching my feet as they made contact with the concrete. Anxiety threatened to grip me when I felt him follow.

This is what you wanted, I had to remind myself when I got to the end of the street, trying to calm my natural instinct to hide. Staring ahead, I waited until I felt him near, then I darted across the intersecting street.

On the other side was my sanctuary.

Summer had taken hold, and only a couple families braved the blistering heat. A mother pushed a small child on the swing, and two older children climbed the stairs to the slide. I slinked behind them unnoticed, following the path that ran to the back of the playground. At its end rose a wood. It was dense and thick from the small river that ran deeper in the thicket.

I felt William at a distance behind me. His own apprehension was radiating in every step.

The ground softened beneath my feet when the path ended, and I traipsed through the wild grasses. The air shifted and cooled as the sun's rays were blocked by the trees overhead. Children's laughter filtered through the branches and leaves, obscured and distorted.

I sank down out of view behind the massive fallen oak. Velvety moss blanketed its sides, padding my back as I leaned heavily against its safety. Soft grass cushioned the ground floor, and lush-leaved branches created a canopy overhead.

Closing my eyes, I released a relieved breath into the welcomed seclusion.

I didn't need to open my eyes to know he was there. I could feel him standing above me.

Allowing my eyes to drift open, I watched in my periphery as he settled facing me, just off to the side. He left a small space between us.

Minutes ticked on as we sat in the stillness. The only movement was the birds flying overhead and rustling through the leaves.

"This is where I come to hide from my father," I finally said, still staring out into the distance, though I felt him stiffen with my assertion. I plucked a blade of grass and rolled it to a wet pulp between my fingers. "I always feel safe here...even at night."

A weighted silence followed my admission. In it, he waited, seeming to understand I needed time. I'd never admitted it aloud, and even though I was aware everyone suspected it, making it form on my lips felt like the hardest thing I'd ever done. Funny how the lies bled so easily from my mouth but the truth fought to remain hidden. But the lies had been ingrained so deeply through fear and shame they'd almost become my truth.

I hugged my knees to my chest. He'd asked about my family, and I was going to tell him.

"My father," I began, squeezing my eyes shut, "he's...sick." William inhaled sharply beside me, but I continued on, "So angry." I glanced in his direction as I wet my lips. "I don't understand it...how...how someone can find satisfaction in hurting someone else. When he hits my mother, it's like...like he gains strength from it." I shook my head to shake off the chills that flashed over my skin, and I couldn't stop tears from gathering in my eyes.

William drifted a little closer. I could feel the heat from his skin, but he still wasn't close enough to touch.

I choked over the sob in my throat as I tried to speak, completely unprepared for the onslaught of emotions that came with finally telling *someone*.

"He feeds on fear...on my fear...my sister's fear...my mother's fear." I wiped the tears from my eyes and rubbed the wetness onto my shorts. A fresh round took their place. "For my mother, it's his fists, his words. With me and my sister"—a shudder racked my chest, the words ripped from my mouth— "he touches."

I swallowed and looked at William through bleary eyes, seeing the shock and disgust he tried to mask on his face. "It's like he needs the control...the reaction...to see us cry."

Unbridled emotion rushed from his mouth, like he couldn't contain the thought. "Does he—"

"No," I shot out faster than he could finish, knowing from the horrified expression on his face what he was going to ask. I pinched my eyes closed and forced away the image of my greatest fear—my father climbing into my bed rather than getting onto his knees beside it.

For the longest time we sat there, until he finally asked the one question I knew was inevitable. "Why haven't you told anyone?"

I'd expected it to feel like an accusation, but somehow coming from William, it didn't. I bit at my lip and kind of shrugged. "When you're raised the way I was, everything is a secret. It was a secret before I knew it was wrong."

"God, Maggie. I can't stand that this happened to you." He stretched a tentative hand toward me and seemed to search my face for permission.

I lifted my eyes to him. For the first time in my life, I was completely open, hiding nothing. I wanted him to know *me*. When he gently spread the palm of his hand over my knee, it jarred another part of my guarded heart loose. I could feel it—his compassion—his sorrow—his anger as it seeped against my skin.

"I didn't want to believe it. Or..." He blinked for a long second, and then he forced out the words, "I guess I just hoped it wasn't true."

Most people didn't want to believe it. I figured that was why they accepted the lies so easily. The few times the cops had shown up at our door after Mom had been screaming, they'd just swallowed the ridiculous stories she stuffed down their throats. It seemed easier to believe them than to deal with the truth.

Aside from William, I could remember only one time when someone had really cared to know. I was in third grade, and I'd been called to the office. I was shaking, petrified I'd done something wrong and I was about to get into trouble as I made my way to the front office with the pink slip in my hand. But instead of the principle being in his office, a woman was there, her voice soft as she asked me questions. I realized now she was a social worker, though I hadn't understood at the time she was there to help me. The one chance I had, and I'd blown it. I'd been too scared to even open my mouth and had shaken my head vehemently with every question she asked. Had I just nodded once, maybe our lives would have been different. Maybe I'd have saved my sister, my mom, myself.

Of course, that was when the rumors started and the girls at school began to look at me like I was different.

And the other was William. He had asked, and somehow he made me brave enough to tell. Maybe it wouldn't change our lives, save my mom and my sister from the secrets that happened within the walls of our house, but somehow I felt changed. I didn't know...relieved? And right then, I felt...safe. No other man had ever made me feel that way. But William did.

I focused on the spot where his hand met my skin. I couldn't comprehend the connection we shared, and I couldn't understand why this felt so right. Some of the thoughts I had about him terrified me. They were so foreign. I gulped for the air his caress seemed to have stolen and whispered toward the forest, "I, I've never had a friend before."

I risked a glance in his direction.

His eyes overflowed with emotion, so much I had to look away. He squeezed my knee, and I knew he understood.

Because I did *feel* it, too. I was just too scared to give myself over to it.

"Come here," he said, and he pulled me against his chest and rested me between his knees.

I twisted and buried my face in his shirt, allowing myself to cry. But this time it wasn't for fear or pain. It was in release. His hold was soft but secure. He kissed the top of my head and mumbled, "I'll be whatever you need me to be."

He held me for what seemed forever, but when he released me, it hadn't been nearly long enough.

೧൫

Maggie ~ July, Six years earlier

I crept below the midnight sky. My movements quickened in anticipation. Ghosting along the line of trees, I checked over my shoulder to be sure I remained unseen, before I slipped into the darkened forest. Twigs snapped below my feet and bushes brushed across my bare legs.

My heart beat fast. Too fast for what I'd convinced myself *this* was.

Moonlight leaked between the twisted branches and struck as a radiant glow over William's face when I stepped out into our spot.

My thrumming heart fluttered.

"Hey you," he said into the muted light. A smile spread over his beautiful face. He was propped up against the tree trunk, and his legs were stretched out in a V front of him.

"Hey," I exhaled in a whispered breath.

For the better part of a month, we had been meeting here, stealing away every chance we got. Each day, while Troy and my father worked, we were here, and each night, long after our families were asleep, we would lie beneath the cover of trees and talk for hours.

It'd become all I looked forward to. My nerves raced as I waited for the moment to arrive, and those same nerves were soothed with just one look from William.

As I walked toward him, he raised both arms up to me. I didn't hesitate to climb down in the refuge I found in them. I exhaled in what sounded like relief when I was nestled in his arms. Tingles spread and butterflies tumbled in my stomach when our skin met.

"How was the rest of your day?" he asked.

"Good," I said with as much enthusiasm as I could find, sensing the little tic of worry that came with his question—his worry that I'd been hurt in some way since we'd seen each other earlier that day. I didn't mention Troy had shown up at my doorstep at six, insisting on taking me to dinner. I couldn't stand the look on William's face whenever he knew I'd been out with Troy.

The only thing I hated worse was his reaction when he actually saw Troy and me together, the cloud that would gather over him, that cloud that crowded out his warmth. I knew it was my weakness to completely end things with Troy that put it there, but the further I tried to push Troy away, the more possessive he became. I kept trying to end it, but my mouth didn't know how. I knew he was going to be angry, and when he stood in front of me, the words I rehearsed at home died on my tongue. Confronting him with what I wanted was what scared me the most. But I knew I had to do something. I couldn't continue on like this...feeling like this about William and having Troy my boyfriend.

For my sake, William and I had labeled ourselves friends, but I knew what we shared was so much greater than friendship, and that the sanctuary I found in this quiet place had slowly become him. I couldn't bear the thought of someone taking this away from me, so I kept it inside and hid the one thing I had in my life that was of any importance. *William.*

Shifting, William pulled me down to lay beside him. Dampness seeped through my shirt and shorts from the cool grass below, and I burrowed into William's side, somehow completed in his comfort.

"What did you do tonight?" I asked, gravitating toward his warmth.

He somehow managed to pull me closer. His mouth tickled the skin just below my ear, and he had his hand splayed across the small of my back.

I tried to hide the way my body trembled. I wondered if he noticed the effect he had on me.

"Hung out with my family, mostly. My Aunt Lara was over, and my dad's changing shifts, so he didn't have to get to bed early, so we ended up having a little barbeque out front. Grace was there. It was pretty cool." He nuzzled his nose in that sensitive spot at my jaw. Goosebumps sprung up along my arms. "It would have been better if you were there," he murmured.

What I wouldn't give to have something like Blake and Grace, to be normal and free. Free and with William.

"Yeah, I would have really liked that. You have a good family, William." I threaded my fingers through his hair and played with the ends, thankful someone I cared about this much had the things he deserved.

He leaned up to look at my face. His expression was soft, like he was aware of the things that made the two of us so different. "I know I do. I'll never take them for granted."

I felt a wistful smile tremor at the edge of my mouth, and William drew me close again.

He told me about the rest of his evening, the show he'd watched while he waited for our time to arrive and the magazine he'd read. Every word he spoke, even the most trivial, seemed like the most important thing. I listened to his voice, got lost in him — lost in his light.

"Tell me about L.A.," I said. We'd spoken of so many things, but never about the future. Summer had begun to speed away, each day shorter than the last, and the cruel reality that I was going to lose the first joy I'd ever had was slowly creeping into my consciousness. I couldn't begin to imagine what my life was going to be like once he was gone.

William propped himself on his elbow, and I rolled onto my back. He looked down at me as he ran his fingers through my hair with his free hand. The gesture warmed me all the way through.

"It's...huge. Crowded, but kind of open at the same time." He smiled, and with the tilt of his head, an errant lock of hair fell over just one eye.

I brushed my fingers through it to push it back.

"The people out there are so different...you can have a table of men in business suits and a guy completely tattooed and pierced sitting with them and nobody seems to notice. There's always something to do." He chuckled and caressed his knuckles down my jaw. "You would never get bored there."

I grinned and leaned into his touch, trying to imagine a place where nobody cared about another's business. It sounded pretty amazing. Somehow the thought also made me incredibly sad.

"Are you going to stay there?" I asked, knowing in the way my voice faltered I'd given myself away.

"I..." He hesitated as he glanced askew before he looked back down at me. "I used to think so, now I'm not so sure."

He placed his palm flat across my stomach. The contact scorched all the way through my shirt. Weeks ago, when Troy had kissed me and slid his hand under my shirt, I'd nearly had a panic attack. It'd felt too familiar and wrong. Now I couldn't help but wonder what it'd feel like if William did the same.

I shivered, scared that I wanted him to try.

I closed my eyes and found my voice. "Is there...someone...out there?"

I opened them to find him staring down at me.

He drew his lips together and shook his head. "There was a girl I was kind of seeing. We broke it off when I left."

"Did you..." I trailed off, biting at my lip in embarrassment. I didn't even know why I felt compelled to ask, but the thought had been plaguing me ever since I'd kissed him.

"Well, yeah," he said, almost as if he were surprised by my questioning, as if it were ridiculous to think otherwise.

Of course it would be ridiculous — to everyone but me. I suddenly felt small, naïve, sheltered inside my messed-up little world. I screwed my face up to block out the overwhelming jealousy I wasn't prepared to feel.

Behind my lids, I saw visions I didn't want to see. In the nonchalance of his words, I knew there'd been many more than this one girl. An agonizing pain stabbed itself somewhere deep in my chest.

William suddenly wrenched himself away and sat up. He swore into the distance and dragged his hands through his hair before he cut his eyes back down to me.

"Do you think it doesn't *kill* me to think of you with Troy?"

Sickness at the thought clawed its way up my spine and settled on my face as I locked my lips together and shook my head.

"Never," I forced out, unable to even imagine giving that part of myself to Troy.

"What?" William jerked around to completely face to me.

"Never." This time I whispered the word and answered the charged question for what it was.

Never. No one.

"Shit...Maggie."

I startled when he lunged at me, and then I sank into his warmth when he pulled me close and covered me with his body.

"What have you done to me?" he said. It sounded like a plea where he caressed his warm mouth against my jaw and mumbled the words, desperation in the affection that wasn't quite a kiss.

My stomach tightened and my heart beat fast.

I couldn't speak because it was him who had undone me.

Chapter Twelve

William ~ Present Day

The day after I asked Blake if his offer on the guesthouse still stood, I pulled into his driveway. Here the houses were smaller than in our parents' neighborhood, some beginning to appear rundown, though most were well-kept. Trees stretched from one yard to another across the narrow road. Blake had always been a hard-worker, and his home bore the evidence of that. The bushes were trimmed and the grass mowed, the paint on the front porch fresh and bright.

Emma ran down the porch steps and across the front lawn. I couldn't help but think how cute she was with her black hair flying behind her. I could see her excitement with my arrival through the wide-spaced slats of the white wooden fence.

I smiled when I stepped from my car. "Hey there, Emma. How are you today?"

She peered at me with one eye through a slat. I could tell she was grinning.

"Hi, Uncle Will."

I looked down at her from over the fence.

"Guess what? I helped Mommy get the little house all ready for you. We cleaned it *all* day, and Mommy let me use the duster."

I felt the tug, rubbed my hand over my chest.

"You did?" My voice lightened into a tone that should have felt unnatural, but somehow it didn't. "That was very nice of you, sweetheart. Thank you."

She released an abashed giggle as Blake crossed the yard and unlatched the gate.

"You made it." He still seemed a little surprised I had carried through with my plans to stay.

Releasing a long breath through my nose, I roamed my eyes over my brother's home—now my home. "I'm here."

Blake laughed and clapped me on the shoulder as he passed, walking toward the rear of my SUV. "Why are you so serious all the time, Will?" Blake glanced at me as he lugged the one suitcase I had out of the tailgate. "To think Mom was worried she was sending her youngest son off into the land of drugs and rock and roll, and you came back the lamest person I know."

"Shut up." I shook my head and chuckled as I grabbed my suitcase from him.

Blake grinned that same shit-eating grin that he'd taunted me with since we were boys, the one that said he'd gladly kick my ass if he needed to, the same one that said we'd always be the closest of friends no matter what happened in between.

I smiled back.

CRS80

I grabbed a couple of shirts from the suitcase I had laid out on the bed and turned toward the closet.

Blake hadn't been joking. The guesthouse was small, basically encompassed in one room except for a tiny bathroom in the back. The head of a large bed was pushed up in the middle of the right wall, and an oversized cushioned chair sat in the corner beside it, angled to face the built-in fireplace by the door. What could barely be construed as a kitchen was tucked in the far left front corner, and an armoire closet ran along the back wall.

But Blake was right. It was better than being cooped up in my old bedroom at my parents', and it felt like paradise compared to the house I'd lived in for the last six years. I knew I was unhappy there, but distancing myself from that world made it clear just how miserable I'd been.

There was a small rap on the front door.

"Come in," I called as I pulled a hanger from the closet and slipped a shirt on it.

All afternoon the girls had run in and out without knocking, and Blake had waltzed in unannounced several times, so I already expected it to be Grace. From the sound of the cautious footsteps on the old hardwood floors, I knew I was right. I glanced over my shoulder at my sister-in-law.

"These just came out of the dryer," she said when her wary eyes flicked up to meet mine. She set a pile of folded towels on the bed. "Sorry I didn't get them out to you sooner. There's no laundry out here, so you're going to have to do it inside." She scooted back toward the door. "Let me know if you need anything else."

That was something I'd always liked about Grace. She was genuine, never fake. That honesty was still apparent, though now it filled the room with her distrust. I could tell she was struggling to overcome it, to accept me back, the same way Blake had.

"Thank you, Grace," I called quietly from across the room. I glanced around. "The place is great. I hope you know how much I appreciate all of this."

She paused in the doorway and looked back at me as if she still couldn't understand, though she offered a small nod. "You're welcome, Will."

After I unpacked, I lit a fire and closed the door to shut out the slight chill that filled the air as night approached. I stood at the window, staring out over Blake's backyard and to the rear of his house. Sound traveled from within, Emma crying, the clatter of pots in the kitchen, an echoed voice.

I was incredibly thankful for what Blake had done for me, the way he'd welcomed me in and given me a place to stay. Still, I felt utterly alone.

I wished for a way to ease the isolation, a way to ease the fear. Wished for an answer.

I dropped down into the chair with my elbows on my knees, held my head in my hands.

My first instinct was to go to the police, but what would I say? That I believed someone was in danger? Someone I hadn't spoken to in years? Someone I was certain would deny it if I did try to report it?

When I left for California that final time, my goal had been to put as many miles between Maggie and me as possible. To separate myself from the life she had chosen. I'd been so angry. After everything, how could she have picked Troy over me? But at the heart of it had always been my worry for her, the fear she'd traded her father's savage hand in favor of a brutal one.

Her reaction in front of my parent's house had proven it.

God. I was so stuck.

Blowing the air from my lungs, I slumped back in the chair. I knew something had to give. I couldn't just stand by — stay here and do nothing.

Flames flickered and cast shadows across the tiny room, warmed my face. I closed my eyes. The fire danced and played behind my lids. There I saw Maggie as I did the first time I'd seen her, when the fire had lit her face and kissed her cheeks. The night my life was permanently changed.

I missed her.

Wanted her.

As the fire jumped and crackled, my breaths slowed and evened.

And I fell.

"Bet you can't find me."

A flash of blond streaked in the moonlight, disappeared in the shadows.

William tried to scream, to warn him to stay. He pushed himself harder than he ever had. The child remained just out of reach, his laughter taunting William's fear.

"Wait," William called. His voice carried on the wind, bled into nothing.

"Jonathan!" he screamed.

The wind shifted and stilled, the roving life of the forest floor stalling under his feet.

The small boy peeked out from behind a large tree trunk and stared back at William with huge brown eyes.

An emotion William had never felt pounded against his ribs, bound with his soul.

The boy cocked his head and grinned, sweet and small. Blood filled his mouth and covered his teeth. The grin faded, and he sniffled, wiped his nose with the back of his hand.

I lurched, body and soul, cried out as I lunged for the boy.

I was on my feet, panting, eyes darting around the small room. Embers smoldered in the fireplace, the fire quelled and lulled to a muted glow, the boy still floundering through my mind. I tasted his fear, felt his spirit needling through my skin, weaving a child's pattern of despair.

I roared—a manifestation of desperate, helpless rage— and hurled the lamp sitting on the small table across the room. It smashed against the opposite wall.

I was losing my fucking mind.

☙❧

"Want another beer?" Blake handed me a bottle from the cooler sitting on his front porch.

"Sure. Thanks," I said. I twisted off the cap and took a drink, looking back over the peace of Blake's front yard.

Late afternoon sun warmed the air, and the girls squealed where they chased each other on the grass. Olivia fell down about every ten steps or so. She'd giggle and get herself back up on her feet without seeming to miss a beat.

Blake wandered out into his yard, smiling as he watched his girls play.

"Whoa...," he said as the girls did a loop around him, their laughter carrying across the neighborhood when he loped after them, not *quite* able to catch them.

Grace was on the porch, one knee drawn to her chest, the other foot swaying her gently on the porch swing.

I found it ironic that everything felt right, just as it should be, except for the one thing holding me in this place — the same thing that had chased me away years before.

For the last two nights, I had called the guesthouse home, though I'd spent most of the weekend hanging out with Blake's family, making bonds I should have made years ago. Grace seemed to be slowly warming up to me. Her smile was a little less tense each time I walked through their door.

"Catch us, Uncle Will," Emma called as she flew in close to the porch steps where I stood.

So unaccustomed to child's play, I felt completely out of sorts, but I found myself powerless to this little girl who had attached herself to me so quickly. Laughing in spite of myself, I chased her across the lawn, two steps behind, before I drew in near enough to sweep her off her feet with one arm wrapped around her belly. I swung her around, and Emma shrieked with laughter.

I hugged her back close to my chest before I set her back on her feet, smiling when she grinned back up at me as she ran away.

Blake's face was soft when I joined him near the fence.

"It's really good to have you here, Will," he said then took a swig from his beer, turned away to rest his arms over the top of the wooden fence. He dangled his bottle over the other side, looked down at his feet.

Drawing in a breath of the crisp evening air, I draped my arms over the fence and gazed out over the quiet street.

"I'm glad to be here." I took a drink and looked over at my brother. "Your girls are...great." I had no other way to explain it. I was really happy for Blake. Almost envious. I guess I'd spent my entire life being *almost* envious of my brother. Maybe that wasn't such a bad thing.

Blake glanced over his shoulder at his girls, then back at me. "Yeah. I couldn't imagine life without them." He shook his head. "It's crazy how you can live for years without them, but the moment they're born, they become your entire life."

Focusing on the toe of my shoe I dug into a bare spot of the grass, I thought maybe I understood what my brother meant.

Blake cut an eye in my direction. "You know, we're all really glad you're back, but I wanted you to know I'm sorry about Kristina. I know that's gotta be hard. You doing okay with it?"

I rubbed my chin and took another sip, releasing a humorless chuckle after I swallowed. "That was over before it started."

Blake frowned. "You were with her six years. How can you say that? Are you telling me you didn't love her?"

I shook my head and looked my brother in the eye. "No…not at all."

Blake stared at me, the air rushing from his nose in disbelief. "I don't get you at all." Disappointment darkened his face. "You disappear for all this time, and now you tell me it didn't mean anything? What was it? The *money*?" he asked.

"Of course not."

"Then what?"

The only thing I could do was allow the heaviness in my presence to speak for me. I had no excuse, my reason a secret I'd never told anyone.

"What the hell, Will? You were gone for years, and now you can't say one damned word about it? We used to tell each other everything."

I rolled my jaw and looked out over the street. "Not everything."

Blake's agitation seemed to subside as his frustration doubled. "Then *tell* me."

I dared to meet my brother's face and clearly saw the damage my absence had caused him.

"Blake..." I swallowed over the thickness that gathered in my throat.

Blake frowned and inclined his head. "Come on, Will. Anything you have to say can't be that bad. That's what family is supposed to be for. It's like I just got my brother back, but a huge piece of him is still missing. We all have shit that happens in our lives...you don't have to hide it from me."

Defeat clenched my hand around my bottle. "I just couldn't stay here, okay?" I wiped my brow that suddenly felt hot. "I got wrapped up in something I shouldn't have, and I needed to put it behind me."

Shouldn't have?

For six years, that's what I'd been telling myself. It'd become an easy lie.

"What are you talking about?"

"It didn't have anything to do with you, Blake."

"When you took off, you think you didn't make it about us?"

"I get it, Blake. I told you I was sorry, and I'm back. Just...forget about it."

Blake released a sarcastic snort. "Sure looks like you've forgotten about it."

"Hey guys," Grace called from the porch, "dinner's ready."

Blake pegged me with a look that told me this wasn't over, before he turned, crossed the yard, and climbed the porch steps. Grace smiled, and he dipped his head to kiss her, then took her hand and led her inside.

Just on the verge of dusk, the mild winter sun still held on at the brink, subtle blue and pink rays casting the day's goodbye.

Dinner was incredible, and after we all wandered back out into the front yard to enjoy the last minutes of the day. The girls settled on the grass, playing with toys, and Grace went back to her favorite spot on the porch swing.

Grabbing another beer from the cooler, I leaned against the fence and watched the girls play. Blake joined me, and he popped the cap to his beer with a satisfied sigh.

"So how's business?" I asked, sinking into the calm of the approaching night.

"Good," he said before he drained the rest of his beer. "This shit-hole town is sure to keep me busy." He grinned, and I laughed low. Blake had been doing construction all of his adult life, and half the houses in town were falling apart. "Every time the wind even stirs somebody needs…"

Part of me understood Blake was still talking, but his voice came muddied and warped against my ears. I could focus on nothing but the van coming to a stop across the street, six houses up.

Blake nudged me on the shoulder, jarred me into semi-consciousness. His words were distinct only because of what he said. "Maggie Krieger. God…that poor girl…I almost slipped up with Mom on that the other night. Too bad you weren't around to protect her when she got herself knocked up and married that asshole. I called that one, though, didn't I?"

My eyes locked on Maggie as she emerged from her van and went to the side to help Jonathan out. My entire being shifted in their direction, drawn.

"Her little sister moved in about a year ago…see Maggie over there every once in a while…little boy sure is cute." Blake continued to ramble, each word striking me deeper than the last.

I held my breath when the two came to a standstill in front of the van. The wind stirred Maggie's hair, large chunks thrashing around her face, the boy clinging to her as he stared in my direction.

I was unable to look away from my heart—my life. There was no way I could let either of them go. As if they felt it too, they remained unmoving, frozen, as if the space between us had dissolved.

My fingers twitched their direction.

"Oh my God." I was knocked from the place I'd gone by Blake's voice, low and disgusted. "You fucking asshole." I turned to see Blake stumble back as if he'd been punched in the gut. "I can't believe you…*this* is what you shouldn't have gotten wrapped up in?" He gripped his head as he looked down the road to where Maggie suddenly turned and rushed Jonathan up the sidewalk and into her sister's house. Blake's face twisted up as if just looking at me sickened him.

"Blake—" I reached out to stop him.

Blake shoved me and pointed in my face.

"Don't you dare try to make excuses for this…I…ugh…" Blake turned and threw his beer bottle across the yard, his muscles rigid and held in restraint as he stormed toward the house.

Olivia cried and ran to her mother, climbing onto her lap. Grace covered Olivia's ear and held her head against her chest.

"Calm down, Blake," Grace demanded beneath her breath, "you're scaring the girls."

Blake said nothing as he yanked the screen door open. It clattered shut behind him.

I wanted to scream. Fisting my hands at the sides of my head, I stole another glance behind me, up the empty street, to the place where Maggie had just stood.

Fuck.

I wrenched a hand through my hair.

"What'd you think was going to happen, coming back here?" Grace's voice was laced with bitterness from where she hissed at me on the porch swing. "Did you think enough time had passed that nobody was going to notice?"

My heart faltered, a rush of fear and nerves and anger slicking like ice just under my skin. "What?" I asked. I turned around and walked slowly toward Grace with my head cocked to the side. "What did you just say?"

She narrowed her eyes at me.

"You knew?" I half accused, half begged.

She huffed and hugged her daughter closer. "I knew the second I saw that baby that he was yours. I thought better of you, Will." Her forehead creased as she glared down at me. "I thought maybe...*just maybe*...somebody would finally love that girl. And you treated her like a piece of trash, just like everyone else. Do you know what it's like to have to keep a secret like that from your husband because you know it's going to break his heart? Blake's always thought the best of you...all that time...always making excuses for you, telling your mom that you needed time to find yourself. Do you know what it feels like to sit there and know the truth, that really his little brother is just a selfish jerk?"

I crammed the heels of my hands into my eyes then dropped them like a brick. "I didn't know," I yelled as I moved across the yard.

She looked down and slowly shook her head. "Don't..."

I took the three steps up to the porch, trying to control the anger Grace had just evoked. No. It wasn't her fault. But if she'd just said *one* goddamned word in six years. I roughed a hand over my face, knowing I looked like a madman because I sure as hell felt like one. "I didn't know, Grace...I swear to you, I didn't know."

Grace tilted her head up, her face a war of disbelief and confusion. Her gaze flashed up the street, back to me.

"Oh God." Her brow twisted as realization flushed her face. "I thought...why do you think I've been so angry with you all this time? I figured she'd told you that night you'd just up and left. Will—"

I didn't know how to deal with Grace, with what she'd said, with what she'd known. I shook my head, opened the front door, and left her sitting there.

Inside, Blake was across the room with his head down. His hands were on his hips as he paced with his back to me.

I raked the back of my hand over my mouth. Blake's shoulders tensed with my presence, his breaths audible in the otherwise silent room.

"Blake."

"You need to get out of my house." When he turned to look at me, every trace of tolerance he had for me was gone. "I don't want you anywhere near my family."

I took a step forward. "I—"

"I'm not playing around, Will." Blake took a step back and put his hands up. "You are a coward, and I'm just...*done*." His tone took on an edge of sadness. "I spent so much time defending you and the decisions you made. I believed in you, Will. But this...leaving her like that...it's unforgiveable."

I turned away and faced the wall. I struggled to find the words to speak. Maggie had always been a secret, a secret she'd asked me to keep, and I had no idea how to explain it now.

"I've loved her since that first night..." I gathered enough courage to look over at my brother.

He stared back at me. His eyes were narrowed in doubt, though the aggression seemed to have faded from his posture.

"I never stopped."

A rush of relief covered me when I admitted it aloud. It somehow made it real. Made Maggie real. What we had real. It also somehow made them real—the dreams. A tremor skittered over my flesh. I swallowed.

"She destroyed me, Blake. I left because I couldn't stand to come back and see her with him."

William ~ September, Six Years Earlier

Grace climbed into her spot between Blake and me. What was probably the biggest smile I had ever seen looked to be permanently etched on her face.

"Hey, Will," she said as she put on her seatbelt. She held out her left hand that boasted the huge rock in front of her. As the sun melted from the sky, Grace rotated her hand through its rays, the diamond glimmering and shedding its promise across the cab of Blake's truck. "It's gorgeous, isn't it?" she asked in an awed, appreciative voice, never turning from it.

Blake had proposed the night before.

"Eh...it's okay," I teased her, laughing when Grace slugged me in the arm. "All right...all right." I held up both hands in surrender.

"Don't get on my bad side, Will." She grinned. "You know, I'm family now." The playfulness drained from her voice as soon as she said the word, as if it were sacred.

My face relaxed into a knowing smile. "It's really beautiful, Grace...really. I'm happy for you."

Blake grinned at us both as he turned and hit the long, desolate stretch of road.

Tonight we were celebrating.

Twenty-minutes later, we pulled into the secluded field. In the center, a fire already blazed in welcome.

Grace and Blake were met with catcalls and congratulations when they stepped from the truck, their hands clasped and swinging between them as they walked toward their group of friends. Blake kept glancing down at her. Love poured from him every time he did.

I trailed behind, my hands in my pockets as I internally scolded myself for being such a self-centered prick, continually wishing I could have the same thing.

Things with Maggie had gotten so fucking complicated.

For the last two months, we'd lived in our own little world of seclusion, teetering somewhere between ecstasy and agony. Our relationship was both the best thing I'd ever experienced and complete torture all at the same time.

Friends.

No matter what we labeled ourselves, we were far more than friends. Friends didn't lie for hours wrapped in each other's arms, her heart thundering beneath my hands, her breaths short and ragged as I'd run my nose along the sweetness of her skin and press my lips to her jaw. Friends didn't have that need in the pit of their stomachs, the one that had me twisted up, wishing I could somehow be shaken out.

I wanted her so badly that some nights I thought I might die. Every fantasy I'd ever had developed into making love to Maggie. Every face was hers, every touch, her hand. So many times I'd been tempted to push her past the safe-zone we'd created, this distorted, intimate relationship we had over our clothes.

But I knew she needed that space. She'd confided in me — trusted me — and I wasn't going to be the asshole who disrespected it.

What made my need even harder to ignore was the fact that what I felt for Maggie was far greater than just a physical ache. I loved talking to her, loved that she opened up and shared herself with me, loved how kind she was, loved...everything about her.

I couldn't help but smile now, thinking about it. Nothing was better than seeing Maggie smile. When we'd talk, she would get this wistful expression on her face, her lips parting as *that* smile played at the edges of her mouth while she'd stare up at me.

She'd get lost in my words while I'd get lost in those eyes.

But as close as we were, there was still a huge barrier separating us. Troy was the visible obstacle, but I knew it went so much deeper than that.

Maggie was scared.

Scared of everything.

It was just easier for her to stay with Troy than to risk losing something that meant something to her.

I glanced at my brother and Grace who chatted with their closest friends gathered there, Grace showing off her ring, everyone sharing in their joy.

I was here to celebrate them, so I tried to push aside my inner turmoil.

But it was no use. That yearning I felt whenever she wasn't near, the worry that haunted me every time she was out of my sight, wouldn't let go. The need to protect her was acute.

Almost painful.

Each night I trailed behind her, unseen, unknown to everyone but her. From a distance, I would walk her back to the Hell she knew as home. The second she disappeared from view and vanished into the front door of the shitty house she lived in, fear would grip me. I hated not being there to protect her.

There was no escaping that fear now as I sat down on the ground and leaned against the old tree trunk.

"A toast to the happy couple," Justin, one of Blake's oldest friends and now business partner, said as he raised his beer.

Everyone lifted their bottles.

"May the two of you have the best of lives...and never grow...bored." Justin lifted a suggestive brow, and Grace turned red and buried her face in Blake's neck before she peeked back out at us.

"That, my friend, will never happen," Blake assured him as he looked down at Grace who was clutching his shirt, grinning up at him. He kissed her hard, in a way that told all of his jeering friends to go to Hell.

I laughed and toasted with my near-empty bottle. "Here! Here!"

Blake tipped the head of his bottle in my direction without coming up for a breath.

In the distance, a truck engine whirred and drew near, tearing my attention from my brother and future sister-in-law. It spun a path of anxiety through my muscles.

No one should have mentioned this gathering to anyone else but this small group, but there was no mistaking what I heard. Over the summer, I'd memorized the sound of Troy's truck. Every time Troy would barrel up to wherever I happened to be and I had to prepare myself to sit and watch Maggie with him, the distinct hum of that engine had been etched deeper and deeper in the recesses of my brain. It was almost Pavlovian, the instant anxiety, the hatred that surged and constricted my lungs.

I wanted her here, but not like this.

Dropping my head, I tugged and tore at the lone tuft of grass growing near the fire pit. I fought the urge to look up when I heard her soft footsteps out of sync with Troy's.

Shit.

I jerked my head and rubbed my eyes with the back of my hands, trying to get myself under control, knowing I had to play it cool or one of these days I was going to give us away. I just didn't know how much longer I could take this before I snapped.

And somehow I knew when I did, I was going to lose her.

I pretended I couldn't sense the smirk on Troy's face when he looked in my direction as they came up to the group. It was like he knew exactly how much it hurt me to see her with him and was happy to rub it in. He'd seen the way I looked at her. I wondered what he'd think if he knew she was sneaking out at night to see me rather than him.

From across the fire, I felt her, could sense the way her body settled onto the dirt floor. This time I couldn't stop myself from looking up and searching for the solace I found in those sweet brown eyes.

Through the writhing flames, I met her gaze.

Did she see how this affected me? Did she understand that every second she wasn't mine was torture?

Her eyes drifted closed as her head lolled to the side. The motion was soft and laden with affection.

I closed my eyes and coaxed myself down from the instinct to rip the possessive arm Troy had wrapped around Maggie's chest clean from his body.

Instead, I pictured her in our spot, snuggled against my side where she was safe and protected. I imagined the smile that she reserved for me and the way her fingertips felt as she ran them down my face and across my lips.

Pictured her where I was sure she was imagining we were now.

I sensed the shift, the rupture in our peace.

"Knock it off." It came out hushed, meant for no one but Troy, but with the sound of Maggie's voice, I yanked my head up and found them in a position so similar to the one they'd been in the first night I'd seen her. Troy's mouth was at her neck, kissing the same spot I had just imagined my mouth to be — the same spot where my mouth had been last night.

Possessiveness turned my stomach, and as desperate as I was not to witness this, I couldn't tear my attention away.

Troy laughed against her skin and grabbed her breast over her shirt. "C'mon, Maggie...why do you always have to be like that?"

Hatred burned hotter than the fire that thrashed between us, savage flames that swept through my blood.

No. This I couldn't handle. I dug my nails into my palms and tried to sit still.

Maggie threw Troy's hand off and stood, stumbling away from the group. She hugged herself across her middle, her head hung.

I sat in chaos, my mind and spirit screaming that I defend her while everyone else carried on as if nothing had happened. A lover's spat paid no mind.

Troy got to his feet, standing with his fists balled at his sides, glaring at Maggie across the space where she faced away from the fire not more than twenty feet away.

"Stay away from her," I said too low for anyone else to hear when Troy began to creep up behind her.

Their argument was low and one-sided, Troy's words unclear as he breathed more poison into her mind, as she cowered and slowly turned around to face him. I sat frozen as I watched her take one step back, shake her head hard, and squeeze her arms tighter around her body.

I was ready to spring into action if he moved one inch closer to her.

But instead, I froze. The words she spoke next should have been indistinguishable, but I heard them as if I'd been standing at her side.

"I don't want to be with you anymore...I never have. Please, Troy...just...leave me alone."

For a moment, I rejoiced, before the crack of Troy's hand across her face rang out in my ears, blurred my vision—though somehow I'd never seen anything clearer than the shocked, horrified expression that took over Maggie's face.

Then something snapped, and I saw nothing except the bastard who'd hurt her.

Troy spun around just as I rushed up behind him. In the same motion, I cocked my arm back and hit him under the jaw. Pain exploded in the bones of my hand, and with it, I felt a thrill of satisfaction. Troy's head rocked back.

Maggie screamed.

As Troy righted himself, he swung, catching me against the right temple. The blow split my vision, my consciousness tossing in a bid to concede. I shook it off, remembered why I was here. I would fight for her. Die for her if I had to—if it would make her better—if she would live.

"You piece of shit...you want to hit a girl?" The words scraped from my throat, raw and abraded. I wheezed as I sucked in air, pulled back then rammed my fist into Troy's nose. Blood gushed as the tissues gave and Troy fell to his back on the ground.

I lunged at him, fisted Troy's shirt in my hands. I yanked him up and slammed him back down. "Huh? Answer me...answer me!"

Troy spit a mouthful of blood in my face. "What do you care? She's just a trashy little cock tease."

In a violent explosion of pent-up fury, I felt my sanity slip. My fists landed in a constant barrage of blows to Troy's face.

"You fucking asshole...I'll kill you...touch her again, and I swear to God, I will kill you." Beneath my hands, I felt skin tearing, bones buckling. Foggy voices pressed into my awareness, imploring.

A scream.

Shouting.

I didn't care.

I drew my arm back again, struggled against the hands holding it back, fought against the arms around my waist. I kicked as I was pulled off of Troy. My shoe grazed the asshole's face.

"I'll kill you," I screamed again, my legs flailing as I was dragged back and thrown to the ground beside Blake's truck. "I'll kill you." This time it was a whimper.

Around me, there was so much movement, what felt like horror and panic.

In the fog, I heard Blake shouting. "Justin...get Maggie out of here."

Above the chaos I heard her sobbing.

Suddenly Grace filled up my vision, kneeling in front of me, whispering words I couldn't comprehend. Through the haze of adrenaline, I tried to focus on Grace's face. She brushed my hair back.

"Shh...Will...it's okay...it's okay."

It wasn't until then I realized I was mumbling, incoherent words pouring from my mouth, words that only registered in my mind.

I lost her.

"Get him in the truck." Blake grabbed me under the arms and hauled me to my feet, his movements frantic as he pushed and pulled at me.

Grace crawled in beside me, cradled me in her arms, and rested my head in her lap. I twitched uncontrollably as the flood of adrenaline wept from my body.

I lost her.

I'd become that person, one who couldn't control their fists or their rage. Someone to fear.

Blake gunned the gas, flew into a tailspin as he whipped the truck around in the dirt clearing. We slid before the wheels found traction. The truck rocked as it centered and Blake bolted down the narrow road.

Tires squealed when they hit the pavement, the engine roaring as Blake pushed it as fast as it would go.

"Shit," Blake screamed and punched the steering wheel. The sound hung in the darkness of the cab as we sped down the road. "Goddamn it, Will!"

I felt Blake shake himself off, his eyes landing on me. "Is he okay?"

Holding me closer, Grace ran her fingers through my hair again. "No...I don't think he is."

Somehow I knew the words were directed at me and not to Blake.

"Here." Grace led me to a chair at the small kitchen table and placed an ice pack against my eye. We were all whispering, our movements checked and subdued in the quiet house. The last thing we needed was for Mom to walk in on this.

"Thanks," I mumbled as I held the pack to my eye and slumped over in the chair.

I looked up at Blake who stared down at me, standing two feet away, his face contorted in worry. "Are you sure you're okay? I really think we should take you to the emergency room."

"I'm fine," I said for the fifth time in about four minutes. I dropped my attention back to the ground and released a weighted breath.

"You lost your damned mind back there, Will...I'm worried about you."

I looked up. "He hit her."

Blake ran his hand through his hair and shook his head. "I know, but—"

Grace cut him off. "He stood up for a girl who needed help, Blake. He doesn't need to apologize for that."

Blake shook his head again, paced back and forth in the same two-foot radius before he exhaled. "I have to get Grace home. I'll be back later. You sure you don't need anything?"

"Yeah...I'm fine."

Blake headed out the back door. Grace hesitated in the doorway, studied me in a way I didn't quite understand. "Goodnight, Will," she finally said before she followed Blake out and closed the door behind her.

I dragged myself upstairs to my room and quietly latched the door. I lay back on my bed and held the ice pack to my throbbing eye.

Everything throbbed, really.

My knuckles, my face, my heart.

I'd fucked it all up, losing it, scaring Maggie the way I had.

The most terrifying thing was I knew I wouldn't have stopped.

I dropped the ice pack to the floor and turned to my side, facing the wall.

Moonlight soaked the room, the shade open wide. Shadows from the tree outside played across the walls.

Even though it was still hot and muggy outside, I felt chilled. Cold. I curled up. Hated Troy. Hated she wasn't mine. Hated that I'd probably ruined any chance that she'd ever be.

I thought maybe I dozed, but I wasn't sure, when I was stirred by the tapping on my door. I groaned and rolled to my stomach, mumbling into my pillow, "I'm fine, Blake. I'm trying to sleep."

The door creaked when it was opened. I looked over my shoulder, frustrated Blake wouldn't just leave me alone.

"Maggie," I whispered and rushed to sit up. She took a tentative step forward and latched the door behind her. In the dim light, she stood across the room from me. Her face was streaked in tears and dirt, her hair a mess, her eyes—I swallowed, wishing I didn't have to witness the sadness found there.

"How'd you get in here?" I asked as I slowly got to my feet, my movements calculated, worried she might run if I made the slightest wrong move.

She averted her gaze to the tree just outside.

"I waited for you." Her voice was all wrong, strained, nothing like my Maggie. She still wouldn't look my way.

"Maggie..." I moved in her direction.

A sob tore up her throat. "I waited."

171

"I'm so sorry. I thought...I didn't think you'd want to see me," I pled as I took another step. "You know I would never—"

I couldn't stand the thought of her being scared of me.

She squeezed her eyes shut. Her movements were small and jerky when she shook her head. "You think I don't know that?"

With one last step, I backed her into the door, unable to resist the comfort of her presence. Her hands were flat against the wood, her head turned the farthest to the side and downcast. "Maggie, look at me."

"Did he hurt you?" Her abrupt question was a whimper, her watery eyes darting up to meet mine before they searched my face.

I slowly shook my head, tilting it to the side.

Her hand trembled as she reached out to touch my tender eye.

Warmth sped across my skin.

"It's nothing." *Nothing.*

"I can't stand the thought of you getting hurt for me," she said, her expression pained, telling me the very opposite of what I felt. *I'm not worth it.*

I brushed my fingertips over the small cut to the side of her bottom lip before I pushed past our boundaries and brushed my lips over it.

Did she understand? Did she feel anything close to what I felt when our skin met? Did she understand, to me, she was the only one who *was* worth it?

Maggie gasped, sagged against the door as she twisted her hands in my shirt. "William."

"I'm so in love with you, Maggie." I hesitated, both palms inches from her face, before I took her face in my hands and kissed her again. "I love you so much, I can't see straight...can't think straight." I braced myself with one hand against the door and wrapped the other arm around her waist to bring her flush. I'd held her close, so many times, but never like this.

My mouth captured hers, and I coaxed her lips apart. I swept my tongue across hers. So sweet. Everything I imagined Maggie would be. I dove in, sure I would drown. I'd waited so long to kiss her like this, to taste her warmth.

A moan lingered deep in her throat, and her fingers dug into my hips as she tugged me closer.

My body reacted, hit with a need unlike anything I'd ever felt. I pressed her against the door.

"Tell me," I begged against her mouth, kissing her hard. "Please, Maggie…tell me you feel the same."

Her hands slid from my waist and up to my chest. Then she nudged me away.

I reeled back. I'd pushed her too far. Violated her trust.

"Maggie, I…"

The words died in my mouth as I watched the motion in front of me. She held her breath and closed her eyes, trembling as she reached down and grabbed the hem of her shirt. She pulled it over her head and dropped it to the floor.

"Maggie…no." I tried not to look, didn't want to take advantage of this screwed up night that had spun out of control. I was desperate for her, but not like this.

"Please," she said, "I love you, William. You're…everything." She swallowed and blinked. "Please…I want it to be you."

Desire tripped through my body, and I dropped my gaze to her plain white bra, the soft swell of her breasts exposed, the creamy skin of her neck a milky glow in the moonlight.

"Please," she said again.

"Maggie." It was a plea. *Please stop*. It repeated as a chorus in my head, though I knew there was no way I could resist her. She was all I wanted. Everything.

Maggie.

I was shaking as badly as she was when I stretched out a trembling hand and touched her, ran my fingers from her chin and down the length of her delicate neck. I splayed my palm flat across her chest—searched her face as I did. A shiver rolled through her body, and her heart thrummed against my hand.

"Is this okay?" I asked, moving a little closer and my hand a little lower.

"Yes," she breathed.

My fingertips grazed over her breast and down her stomach, before I flattened my palms against her skin and slid them around to wrap my arms around her. My body was flush with hers, her bare skin singeing me through my clothes. I wanted her so bad it ached, but I couldn't stand the thought of becoming another mistake for Maggie. I moved my hands to cup her face, and I pulled away and stared down at her.

"Are you sure?"

Those eyes filled with the complete trust she'd given me over the last two months—filled with the love she felt for me.

"I want it to be you," she repeated.

Maybe it was wrong. Maybe she needed more time. Maybe there was no amount of time that could ever make this fucked up situation right.

But what I did know was there was no amount of time that could ever change how I felt about her.

I rested my forehead against hers, breathed her in. Then I kissed her. Our mouths moved slowly, learning the other, steadily building in intensity. My fingers traced up and down her arms. Her hands fumbled under my shirt and pressed against my stomach.

"Come here," I whispered, stepping back to lead her by the hand to sit on the edge of my bed. "Lay back."

Maggie bit her lip and her face flushed, but she didn't hesitate to scoot back into the middle of my bed. She rested on her elbows, watching me.

I never took my eyes off of her as I knelt on the floor and tugged her shoes from her feet. That tenderness was there, shining in her eyes, mixed with a disquieted apprehension.

My head spun with the magnitude of this moment, with what she was trusting me with.

"Promise me you'll tell me if you want me to stop," I murmured. I placed my hands on the outside of her calves and ran them up her legs as I crawled onto the bed.

Her skin prickled and she quivered beneath me, but she nodded and whispered, "I promise. But I want this, William. I want you."

I undressed her slowly, taking my time — giving her time.

I slid my hands under her back and unfastened her bra. I pressed my mouth to her shoulder, my fingers playing at the straps. Sitting back, I slowly dragged them down her arms and dropped her bra to the floor.

The softest hue of pink spread over her creamy skin.

I watched her face, the modesty in the way she blinked, waiting for my reaction. "You are so beautiful, Maggie."

Her expression told me it may have been the first time she believed it.

I kissed the blush, soothed away her fear of the unknown. A brush of my lips across her belly, gentle fingers in my hair, a soft sigh from her mouth.

Rising up on my hands and knees, I hovered over her and dipped my head to kiss her mouth. Our tongues danced, slow and long. My lips traveled to the edge of her mouth, her jaw, and down her neck.

"William." Her hands fisted in my hair.

I gently took the rose of her breast in my mouth.

Maggie's breath caught. She slid her tentative hands down my neck and shoulders, wandering my body. My muscles twitched and tensed. Nothing had ever felt so right.

An unknown hunger rippled through me like shockwaves when she ran her hands up the planes of my back and pulled my shirt over my head.

I leaned back on my knees and hooked my fingers in the sides of her panties. "Are you sure, Maggie? We can't take this back."

Her brown eyes warmed in the moonlight. She touched my cheek. "I will never regret you."

Swallowing, I slid off the bed and watched as I peeled them down her legs. My gaze swept up her body, my voice rough when I uttered her name.

"Hold on a second," I murmured in quiet reassurance. I hurried to the closet and dropped to my knees. I dug through the duffle bag stuffed in the back corner on the floor. Grabbing the box, I tore it open, realizing how badly my hands were shaking. I glanced back at Maggie who watched me, shy but curious.

Completely bared to me, she waited, her hair spread out around her face, spilling over her shoulders and onto my sheets, and again, I was hit with awe with what this meant to her—with what this meant to me.

I smiled softly at her as I stood and made my way back to the bed. I shrugged off my jeans and underwear while watching her for any sign of discomfort, anything that would give me an indication to stop.

But there was none, just a vulnerable trust alight in her eyes as she looked up at me.

I rolled the condom on and slowly climbed back between her legs.

She sank back onto the bed as I did, reached for me. She whispered, "William," as our mouths met.

She was panting by the time I pulled away, and I snaked my arm behind her back and up her spine to hold her head in my hand, the other propping myself up. "It might hurt."

She kissed my neck, trailed her mouth up my jaw, and then rested her cheek against mine as she anchored her fingers in my back. "I know. It's okay...just...please."

Emotion rushed me, love and lust and fear.

She whimpered when I pushed into her, her eyes squeezed shut, tears gathering at the corners. Her nails dug deep, drawing blood from my flesh.

I shifted to my elbow, swept her hair away, kissed her tears.

"Shh...shh...Maggie, I love you...I love you...baby, please don't cry," I pled as I brushed my lips across her face, as I urged the tension away, hating that I caused her even an ounce of pain.

My body burned in restraint as I held her and let the shock pass.

She released the breath she'd been holding across my face and wrapped her arms around my neck, pressing her chest to mine. "Love me."

I kissed her, loved her. Every touch overflowed with devotion, repressed emotions that could no longer be contained. Our bodies moved as if they knew the other, perfection, the best thing I'd ever known.

"Maggie." My breaths came in short gasps, and I wove my fingers through hers, pressed her hand to my lips.

Maggie.

This girl who had undone me, tossed me from my foundation, shattered every belief.

Maggie.

The only thing I knew.

"Maggie."

I let myself go.

William ~ Present Day

I turned back to face Blake where he stood across the room. He was right. I was a coward, but not for the reasons he'd initially believed.

I was a coward because I ran.

I never should have gone. Never should have given up. But I'd never lied.

There was no amount of time that could change what I felt for Maggie.

Chapter Thirteen

William ~ Present Day

I sat on the edge of my bed, facing away from the door when the small knock sounded against it. I didn't respond, though I wasn't surprised to hear the sound of it creaking open, the guilty presence emerging behind me. Her short breaths filled the room.

"Do you mind if I come in?" Grace asked.

I shrugged, but didn't look her way.

"Blake's really pissed off at me right now." She said it almost casually as she moved across the small space. She fiddled with the faucet on the kitchen sink, grabbed a sponge and began wiping down the miniature countertop, an obvious distraction from her discomfort. "Guess you probably are too." This time the words didn't sound so casual.

I finally looked over my shoulder at my brother's wife. "I just don't get it, Grace. You know me...how could you believe I would have pulled something like that?"

From behind, I watched as her shoulders sagged, her head drifting lower. Her voice was soft when she spoke.

"You don't know what it was like here, after you left. You didn't come home for Christmas, you stopped calling, made excuses when Blake begged you to come back for the wedding the next summer. I was so angry at you for doing that to him. You hurt him, Will." She paused, seeming to search for the right words. "Jonathan must have been about five months old the first time I ran into Maggie in town. I swear to God, my heart stopped in my chest. I'd already chalked you up to being an asshole who cared nothing about anyone but yourself. It was easy to add that to it. I tried to talk to her...tried to dig for answers and asked her if she needed help." Grace peeked over at me. "Of course, she said she was fine. I should have known better than to have even tried." She blew the air from her lungs.

I fought against the bitterness and resentment that worked to take hold of my heart. I'd considered Grace a friend — considered her family.

"Will, I'm so sorry."

I nodded, facing away. "So am I."

I stepped out the front door of the little guesthouse and into the darkness. The night was suffocating, heavy and dense, the world quiet and still. Breathing in the silence, I stuffed my hands in my jacket pockets and wound around the side of Blake's slumbering house. Gravel crunched beneath my boots, echoed as isolation as I made my way to the sleepy street and walked to its end.

Sucking in the cool night air, I took in my surroundings, the town asleep, and gave heed to the longing in my chest.

Stupid, I knew. Torturing myself this way. But when it came to Maggie, I always had been. Stupid from the moment I'd seen her. It was crazy how, for years, I had lived in denial, pushed it all aside, and it had just taken me coming back for it all to take hold, to take me over. I snorted at myself. More like it had come after me when I'd refused to listen.

Running a hand through my hair, I contemplated for only a second before I slipped into the darkness behind the lumberyard and into the lush woodland that always seemed alive, no matter what time of year it was. We'd taken this shortcut what felt like a million times, so many of them walked in our own denial, as two people who could never stay away, even though neither of us had been brave enough to give in.

But for two weeks, she had been mine.

I passed the immense tree growing just off the worn path. It stretched to the heavens, lost in the canopy overhead. I imagined her pressed up against it, her heart pounding with mine as our worlds spun with desire and laughter and a future we'd been foolish enough to believe we'd have.

Pushing myself forward, I glided through the trees and underbrush, felt her spirit suck the air from my lungs, the memories so thick, I felt as if I could no longer breathe. Just at the edge of our sanctuary, I stood frozen, held captive in the echo that had once been my freedom. This once trampled refuge was now dense and overgrown. With heavy feet, I forced myself forward and folded myself onto the soft, high grasses slicked with dew.

I thought it might be too much when I leaned against the fallen oak. I could almost feel her resting against my chest, her fingers woven with mine, the freest smile on her face.

In the calm, I could hear her laugh.

William ~ September, Six Years Earlier

I held her, never wanted to let go. Her body burned into mine, the warmth of her bare skin a blanket that covered me whole. So many months had been spent dreaming of this, of what it would be like to make her mine, imagining what it would feel like when I heard *those* words fall from her mouth. I knew now those dreams meant nothing compared to this truth. Our connection was perfection.

Maggie shifted closer beneath the covers of my small bed and drew my arm tighter around her. A shiver rolled through her body.

I buried my nose in the vanilla warmth of her hair, then laid my cheek against hers as I hugged her to me from behind, brushing my lips just under her ear. "Are you okay?"

She rolled to her back, and I propped myself on an elbow to look down at her. Her eyes swam with affection. I touched her cheek, felt the hint of a smile beneath my skin as she slowly nodded. She swallowed, her gaze wandering over my face. Chewing at her bottom lip, she seemed embarrassed, before she soothed my worry with hushed words.

"I never imagined it would be that way."

I leaned down to kiss her, a gentle brush of my lips against hers. Sliding my hand down, I cupped the back of her neck.

It was everything that I wanted her to know, that it shouldn't hurt to be touched, that it was okay to be adored.

"I love you, Maggie," I murmured at the edge of her mouth as I wound my fingers through her hair.

A soft hand wrapped around my neck, and she kissed me back.

⊙⅀☉

The next day dragged by at too slow a pace, the hours agony as I silently begged them to pass. Grace and Blake had stayed near me the entire day. I knew Blake was standing guard as my protector, ready for the backlash he was sure was going to come. He continually looked out the front window as if he were expecting an attack.

Yeah, I had woken this morning with my eye throbbing, the flesh black and blue, but I couldn't even bring myself to care about Troy or any threat he might make. The only thing that mattered now was Maggie was free — and she was mine.

It was really hard to find anything negative in the situation when I was just so damned happy.

I couldn't wait for the moment when I could sneak from this house to see her again. Anticipation wrapped me tight, thoughts of what tonight would be like now that our walls were down and admissions had been made.

Grace was curled up on the opposite end of the couch from where I sat. Her knees were bent with her feet on the cushions, her head supported by her hand with her elbow on the back of the couch. She searched me as if she could reach out and pluck the thoughts from my mind.

"Would you sit still, William? You're making me nervous. Are you sure you're okay?" she asked.

I sighed. "I'm fine, Grace...really." I looked at my brother who pulled back the drape to peer down the road again. Apparently the two read my anxiousness as something else entirely. "Blake, would you just stop? Let the asshole come. I don't really care."

Blake turned around. "You don't get it, do you, Will? You've just created a shit storm, and you're sitting there acting like it doesn't matter."

I scoffed. I would be happy to take anything Troy brought my way. Welcome it. He *hit* her, and as far as I was concerned, the broken jaw and fifteen stitches weren't nearly enough. In the light of day, the really sick part of me wished I'd just finished it.

"What do you want me to say?" I inclined my head when I spoke. "Because I don't regret anything about what happened last night." Not the part Blake knew about and definitely not what happened after.

"I want you to say you get that Troy isn't going to let this go. He will find a way to make you pay for what you did."

"I'm not twelve, Blake. I don't need you to protect me anymore."

Blake dropped his head and released a small laugh under his breath. "Well, you made that pretty clear last night." When he looked back up, his expression was once again urgent. "Just lay low until you're out of here, okay? For me?"

My nod was pensive. I really didn't need a reminder that I was only here for two more weeks. "Yeah, don't worry about it, Blake. I'll be careful."

Just before ten, I slipped out the back door. Impatience quickened my steps—quickened my pulse. I couldn't wait to see her.

Mom and Lara had cornered me a couple of hours before, ambushed me with questions about my eye, demanding answers there was no way in hell I was going to give. I'd made up some convoluted story that was barely believable about some guys I'd never seen before at the next town jumping me when Blake and I had stopped for gas. Only after I'd convinced my mom and Lara that I was fine and I'd spent the next two hours listening to them chat over hot tea was I able to escape. I imagined the late hour was my only salvation.

Besides, I figured this town had enough gossips that either of them could have just asked and they'd find the answers to their questions. As it was, I was wondering why they hadn't already heard. I guessed since the only ones who had been there last night were Blake and his small group of friends and that fucking coward Troy, no one had uttered a word. A part of me wanted the whole damned town to know what Troy had done, even if it meant I would bear the consequences of it, while the other part of me wanted to protect Maggie from any more shame.

I tried to push those thoughts aside, told myself, *it's over…it doesn't matter*. Maggie was mine. Now I just had to figure out how to get her out of that house so she'd be completely safe.

Maggie was already there when I emerged at the outskirts of our refuge. Her head snapped up when she heard me approach, *that* smile lighting her face when our eyes met. There was no hesitation as I rushed to her. I sank to the ground and pulled her into my arms.

"Hi," I mumbled between our frantic kisses.

Maggie gasped then giggled against my mouth when I spun her and pressed her into the cool grasses.

"Hi," she said, grinning when I finally pulled away to let her up for air. The moonlight seeped through the ceiling of leaves and illuminated the joy on her face. That joy faded when she focused on the mark above my eye. She reached out and ran her fingers over it.

I grabbed her hand and brought her fingers to my lips before she could say anything.

"It was worth it, Maggie…you're worth it. I need you to believe that." I'd do it a million times over if what happened last night had set her free.

I watched as disbelief and uncertainty twisted her face, and she closed her eyes and seemed to struggle against her past before she nodded her head as if maybe she understood.

Her eyes fluttered open. "I love you, William."

"Do you know how long I have been dying to hear you say that?" I almost teased as I settled myself between her legs and hugged her closer. I felt the heavy breath ease itself from her lungs and her spirit sink into mine as she relaxed beneath me. She smiled at me, her eyes wide and awakened. I loved the way she looked right then, like the girl I'd fallen in love with over the last three months, although now exposed and without the barriers she'd erected between us.

"I think I've known it for a long time," she finally said, her fingers playing with the hair at the nape of my neck. "I don't really know why I felt like I couldn't admit it." Maggie wet her lips, glanced into the distance before bringing her attention back to me. "I'm scared of *this*, of finally having something I've wanted so badly, but I'm more scared of losing it."

I squeezed her, a gentle encouragement. She was never going to lose me.

"I'm not a normal girl, William." When she said it, her eyes burned into mine, as if warning me, giving me an out.

I brushed the bangs from her face. "You think I don't *know* you, Maggie?"

Yeah, I knew she was broken, knew no matter where she ended up in life, her past would always be there to haunt her, knew she had so much to overcome. But I also knew, underneath it all, she was strong. I saw it in her eyes and felt it in her spirit. I knew she was kind and good, knew she was beautiful. And I knew I was never going to stop loving her.

"I fell in love with *you*."

A tremor of a smile tugged at one side of her mouth. "I guess that's the part I really don't understand."

"Maggie," I said as a whisper as I leaned down to kiss her. I pulled back. "You deserve to be happy." And I'd do whatever it took to be sure she was.

Cupping my cheek, she ran her thumb beneath my eye. "You make me happy."

I didn't even try to contain the smile that spread over my face.

With fall's approach, the air had cooled, a tepid breeze winding itself through the trees. Leaves rustled, and the Mississippi night hummed low. I thought I might have found paradise when I leaned down to capture her mouth with mine, as our mouths danced in a languid fluidity and I undressed her in this place that was only ours, as I held her in our sanctuary. As I loved her and promised that I always would.

I dug my fingers in the dirt where I braced myself with one hand. The other was flattened across the small of her back where I held our bodies close. Maggie cried out in a pleasure she had never known, her eyes squeezed shut tight before she opened them wide with shock.

Her expression would forever be etched in my memory. I was sure it was the most beautiful thing I'd ever seen.

I had spent my life believing I was happy. Satisfied. Until the day Maggie Krieger sent my world careening out of control. I knew then that having her was the only thing that could ever right it.

William ~ Late September, Six Years Earlier

Almost two weeks had passed. To me they felt like a day. Time sped in a blur of laughter and kisses, in a haze of tender touches and even softer words. The grasses had been crushed and flattened from the countless hours we'd spent there, every second we could find to sneak away. For me, they had been the best two weeks of my life.

Lying on our backs, Maggie was nestled in the crook of my arm with her head resting on my shoulder. We stared up at the shelter of leaves partially obstructing the blanket of stars.

"I could lie here forever," Maggie whispered into the night.

I pulled her closer, kissed the side of her head. "Me, too."

Her palm rested flat across my stomach, my hand holding her firm at the hip.

"I can't believe you have to leave in two days," she said. Heartbreak flowed through each word. "I don't..."

I looked down to see her mouth trembling as our reality took hold. Burying her face in the side of my chest, tears broke free, and she slid her hand to my side and clung to me.

"Shh...baby...don't cry." I only had one year of school left, but even to me, that felt like a lifetime. I couldn't imagine being separated from her for so long, even though I'd come back to visit every chance I got. "Will you wait for me?" I murmured into her hair.

Maggie slowly shook her head through her tears, shifting so she could look up at me.

"Do you think I couldn't? I...I—"

In her expression, I saw everything I felt.

I cut her off with a kiss, unable to bear the thought of being separated from *this* girl for so long. I couldn't fathom how lonely my nights would become or how the worry for her safety would torture me while I was away.

I wanted to consume her, every inch, every day.

Maggie gasped when I abruptly tugged her on top of me, her eyes wide and surprised as I held her face. Those warm eyes were so beautiful, still so sad, but so different than when I'd first been plowed over by them from across the fire. Now they shone with love as she looked down at me. With a measure of joy. With the beginnings of *life*.

"Marry me," I whispered urgently, increasing my hold as her eyes flooded with confusion before they grew wider with shock. She tried to scramble back, but I refused to let her go, said it again, "Marry me...let's get the hell out of here. We can get a little apartment or something while I finish school."

"Are you insane?" she asked, her hands flat on the grass on either side of my head, her hair falling around her face and down my arms.

I grinned. "Completely."

She smiled, but shook her head. "William..." My name was the sum, in it how much she really loved me, how scared she was, the sadness that she believed the idea of us only a fairytale. "My mom and my little sister. You know I can't leave them." Loyalty and fear sogged her spirit and made her twitch in my hands.

My voice softened. "I'm serious, Maggie. Marry me. I love you, and I can't stand the idea of being away from you, even if it's only for a few months at a time. I *can't* leave you here. I know you love your sister and want to take care of her, but what about you? Tell me what *you* want."

Tears welled in her eyes, and she bit at her lip.

"You really are insane." This time when she shook her head, she released a low, dubious laugh.

I smiled up at the girl I knew I'd never stop loving and asked her again, "Maggie, marry me."

She threw herself at me, her mouth frenzied. I was nearly delirious when she murmured, "Yes," against my lips. It shot straight through me, rushed as commitment through my veins where it grounded in my heart.

Yes.

We were laughing as we stumbled through the woods, a whirlwind of expectant hands and excited words. I pulled her into the shadows and pushed her up against the nearest tree. My mouth descended on hers, my spirit fevered and roused. Maybe I was insane, because I couldn't focus, could see nothing but *her*.

"Oh my God, Maggie," I murmured. "I love you. Do you have any idea how much?"

Her fingers burrowed deep in my skin, "Yes," her only reply.

I smiled at the word again, slowed my movements, and kissed her softly. I ran my fingers through the length of her hair framing her face, and whispered, "Yes."

Taking her hand, I snaked us through the hollows of town, along the sides of darkened buildings and obscured alleys. Hidden at the end of her street, I kissed her goodbye, and watched her sneak in the front door of her house one last time.

Tomorrow night, she wouldn't go back.

I sucked in a deep breath of relief and overwhelming joy.

I tracked back the way we'd come and hopped on the sidewalk halfway home. My mind was with tomorrow when I noticed the truck trailing close behind. My feet slowed as hatred flared.

Looking over my shoulder, I was blinded by headlights that sprayed out from a truck not more than fifteen feet behind me. I squinted, nerves zinging as I prepared for a fight. It was after three in the morning, and the town was dead. I could only hope Troy was alone because I was going to be in a ton of trouble if he wasn't.

Blake's warning flared in my head. *He will find a way to make you pay for what you did.*

I braced myself. Like I'd told Blake then, I'd take anything Troy brought my way.

I jumped back when the truck accelerated and swerved my direction before it righted and sped down the street.

Fisting my hair in my hands, I watched the taillights fade in the distance, trying to get ahold of my pounding heart and make sense of what had just happened.

Shit. That was stupid. Maybe I should have given Blake a little bit of credit, laid low like he'd asked me to, instead of traipsing down the center of Main Street in the dead of night.

I climbed in bed, thanking God tomorrow all of this shit would be over with.

William ~ Present Day

Fatigue pinned me to the forest ground, chained by confusion and the unknown, by the memories of what had been created in this place. I ran my palm over the cool grass. Maggie and I had shared so much here, my greatest joy and the worst heartache I'd ever known. I didn't know how much of this I could take. All I wanted was my family, wanted them safe. I sagged further as the emotional exhaustion took me over, curled onto my side. Wished I could go back six years and she would be here.

A flash of blond streaked in the moonlight, disappeared in the shadows. William lumbered over the earth, a tangled web, a snare underfoot. "Wait," he called, reaching into the shadows, grasping at nothing at all.

Despair clung to him, clawing at his skin, burrowing itself deep. He pushed forward, lost in the thicket and haze of night.

William stumbled when he came upon a clearing.

Beneath a tree, the boy rocked himself, soft cries buried in his knees.

"Jonathan," William whispered.

Startled, the boy looked up. William gasped for air, the boy's face covered in blood. "My daddy is so mad."

I woke up gasping for the same breath, gripping my head.

On my hands and knees, I pushed myself onto my feet. I jogged back through the forest trail, materialized on the edge of Main Street of the sleeping town. Chills rolled down my spine as I forged ahead. I passed Blake's street, rushed across the road, and took the third right down.

There was no other place I could go.

I stood in the middle of the road, staring. It was a tiny house, painted a dingy blue. Night wrapped it in silhouettes. I crept forward, light underfoot, slinked along its outer walls. I placed my hand flat on the side window. I felt the sadness within those walls, the ache of a home where no joy lived. It lit a seizure of emotion, anger and hurt and an old devotion I'd hidden deep.

The boy's face swirled behind my closed eyes.

I lowered the gates and let the anger well.

By the time I forced myself away, I was swimming in it, in the same fury that had overpowered me six years before, the same that had wanted to see him die. I waded through the storm, fumbled my way back to Blake's house, and collapsed onto the unmade bed.

Chapter Fourteen

Maggie ~ Present Day

With the snap of my wrists, the blanket unfurled, billowing out in the wind before it settled to the grass floor. Just a mild chill still hung in the air. I lowered myself onto the blanket and drew my legs up under me.

The children ran to the playground. Amber's two small children toddled out over the field and to the sand. Jonathan trailed awkwardly behind. He looked back over his shoulder, as if asking for guidance. I gestured with my chin for him to go on.

I hated he was always this way, shy and unsure.

Amber climbed down beside me with a big, bulky camera in her hands.

"God...they are just *incredible*, aren't they?" she said as she focused the long lens, snapping picture after picture of the kids as they played. A shrill cry of giddy laughter rose up from her eighteen-month-old daughter, echoing over the play yard. "Sometimes I still can't believe they're mine."

Jonathan flashed proud brown eyes back at me and a timid smile crept over his face, but it was one that spoke of joy as he cautiously found his footing on the jungle gym and wove his way to the top. Incredible didn't begin to describe the way my son made me feel.

I moved to hug my knees, before I looked over at my little sister who continued on in a constant barrage of clicks.

I couldn't help but smile.

My sister had escaped.

Amber caught me staring, her mouth twisting up in a little half smile as she blew back a thick lock of brown hair that had fallen in her face.

"What?" Her dark hazel eyes were wide and playful.

"I'm just happy for you," I said.

Amber had a husband who loved and respected her and two children who were—just as she'd said—incredible.

Amber glanced over the kids, before she turned her attention back to me. "It's because of you, you know."

I knew what she was saying, and I bit at the side of my bottom lip and shook my head. "That's not true, Amber."

She scowled. "You think I'd be here right now if it wasn't for you? Do you really think I would have survived?"

I was suddenly back in our little room, and I knew she was too. The fear. How it had crawled thick and menacing along the walls and hung heavy in the air. Suffocating and pressing down.

I could almost feel the little girl climbing into bed beside me, the way Amber would bury her face in my side when I wrapped her in my arms, could feel her shake as she cried. I could almost hear myself whispering to her that it was going to be okay.

I hugged my knees closer and looked away.

"I survived and you didn't." Amber's presence beside me was overwhelming, the urgency in her tone, even though the words were said in no more than a whisper.

Forcing a smile, I turned back to her. "I'm still alive, Amber."

"Only part of you." Her face was sad. I was sure mine was too.

That small flame that had lived inside of me had burned out that night—the night when the fantasy William had painted and I'd been foolish enough to believe was shattered when *my* reality came crashing down. I'd been...nothing. Empty. Dead. The only evidence my heart still beat had been the ache William had left behind.

Only Jonathan had set it aflame. Now it smoldered somewhere deep, kept hidden with the memories of the treasure I'd let slip away.

"You were strong enough for us both." Amber glanced in Jonathan's direction. His hair whipped around his face as his younger cousin chased him. He laughed, stumbling through the sand on unsure feet.

"Do you really think you're going to be strong enough for the both of you to make it through again?"

It wasn't as if I didn't know this. Understand it, even. Every day, I imagined my escape. What it would be like to finally be free. Every day, it seemed just a fantasy, just like William holding me was every night. I knew something had to give. Cracks only deepened, widened, and eventually buckled. One of *us* was going to fall.

I just prayed to God it wasn't me.

"You have to do something, Maggie. I can't watch you live like this anymore."

"It's not that bad." The words came naturally and without thought.

Amber tilted her head and shook it sadly as if she couldn't believe I'd just said what I did.

She suddenly twisted her head around and rested her chin on her shoulder.

"God, that guy is such a creep, isn't he?"

I followed her line of sight to the black SUV parked directly on the other side of the street.

That hidden flame burned, though my stomach clamped in apprehension. My eyes flicked to Jonathan then back to him, gauging William's purpose.

I shouldn't have been surprised he was here. Since seeing him in front of Amber's last night, I'd caught him following me twice, once after dropping Jonathan off at kindergarten this morning and again when I was leaving my mother's house. Part of me was terrified of his intentions, of what he may be planning, while another part of me felt safer under his watch than I had in years.

Amber was too young to really be able to remember William, the years apart leaving them with no connection.

Just like me, William had become a rumor.

I stared back at him. Protective affection radiated in his posture as his eyes left me to find my son.

An old comfort rose.

The same affection had been there in his unwavering gaze when I'd walked into the restaurant on Thursday, even when mine had fallen. It had been even stronger last night when I'd stood in front of my sister's house, again lost in William, staring at what should have been.

"Apparently, he didn't get the memo that it's kind of weird for a guy to just sit in his car alone and watch kids playing in the park," Amber said as if a joke, though the strain in her voice belied her true unease. "Did you know he moved into his brother's guesthouse down the street on Friday? I've seen him a few times, and he always just...stares." She exaggerated a shudder.

I was unable to look away from William when I spoke. "He's a good man, Amber. You don't need to be frightened of him."

I sensed the pause in my sister, the trip in her thoughts.

"You know him?" Amber asked.

I glimpsed the confusion on her face.

William.

My secret, my heart.

The beautiful man I'd lain with for hours under the stars, our lives poured out in a torrent of stories and words. The way he held me while I shared the ones that hurt me the most. How he touched me, the way he made me feel incredibly safe. How that hold had escalated from safety to ecstasy as the soft pads of his fingers would dance across my lips when he locked himself to me, the perfect weight of his body, the expression on his face when he came.

The heartbreak in his eyes when I told him goodbye.

I knew it all.

"Yeah." My voice was soft. "I know him."

I waved from the driver's seat of my van as Amber pulled out onto the street, the tranquil spring day drawing to an end. Our kids had played the entire afternoon while we watched over them. I had savored the time. It felt amazing to see my son run and soar on the swing on his belly, laughing uninhibited. For a few short hours, he was free. I'd basked in the warmth of the new sun, the cool breeze its perfect companion.

And I reveled in *him*. Even in the whirlwind of emotions his reappearance incited in my life, William's light was inescapable.

He sat there for close to an hour, and I wondered if he could feel it too.

Did I wrap him up in comfort, like a familiar embrace? Did I stir him up, a welcomed chaos that stole his breath? Did he feel himself just on the cusp, that churning intuition that things were about to change?

Did it scare him, the way it scared me?

But God, I wanted it.

Fairytales had begun to knit themselves through my heart and mind, ones that no longer seemed so distant, now only just out of reach.

I looked back over the playground to its edge, to where the trees grew tall and tangled. Our sanctuary was buried just inside. I hadn't been there in years. I'd gone once, seeking refuge in its seclusion. Without him there, I'd never felt so alone. In six years, I'd never gone back.

Now...

I shook my head from the dangerous thoughts and glanced at my son in the rearview mirror.

I knew my judgment was skewed. I'd lived in step with the fear, surrendering to its demands. I'd done it believing I was protecting Jonathan and protecting myself. The hardest to swallow was the reality that part of my reasoning was true, but our situation was never going to change until I did something about it.

Shifting the van into reverse, I slowly backed out onto the street and headed to the house. Troy's truck was parked in the carport. I pulled in beside it and took the key from the ignition.

During the short trip, Jonathan had fallen asleep in his car seat after the long day of play, his head lolling to the side. I smiled as I quietly unbuckled him and picked him up.

He felt so good in my arms, like everything that was right. I nuzzled my nose into the hair that hung over his ear, his breath thick on my neck.

That internal chaos quivered and rose.

I jerked to look behind me. Craning my head, I squinted my eyes, scanning the empty street.

Comfort surged and wrapped me tight.

Shaking myself from it, I forced myself inside, glancing once more over my shoulder before I shut the back door behind me.

"Where the fuck have you been?" Troy demanded before he tipped a can of beer to his mouth. I knew his tone, filled with accusation and blame that was never mine, as if I were to blame for how miserable he was inside. He sat at the table, shirtless, his eyes scrutinizing as they looked me up and down.

"I was with Amber and the kids…at the park." I crossed the kitchen, hugging my son closer. I paused and looked down at the man who had stolen my life. "I told you where we were going."

I wondered when I'd begun to think of him as weak, just a sick, pathetic man, just like my father. I'd allowed him to control me for so long, and he did it well. He always knew exactly where to get me and exactly how to hold me.

His face twisted in a sneer, but he didn't move.

He'd wait.

I turned away and left him there while I took Jonathan to his room. As gently as I could, I pulled his shoes and socks from his feet. He stretched and snuggled under the covers, but the movement never broke into his sleep. Brushing back his hair, I kissed him on the forehead. "I love you, my sweet boy."

Then I stood and went to face what I knew waited for me outside the room.

Walking into the kitchen, I went straight to the sink and began washing the few dishes left there from this morning. It bore down on me — the anger that had been bred into Troy by his father. I fought the fear that had been bred into me by my own.

He approached like the stillness before the storm, his words a perverted murmur near my ear. "I'll kill you, Maggie...I'll find you, and this time, I'll kill you."

I pinched my eyes shut and bit my bottom lip to suppress the cry I bottled in my throat.

My head spun and my stomach turned.

Maggie ~ Six Years Earlier

My heart was still thundering, and laughter still danced on my tongue when I snuck into the darkened house. I leaned back against the front door, trying to calm my pulse, trying to slow my mind. Touching my lips with my fingertips, I smiled.

William loved me. Wanted me with him forever. Sometimes I still couldn't believe how my life had changed over the summer.

At the bonfire for Blake and Grace two weeks before, standing in front of Troy and telling him I didn't want him and I never had had been one of the most frightening things I'd ever done. Never before had I stood up for myself. But I'd looked to William for strength, to remember the way he made me feel as we spent those long hours alone in the woods.

I hadn't expected Troy's reaction and was shocked by William's. It had all been as if in slow motion, the fists, the blood. All I could think was I would never forgive myself if something happened to William because of me.

It was then I finally admitted it to myself.

I was in love with him.

The second Justin had dropped me off at the front of my house, still shaking but promising him I was fine, I rushed to our spot. William never came.

I'd paced, every worry I could have had twisting its way through my heart and mind, William was hurt...William was angry...William finally realized I wasn't worth all the trouble.

When I could take it no longer, I found the hidden key Mrs. Marsch had shown me under a pot on their back porch and slipped in the back door. I'd known I was crossing a line, acting completely out of character, but William made me forget who I was.

I told myself I'd go to be sure he wasn't hurt, never anticipating the heartbreak I felt when I entered his room and found that he just hadn't come.

Not once in three months had he not, until that night. Rejection had poured from me as a grieved accusation.

Then he'd uttered the words and told me he loved me, and for the first time in my life, I felt worthy of it.

It was everything I'd ever wanted. Someone who really loved me. I knew I was naïve, but I was wise enough to know this wasn't just a reaction or a desperate appeal for affection.

I loved him.

Giving myself to him—I shook my head because I still didn't understand it—I guess I thought it would be some sort of sacrifice for the one I loved. Or maybe I'd been looking to build a memory, something to hang onto once he was gone. What I never could have imagined was the way he would feel, like life and joy. Above it all, there'd been no shame.

I looked around the tattered living room I'd grown up in, completely dark save for the faint slivers of moonlight leaking in through the windows.

There'd only be one thing I would miss.

Creeping upstairs, I let myself into my childhood room. Amber slept buried beneath the covers in her tiny twin bed.

On a heavy sigh, my gaze wandered over the bump where my little sister lay. I couldn't imagine leaving her in this place. I crossed the room and crawled into bed with her.

For so many years, it had been the other way around.

I wrapped her in my arms. In her sleep, Amber tensed, before she relaxed into my hold. I lay awake, thinking of William's words. It was time I did what was right for me, even though I knew my leaving was going to hurt my mom and devastate my sister.

I hugged Amber closer and whispered, "I'm so sorry."

But there was no way I could live without William.

CK280

Twilight approached. The humidity was still present, but the air wasn't nearly as muggy as it had been just a couple of short weeks ago.

And how short those weeks had been.

I smiled to myself as I hugged my arms across my chest, this time, not as a way to hold myself together, but in memory of the way I felt in William's arms and in excitement for what was to come.

I was going to marry William.

I'd just been to the ATM on Main Street and emptied my bank account of all the money I saved over the summer while working for the Marsches. I stuffed the small wad of cash in my back pocket. It wasn't a whole lot, but it was every penny I had to my name.

I crossed the street and headed toward home.

It was time to tell my sister goodbye. I contemplated what I would say as I walked with my head hung low. I was going to miss her so much, and I prayed she'd be safe.

Turning right, I cut across the far end of town, taking the long road that wound around before it crossed with my street. My footsteps echoed in my ears as I counted them, my nerves increasing as I imagined leaving my house for the last time tonight. I still couldn't believe I was actually leaving. I lifted my face to the cooling air. Night crawled its way westward and a lone star dotted the sky.

Dread twisted a knot in my stomach when I heard the sound of the engine behind me. I hadn't seen him since that night. I dropped my head further and increased my speed. Troy was the last person I wanted to deal with right now.

The truck slowed as it came up behind me. He cut over into the wrong lane and came right up beside me. I didn't look up.

"I wanna talk to you, Maggie," Troy said, his voice low and simmering with hatred.

That hatred rushed over me as chills, an internal warning flare. I squeezed myself closer, as if somehow I could twine myself so tight I would disappear.

"I said I want to talk to you."

I began to walk so quickly I may well have been running. I guessed Troy knew that was exactly what I was doing.

The truck inched forward alongside me.

"Maggie…I'm not fucking around with you. Get your ass in the truck."

As hard as I fought it, my eyes darted over my shoulder. They went wide when they met with Troy's face. I was completely unprepared for the destruction evidenced there. Bruises still marked him beneath both eyes and ran across his nose. Rows of stitches had been removed from above one eye and at his jaw. In their place were angry, puckered scars.

Troy noticed my reaction. His nostrils flared. "I'm warning you, Maggie...*get in the truck.*"

I couldn't...wouldn't give in. I pinched my eyes shut once more, sucking in a deep breath as something inside of me snapped.

I ran.

The rubber soles of my tennis shoes slapped against the concrete as humid air slapped across my face. I just had to make it to the end of the street.

The truck lurched forward before it jerked to a stop beside me. The door was thrown open, and Troy was right behind me.

My heart pounded in the worst way. A flood of terrified adrenaline thundered through my veins and roared in my ears. A slew of curses were unleashed from his mouth, hatred and corrupt thoughts.

He yanked me back by a handful of hair. My knee twisted and buckled beneath me. The joint felt as if it burst as it erupted with a red-hot, lancinating pain.

A scream tore from my throat.

Troy clamped a hand over my mouth and jerked my back against his chest. "Shut the fuck up, you stupid bitch."

I tasted the vile skin of his hand as he held his palm harder against my mouth, dirt and oil and sweat. I gagged and bile rushed up to take the place of the scream still rattling in my throat.

I struggled against the arms caging me. My deepest fear gripped me when he began to drag me back between two houses, where we blended into the dusky shadows.

Grass and dirt slicked beneath the rubber soles of my shoes as I fought to dig my heels in, fighting to break his hold. I clawed at his hands and bit at his palm.

"I will kill you, Maggie," he threatened in a low growl at my ear.

I flailed more.

"Help me...please...help!" My pleas were lost in the palm of his hand.

We broke from the secluded walls of the houses and to the wide, unfenced backyards. A dog barked, viciously straining against the chain that held it back by its neck. A solitary light gleamed from the back porch, although the movement from inside that I begged for never came.

I knew where he was taking me. As a child, I'd played in these woods a thousand times.

Tears broke free and streamed from my eyes. My vision blurred in both fury and dread as the glimmer of light faded in the distance. Trees rose up like walls on every side, darkness swallowing us whole.

I cried out when Troy threw me to the ground. My back slammed against the forest floor with a painful thud, followed by my head. I dug my elbows and heels into the slippery soil as I fumbled my way backward, desperate to get away from the man who stared down at me with a twisted revulsion, like he hated me and had to have me at the same time.

I couldn't allow this to happen. Not after William had fought for me. Not after he'd *loved* me.

Flipping myself over, I crawled along the ground. Twigs snapped beneath the weight of my knees and pierced my skin. In the humid late-summer night, the dirt and leaves somehow felt cold where they burned and scraped along the abrasions. The acrid air filled up my nose with the smell of rot and decay.

Gathering all my strength, I labored to my feet. A hand descended on my shoulder, pitching me to the side. I landed on my right thigh and skidded across the ground.

Troy laughed. "Where do you think you're going, Maggie?"

He lunged at me, forcing his knee between my thighs. A heavy arm pinned me down across the chest.

No. I spit in his face. "You asshole."

Troy roared. He swiped the wad from the edge of his mouth and looked at his fingertips. "You little bitch." The blow came to the side of my face. "Did you really think I'd just let you talk to me that way…make a fool of me?"

He fumbled at the buckle of his pants. Metal clanked as he tore it free.

"No," I whimpered, turning my face to the side and squeezing my eyes. *No.*

I thrashed.

No.

"Please." *Oh my God. Please don't let him do this to me.*

He tore at my shorts, shoved them down to my ankles and off one leg, and ripped my panties from my body.

I tried to press my knees together. They only pressed into Troy's bare thighs.

I fought him until the moment he took me, until the moment he stole the beginning of life that had been planted in me, the small flicker of light that had begun to glow, the spark that had told me I just might be worth it.

The tears of dread gave way to a flood of submission.

Still, I whimpered *no* as I pinched my eyes shut in a bid to remove myself from the torture Troy inflicted.

"Look at me."

I squeezed my eyes closed tighter.

His hand went to my chin where he dug his fingers deep into the skin. "I told you to look at me."

In the faint light, my eyes opened and met with the same sickness I'd witnessed my entire life.

"I want you to remember this, Maggie...the next time you try to run from me...you...remember...this."

He clenched my jaw harder as his face twisted, his body hurried in anticipation.

I fought him one last time, and a wrenching cry came from deep within my shattered soul.

Troy's body jerked. A vengeful grin spread across his face and malignant satisfaction flashed in his eyes. He collapsed on me, cupping my cheek while he whispered in the opposite ear. "Don't forget it."

When he pulled away to stand, I curled in on myself and wept as grief took over. It coiled as misery and loss in the pit of my stomach and erupted as anguish from my mouth.

Troy glanced over his shoulder into the still night, before he turned and kicked me in the stomach. It wasn't hard enough to hurt, just hard enough to remind me of the trash I was.

"Get up." He leaned down and tossed my shorts toward me. They landed in a tattered, stained wad in front of my face. "Get dressed."

I looked up at him as he buckled his belt and smoothed his hair back with both hands.

I hated him...*hated* him. But not as much as I hated myself.

Wincing, I sat up and pulled the torn shorts up my legs.

Oh God, I hurt when I climbed to my feet, an excruciating numbness that seared through my flesh and spirit.

Troy held out his hand and I took it. I had no reason left to fight him.

He wound us back through the quickly darkening night, through the short distance of forest where he'd destroyed me, across the blackened yards, and between the houses. At the street, the door to his truck was still open wide. The cabin light burned bright, and the engine still rumbled low.

No one had even noticed.

Troy wrenched the passenger door open and I climbed inside. I stared out the side window as he drove the quarter-mile to my house. The truck came to a standstill in front of the place I thought I'd finally escaped.

"I'll be here to get you when I get off work tomorrow."

I didn't look up when I reached for the door handle. I froze when he spoke again.

"I'd better not catch you going to the cops and making a bigger deal about this than it is, Maggie. They won't believe you, anyway. Everyone in this town already knows you're mine. But if you do, I promise I'm gonna find out if your little sister feels as good as you do."

I swallowed down his words and took them to heart because I knew he'd make good on them, then I slowly opened the door and climbed out.

Maggie ~ Present Day

Troy breathed down my neck, corralling my sides as he gripped the kitchen counter to trap me, his words replaying in my mind. *I'll kill you, Maggie.*

It was the third time he'd ever given me that threat. The first time had been the night he'd shattered my heart and stolen William from my life. The second time was when I'd *tried,* as futile as it'd been, to save my son from living this way. It was the night I'd actually believed Troy was going to kill me.

And he'd said it tonight. Chills rolled down my spine as his intent finally dawned.

He thought I was getting ready to run.

My eyes dropped closed, William's face in my mind.

The chaos raged, and I felt myself slipping a little closer to the edge.

Chapter Fifteen

William ~ Present Day

On Tuesday, I sat down the road and across from the elementary school where the kindergarten was housed. Waiting. I followed her the entire day yesterday, trying to understand and make sense of the connection I had with the boy, the connection I had with Maggie. After seeing them on Sunday, this need was something I could not ignore. Yesterday morning, I stayed back as I followed her to the school where she dropped off Jonathan and then had gone on to her mother's, not sure how Maggie would react. I'd gotten brave enough to expose myself when I followed them to the park that afternoon. She needed to know I couldn't and wouldn't stay away.

An anxious smile tugged at my mouth when the blue van pulled into the school parking lot. I sat up, straining to see.

Maggie stepped out from the driver's side. The smile on my mouth spread when I saw the ease on her face.

I'd almost forgotten how well I knew her, what I found in her expression, how I could tell exactly how she felt.

This morning she was happy.

Sliding the side door open, Maggie helped Jonathan climb down from his seat. The child grinned up at her when she ran her fingers through the locks of his golden hair. Emotion filled my chest.

I wondered if Maggie was so blind that she really didn't see it or if she was too scared to admit it. I guessed it was probably somewhere in between. Jealousy bit at my nerves. Who knew when that sick fuck had coerced her into his bed. As much as I couldn't stand the thought, I knew it had to have been as soon as I left.

I watched my son scurry behind his mother with his hand in hers through the front gate and disappear into the crowded, narrow hall of the school.

No, being a father had never been something I had longed for, although I'd always figured one day I would have a child, and I'd known instinctively I'd be committed and love my family once I did. With Maggie, it'd somehow never even crossed my mind, my every thought wrapped up in loving her.

What I never could have imagined was that it would come at a distance, a connection on disconnect. Now that longing was there, filling me with loss and lingering thoughts of a baby boy, little joys and small triumphs, experiences I would never know. Eclipsing those thoughts was terror for a child I really knew nothing about, only an affinity in my dreams and a face to match my own. But in the moments when I was able to push that terror aside, it was shocking just how badly not knowing Jonathan hurt.

Ten minutes later, Maggie resurfaced at the gate. She hesitated, scanning the lot, although her gaze never made it all the way to where I watched her from down the street. When she pulled out, I turned around and got in line three cars behind her.

Stupid?

Probably. I just didn't know anymore, and I really didn't care if it was.

I already knew where she was headed. She'd gone there yesterday morning after she dropped Jonathan off at school. I couldn't begin to grasp why. The stories of the torment she'd been subjected to within the walls of that house still turned my stomach. I'd always listened without a word, silently understanding she'd never been able to voice them before, while inside it had torn me apart.

When I'd gone back to California, I'd become so jaded. I'd built up walls to protect myself from thoughts of compassion, chalked them up to a sign of weakness.

I realized now it'd just been a tool of preservation, because it fucking destroyed me to think of Maggie being hurt. Every minute I'd spent back in Mississippi had slowly stripped that protection away.

I inched passed the road to Maggie's old house and turned onto the street behind it.

Yesterday, I had moved on from here after I watched Maggie walk along the backside of her parents' house and had driven by the grungy shop where Troy worked just to be sure he was there, a small assurance that, for the time being, Maggie was safe.

But not today.

I hopped out of my car and pressed the lock on the key fob. The car emitted a low *bleep* and the lights flashed. I cast a furtive glance around, wishing my car sitting on the side of the road in this shitty neighborhood wasn't so ridiculously obvious.

Stupid.

I took the edge of the road at almost a jog. My gaze continually darted around my surroundings, watching for some sign that someone noticed I was here. I jumped when a dog lunged at my side and rammed into a chain-link fence. It snarled and snapped at the metal as I passed.

My pulse thundered, fear and need and perseverance.

I wasn't leaving here until I talked to her.

About a quarter-mile up was an empty lot. With my heart still pounding, I leaned down and pushed the barbed wires apart and slid between them. In my anxiety, I stood and looked around again, then tried to keep my footsteps as quiet as possible as I moved forward, prowling in broad daylight. A jungle of weeds grew to my knees and swished against my jeans as I pushed forward. Old tires were piled haphazardly in the middle, a rotted, flat basketball to the side, a dilapidated swing set falling apart toward the back.

Sadness welled, and for a second, I wished for the walls to be back in place.

At the end of the lot, a row of trees had been planted as a boundary. The trunks grew high and the branches sprouted out about halfway up, reaching out to shade the entire yard. In their shelter, I stopped, bracing myself with a hand on a tree as I looked toward the back of Maggie's old house.

A frenzy of emotions twisted through my consciousness, so many they were hard to discern — sadness and love — pity and lust — anger and a broken heart I'd hidden away because I'd never known how to deal with it.

I slumped to the damp, dirty ground and listened to the indistinct sounds coming from inside. Only a patchy lawn and rickety door separated me from the girl, who, without even knowing it, had captured me the moment I'd seen her. For two hours, I just sat there, lost in thoughts and memories.

I jumped to my feet in a race of nerves when the handle rattled and the back door swung open.

Over her shoulder, Maggie called, "See you tomorrow."

She stepped out and turned around to click the door shut, jiggling the handle to be sure it was locked. I watched her slow, as if suddenly overwhelmed, feet chained to the ground. She stood with her back to me, one hand flat on the door, her head hung and body still.

I wanted to know what she was thinking almost as badly as I wanted to touch her.

From the cover of the trees, I slowly approached. Each cautious footstep I took brought her closer to me. I knew she felt me, knew she sensed my presence in the way she tensed. She sucked in air and dropped her arms to her sides.

She never turned around, only waited.

A foot away, I stopped. Her body rose and fell in sync with mine, her short, gasping breaths matching the jagged ones I forced in and out of my lungs. Strands of auburn ruffled in the breeze and brushed across my face, the sweetness of Maggie filling my nose and overpowering my senses. My fingers twitched forward, remembering just how soft that auburn was when I wove my fingers through it.

God, I wanted her.

The shiver that rolled through Maggie was palpable even to me.

I wound my arms around her and pulled her flush, my palms flat on her stomach.

Cheek to cheek. Skin to skin.

I burned.

I ran my nose up her jaw and whispered in her ear, "I don't know how to stop loving you."

Maggie trembled in my hold. A small cry erupted from her mouth as she covered my hands with hers and flattened her body against mine. Her head tilted away to bring us closer, her neck exposed.

I buried my face in the snowy flesh. My arms tightened around her as every nerve came alive. They'd lain dormant for so long, it almost hurt. Repressing a groan in the haven of her neck, I pressed my lips against her skin.

Maggie whimpered my name.

The last shred of control I had slipped.

In a flurry of movement, I spun her around and pushed her against the door. My mouth met hers, fevered and impatient. I buried my hands in the auburn locks I'd so desperately longed to touch. I wound them through my fingers, tugged her closer, kissed her deeper.

Her mouth opened on a shuddered moan. It was almost a sob. I devoured it. A long-suppressed sob of my own bubbled up somewhere in my consciousness and lodged as a weighted mass in my throat.

I loved this girl so much. Too much.

"Maggie...oh God...Maggie," I mumbled between my desperate play to consume her, to fill up this hole she'd left when she'd broken our hearts. It only expanded when tears spilled from her eyes and over my hands, and for the shortest second, she gave in and kissed me back.

Cupping her face, I pulled away and stared down at her. Her eyes were all brown misery and love and shame, and the most wistful of smiles hinted on her swollen lips. Timid fingertips traced my face, as if to remember—to memorize—something to take with her when she walked away. Chills followed in their wake, an aching loss across my skin, torment I didn't think I'd survive. Her touch spoke of it—of giving in and letting go—but her eyes were so sad, I knew she never would.

"No," I pled as I crushed myself to her, my mouth urgent in its petition, strong and overpowering. I kissed her in a way I should have when she'd let me go instead of walking away from her.

Insistent hands roamed up the softness of her slender arms, palmed her delicate neck, ran down across the exposed skin of her chest, and begged at her hips.

Please.

I couldn't bear it, couldn't let her go, but I knew she was already gone. She was limp, and I knew she had withdrawn to that distant place she'd escaped to that night.

"Please, Maggie," I said, grasping her face, "let me in."

She averted her gaze. "William, you know I can't."

I pushed myself closer to erase every inch of space between us. Holding myself up with my hands on either side of her head, I brushed my cheek across hers. "Why...why not? Tell me why I can't have you." My mouth was back at her jaw. "Why did you choose this life?"

Maggie choked over unspent emotion and hid her face at my throat. "I didn't."

She kissed me there beneath my jaw, a lingering caress as she clung to me by my shoulders.

Then she pushed me away.

I stumbled back. The anguished expression on her face snuffed out the last bit of anger I'd held for her all of these years.

I grabbed her wrist when she turned to run. This time she didn't flinch, though she wouldn't look my way.

"I won't walk away from you this time, Maggie...not you or Jonathan. I will fight for you."

She squeezed my hand as if begging me to keep my word, then she jerked it away and took off with her hand covering her mouth. I didn't chase her. I just watched as she disappeared around the side of the house.

I hadn't thought it possible to hurt any worse than I had. I hadn't believed anything could be more excruciating than walking away from her that night six years ago.

But I was wrong.

My heart and body still sped from her touch, filled with the same intense need that only Maggie had ever brought out in me, although my legs felt weak, my feet heavy as I forced myself back across her mother's yard and out onto the shanty street. As I climbed into my SUV, I didn't look twice at the old woman who eyed me with suspicion while she beat a rug against the railing of her front porch.

I didn't care about anything except for the broken words that had dropped from Maggie's mouth.

I didn't.

William ~ September, Six Years Earlier

"You're awfully happy this morning. Bet you can't wait to get out of here tomorrow morning," my mom teased, although I didn't miss the sadness behind her words. Every time I left, my mother cried. For so many years, I'd believed one day it would be permanent and I would say goodbye and never come back to stay. Sure, I'd visit, but both my mother and I knew it would never be the same.

Now, I had no idea what the future held. I didn't know if Maggie would fall in love with Los Angeles and would want to make it our home, if leaving would help to heal her and distance her from her past.

Or would she miss it here and want to return?

The little tugging in my chest told me I hoped she'd want to come back, but really, I'd be happy wherever Maggie wanted to go.

I smiled at Mom. "I just have some...really good news."

"Oh? And what's that?"

"I'll tell you tonight."

"Keeping secrets from your mom now, William?"

I had the urge to hug her. "I'm really going to miss you, Mom," I said as I wrapped her in a small embrace.

She patted my back.

"You'll be back at Christmas. It'll fly by." She squeezed me a little tighter. "Only one more year." It sounded like a promise to herself.

Guilt fluttered its wings in my stomach. Even though I was sure my mother would empathize, and I knew over the summer she'd grown to really care about Maggie too, I knew a part of her would be hurt I'd kept my relationship with Maggie a secret.

"Love you, Ma."

"You have no idea how much I love you."

Cয়৯৩

There was a rap on the wall next to my door. I glanced over my shoulder.

Blake peeked in with a grin on his face. "What the hell are you doing, man?"

I shrugged and threw a smirk in my brother's direction. It was pretty *obvious* what I was doing as I grabbed another shirt and shoved it into the duffle bag that was unzipped and wide-open on the bed. The rest of my things were in piles around it, everything except for my bathroom stuff and a change of clothes for the morning.

"Running away from Mississippi again, huh?" Blake hopped onto my bed and lay down, pushing a pile of jeans aside with his leg as he stretched out along the side with his hands behind his head. His work boots were smeared with dried mud.

"Dude, get your boots off my bed."

Blake dug them in further, toppling a pile of shirts off the bed and onto the floor.

I shook my head, though I couldn't help the smile. "You're such an asshole."

Blake laughed. "That's why you love me, little brother." He blew out a heavy breath and looked up at the ceiling. "I'm going miss you, Will. It sucks when you're not around."

I stopped packing to look over at him. "Yeah, I'm going to miss you, too."

His gaze shifted to me, his expression intense. "Listen, I've been wanting to ask you something. I want you to stand up for me as my best man in my wedding next summer." He rubbed the back of his hand over his mouth before he sat up on the edge of the bed with his back to me. He seemed to contemplate before he looked back over his shoulder. "You know you're my best friend, Will. It doesn't matter if you're my brother or not...there's nobody else I'd want standing up there beside me."

We'd always been close, but we rarely had conversations like this. I got it. It felt as if everything was changing, our lives speeding up as the days of our adolescence blurred.

"Of course, Blake. There's not a chance in Hell I'd miss it."

We stared at each other for a moment. The secret I was hiding burned on my tongue and another wave of guilt bound its way up my throat. I hated keeping something so important from my brother, but I couldn't bring myself to tell him yet. I wanted Maggie standing by my side when I told my family about her, for them to see how much I really loved her — wanted them to see that this wasn't some little summer fling.

Shifting, Blake drew one leg up onto the bed to face me. His face was almost awed. "I still can't believe I'm getting married. I'm kind of freaked out about it, if I'm being honest."

I frowned. "What do you mean? Are you having second thoughts?"

Blake kind of shrugged. "No...not second thoughts. Just scared, I guess."

Scared. I was no stranger to that emotion, but mine had been born of entirely different fears. Grabbing another pile of clothes and shoving them into my bag, I realized I hadn't had time to *really* think about the future. Every decision I'd made with Maggie had been impulsive...instinctual. I wondered if there was something wrong with me that I couldn't begin to relate to the worries that seemed to have crept up on my brother.

Blake scratched at the back of his neck and turned his attention to the floor.

"But God, I love her. It makes me sick to think of not being with her." He chuckled and glanced up at me.

Now that I could understand.

CR80

The back door clicked behind me, and I was enveloped by the night. Billions of stars blinked down from the moonless sky. I quieted my feet over the wooden planks of the porch, an act I'd perfected over the summer.

I couldn't remember another time in my life when I'd felt more anxious — more excited — than I did now. This would be the last time I'd ever sneak from this house. Tonight marked a new chapter in my life, one in which Maggie was no longer something of the night, a secret without shame, although it felt as if our relationship had somehow been soiled by the way we'd kept it concealed.

In less than eight hours, we'd be on the road, fleeing Maggie's past and running toward our future. We'd never even shared a meal, but I knew Maggie better than anyone I'd ever known, and she'd dug in deep and exposed the real man I was. She made me better. Made me happy.

I smiled at the all-encompassing feeling that danced in my stomach and spread out over every inch of my being as I ran through my neighborhood and darted across the road. Maggie'd been the only one who'd ever come close to creating it, but I'd understood it the moment I experienced it.

The playground was deserted. A hazy yellow glow illuminated the area from the solitary parking lamp. I ran through the playground and hit the trail. I couldn't wait to wrap my arms around my girl, couldn't wait to see the excitement on her face.

I almost laughed because none of it made sense. When I'd left to come home for the summer, I never could have imagined what would take place in three short months. I never could have imagined my life would be turned upside-down, that I'd fall head-first. Trip. Love a girl more than I'd ever thought possible.

I was going to marry Maggie.

My feet quickened at the thought. It didn't matter we had no plans and had no place to stay, because I sure as hell couldn't take her back to stay with the leches I called roommates. All that mattered was I wanted this, wanted her, forever.

Rushing over the trail, I pushed branches out of the way as I hurried to our spot faster than I ever had. In my haste, I almost fell when she first came into view. My feet faltered as they slid to a stop over the dewy ground. A tight band constricted my chest, throbbed as pain where my heart accelerated and beat against my ribs.

"Maggie," I whispered. I slowly approached, the sickest feeling slipping through my veins.

She stood in the middle of the small clearing, facing away, but I knew. She was hiding.

"Maggie, baby, what happened?" Shaking, I reached a tentative hand out to touch her shoulder.

She flinched away.

Taking a breath, I slipped my hand under her hair to the back of her neck in a touch of encouragement. "Mag—"

The word died on my tongue when she finally turned to look up at me. Her expression was like a punch to the gut, enough to knock the wind from my lungs in an audible gush of air.

"Maggie."

I instantly took her face in my urgent hands, my touch desperate to break her from wherever she had gone. In everything we'd been through, I'd never once seen her look this way. Her face was flat, expressionless and pale, though her eyes were crimson red as if she'd spent days crying. Behind the red, in the depths of the warm brown where I'd lost myself time and time again, there was *nothing*. My Maggie was gone.

"Maggie." I tightened my hold and gently shook her. *Please come back to me.*

A flicker of something lashed in her eyes.

"Maggie." Softly I pressed my mouth to hers and held her face, coaxing her back. "Maggie, I'm here. I'm here."

She began to cry.

"Baby...don't cry...don't cry...ssh." Pulling back, I wiped her tears with my thumbs, my smile soft and my murmurs tender. "It's okay, sweetheart, it's okay. Tell me what happened."

She cried harder. I tasted her tears when she suddenly pulled me down by the neck to kiss me. Her fingers dug into my skin as if clinging to a life slipping away. Terror hit me when I realized it was not going to be *okay*. It sunk in that she had none of her things, and I knew then what she had come here to say.

"Oh, God, Maggie, don't do this." I wasn't going to allow this to happen. I tried to wrap her up in my arms to give her reassurance, maybe to give it to myself, but she pushed me away.

"Just go, William," she begged beneath her breath. She was back to hugging herself, weeping toward the forest floor.

"No, Maggie. I'm not going anywhere without you. Tell me what the hell happened between now and last night." I stepped toward her and she shook her head and took a step back.

"Nothing happened." She fumbled over what I knew was a lie, squeezing herself to force it from her mouth. "I...my mom...my sister, they need me here."

"That's bullshit and you know it." Hurt sparked a flash of anger somewhere deep inside of me. I inched closer, struggling to control it, to hold it in and to understand. *"Tell me what happened."* It came out an accusation.

She just hung her head further. "I'm not going with you, William. You deserve so much better than me. You'll figure that out later. You're better off without me."

I knew the only person she was trying to convince was herself.

"You're wrong. You're all I want."

"I'm sorry," was all she said.

"No, Maggie, please. Don't do this."

She backed away. Desperate, I locked her in my arms. She screamed as if she'd been hit. "Let me go," she cried, curling in on herself.

Rejection stuttered my heart and sent me reeling back.

Six feet away, she heaved through the sobs wracking her body.

All I wanted to do was comfort her, make her see whatever had happened didn't matter, didn't change how I felt about her. We could make it through this. But every time I tried to take a step, Maggie cried louder. I clenched my fists as I forced my feet to stay in place.

"I love you, Maggie." My arm flailed out toward her, helpless. "You're supposed to be leaving with me tomorrow morning...you said you'd *marry* me," I said, touching my chest, "and you expect me to just *go?*"

"Yes," she whispered to her feet.

"No." I raised my head higher and tightened my jaw. "I'm not leaving here without you. You love me, Maggie. Don't deny it."

She shook her head, the auburn waves a cascading barrier obstructing her face. "I don't belong with you, William. I belong here. With my sister. With my mom." She sucked in a stuttering breath. "With Troy."

"No," I released on an anguished exhale, my body slumping forward as her declaration ripped through my consciousness. "Please, Maggie." I inched forward. "I won't let you do this."

Maggie took another step back, finally lifting her head to look at me. Tears soaked her face. "Please...just...go." She hugged herself tighter, the words strangled in her throat. "I don't want you anymore."

I flinched and stood up straight. I swallowed down the heartbreak, and the anger flared.

"Fine." I brushed past her, hating the way her skin felt against my shoulder when I did, the way it lit as need and amplified the loss. The loss only increased with every step I took.

"William, wait," Maggie cried out from behind.

I stopped and tried to gather myself before slowly turning back to face her. She stood with her arms crossed over her heaving chest, tears streaming down her face.

The anger tempered, though it was still prominent in the heartbreak that poured from my mouth. "Are you coming or not?"

A fractured sob broke into the night and Maggie shook her head.

Stunned, I turned from the girl I should never have given myself to and let the burning anger bind up my heart as I forced myself away.

Maggie wept from behind me, torment pelting my back as she cried my name again and again.

I tried not to hear, to block out the only voice that had ever accelerated my heartbeat, vowing to never allow myself to be so *stupid* again. Blake had warned me and I hadn't listened. Maggie Krieger was every kind of messed up, and she'd just torn out my fucking heart.

I rammed my fists into my eyes, refusing to give into the emotion welling in them. *Fuck.* I was *not* going to cry over this girl.

A voice screamed in my ear that it wasn't her fault...she was just scared...she'd been hurt...something happened. I stumbled, clutching my head in my hands, before I swung around and punched the side window of an old car parked along the street. Glass shattered and I cried out in pain, barely loud enough to drown out the voice inside my head begging me to go back.

Blood ran from the gashes splaying the skin on the back of my hand and dripped onto the ground as I ran down the sidewalk and around the house. I burst through the back door. My heart slammed an erratic beat, my world capsized. Latching onto the fury, I grabbed a glass from the counter and threw it against the kitchen wall. As it smashed and splintered in a thousand pieces on the floor, I roared to break the unbearable still of the house. The pain ebbed as the fury roiled.

Pounding up the stairs, I tore the door open to my room, ignoring the fucking ridiculous ideas I'd had earlier of knocking quietly at my mother's door, of pulling her out into the hall and telling her I'd fallen in love with Maggie and we were running away.

A bitter laugh bounced off the walls of my room.

Stupid, naïve fool. Did I really think I could have her? That I could whisk her away and make everything better, change her life, love her and she'd love me back?

In the light from the hall, I stuffed the rest of my things into the duffle bag, cursing beneath my breath.

The light flicked on overhead.

"What is going on in here?" My mother's scratchy voice cracked in panic.

I continued to shove the few things I had left to pack into the bag. My tone was vicious, the words bleeding out in rush of hatred. "I'm done with this fucking hick town. I'm getting the hell out of here."

"William..." She took two steps before she gasped. "William! Oh my goodness, what happened to your hand?" She was at my side, trying to tug my arm to her. Blood splattered across the bed and onto the carpet.

I yanked it back.

"Nothing." I zipped the bag closed, slung it over my shoulder, and pushed past my mom, the bag knocking into her side when I did.

She reached out with a desperate cry, "William, please, you're scaring me. Tell me what happened."

Guilt hit me hard before Maggie's face flashed, my words, *tell me what happened.*

I almost sneered. "I just learned exactly why I wanted to get out of here in the first place."

I hit the hall, my feet thundering on the wooden floor. Disoriented, Blake stood in his doorway, blinking as he tried to make sense of what was happening. Grace was in his bed, gripping the blanket to her chest as if she were trying to hide herself.

I felt sick with envy and hurt, my broken heart blotting out what these people meant to me. I plunged forward and ran down the stairs, taking them two at a time.

"Will...what the fuck, man? Wait!"

I had my car in reverse before Blake had time to make it out the back door. I gunned the engine, tires spinning and kicking up gravel as I tore out of the driveway.

"William," I barely heard Blake shout, my brother's face contorting in pain as he tried to chase me down the graveled drive in bare feet. My mom just stared in wide-eyed shock in the halo of my headlights.

Jerking the gear into drive, I floored the accelerator. Sickness clawed its way up as I sped up the street, turned left, and flew down Main.

I fought recognizing the look on my mother's face—tried to ignore what I'd done to the people I loved. I refused to acknowledge the shattered expression on Maggie's face when she'd said the words that had shattered my heart.

Five minutes later, the town I had grown up in disappeared behind me.

I swore I was never going back.

Chapter Sixteen

William ~ Present Day

That afternoon, I dialed my phone, pacing the floor as I roughed a hand incessantly through my hair.

God, what was I doing?

"This is Bergstrom."

"Tom." I cleared my throat. "It's William Marsch." I struggled to keep my voice steady, to slip back into the persona I'd projected for the last six years.

"Will?" On the other end of the receiver, papers rustled and a door clicked shut. Tom's voice dropped to just above a whisper. "What the hell happened to you? Kristina is smearing your ass all over the place around here. She said she fired you."

Of course she'd spread some bullshit like that. It was no surprise her pride wouldn't allow her to admit it I was the one who'd left her. I didn't care to correct it. Let Tom believe whatever Kristina needed him to.

He was one of the few people I had considered a friend in Los Angeles. We'd worked side-by-side, doing the bidding of Kristina and her father. For the most part, he was a good guy, but he was a shrewd attorney who could find a loophole in about any situation, and he wasn't afraid to cut a few corners to get a job done. Exactly the type of guy I needed.

Jonathan's face flashed in my mind and the façade broke. "Listen, I need your help."

I sensed the shift in the air as Tom was hit with the realization I wasn't calling to chit-chat or get the news about things happening in L.A. that I cared nothing about. "You in trouble?"

"Yeah." I ran my hand through my hair again, paced the other direction on the hardwood floor. I didn't know where to start or what to say.

"Come on, Will, you're making me nervous here."

Nervous. I laughed humorlessly. Tom had no idea the severity of what was happening, how I felt my life ripping apart and my sanity slipping.

I squeezed out the words. "I think I have a son."

"What?"

I exhaled and the truth dropped from my mouth. "I have a son...I need you to help me prove it."

"Are you kidding me, Will?" He sounded irritated, maybe skeptical. "You know I don't deal in that shit. What do you expect me to do?"

I rubbed my forehead.

"I don't know, something...Tom, I need you." There was no one else I could trust, no one else who wouldn't write me off as completely insane. I was sure I was going to sound it. I closed my eyes and let the past six years of my life pour out in a plea for help. I told him about Maggie, how I'd lost her, how I still didn't know why, but I was sure it was because of Troy. How I'd known the second I saw Jonathan that he belonged to me. "I know they're in danger, Tom, I just don't know how to prove it."

The entire time, Tom remained silent.

"I *have* to get them out of that house. Tell me you can help me."

I didn't try to hide my desperation. Tom probably viewed me the callused man I'd been all those years, and there was no chance he would fully understand. I could only hope he considered me a good enough friend to put a little faith in my intentions.

"Please, Tom. Just this once. I don't have anyone else I can trust."

Tom released a strained breath into the phone.

"Damn it...this is..." He didn't need to complete the thought. We both knew how messed up it was.

"I know it is. But I can't sit here and do nothing."

"Let me see what I can dig up on the guy. I'm not promising anything. Without the mom asking for help, you don't have much of anything to go on. If the mom isn't cooperating, your best bet will probably be pursuing a paternity test."

I fidgeted, not wanting to go that route, knowing to Maggie it would feel like a threat. But if Tom couldn't come up with anything else, then I'd do whatever I had to do.

He scribbled down the information I gave him.

"Hang tight for a few days, and I'll see what I can do. You need to stay away from them until we figure something out. That kid isn't yours until the State says he is." He hesitated. "You're sure you want to get into this mess?" His tone filled with a warning that told me I was crossing a line.

"I'm already in it."

CRISO

Heat rose to my cheeks. I'd grown so unaccustomed to this type of attention. The voices were off key and loud, echoing around the tiny room. The dining table that was normally pushed into the corner nook of the kitchen at Blake and Grace's house had been pulled out and extended with a leaf. In front of me sat a cake with what looked like an uncountable number of candles blazing on it. Icing of most every color was spread over its top in a jumbled mess of decorations, random swirls and mounds, created at the hand of my nieces. I thought it was the sweetest thing I'd ever seen. My family finished off the last line of *The Birthday Song* by drawing it out in a deafening roar. They were all laughing by the time they finished.

"Happy Birthday, Will. It's great we finally get to spend one with you." Dad sat next to me with Olivia on his lap, his face tired, but relaxed and happy as he held onto his youngest granddaughter.

From behind, Mom squeezed my shoulders and leaned down to murmur near my ear. "Make a wish, William."

This was the first birthday I'd been home for since I was a senior in high school. In my college years, my birthdays had been spent partying with my friends and the last handful had been spent with Kristina over expensive dinners in low-lit restaurants with few words spoken. There'd been no laughter or joy.

As I looked around now at the caring faces of my family grinning back at me, I felt it. Joy. It came with a sadness at its incompletion, but I finally felt as if I belonged.

Sucking in a deep breath, I swept in close to the table and blew out the twenty-seven candles, and with it, made a wish. It would have been easy to have made it selfish, the way I wanted it to be, but it came out simple. *Please just let them be safe.*

Everyone clapped and cheered the snuffed out flames, shouting, "Happy Birthday."

Mom squeezed me in a fierce hug from behind. "Happy Birthday, Will. I'm so glad you stayed."

I glanced back. "Thanks, Ma."

Emma tugged at my arm to get my attention then crawled onto my lap. Blake smiled at me from across the table, pushing his chair back and stretching out in a more comfortable position as he blew out a contented sigh.

"Dinner was awesome, babe." He looked up at Grace who set a stack of small plates and forks on the table. Winding an arm around her, he hugged her to his side. She dipped down to give him a quick kiss and draped one arm around his shoulders when she stood back up.

It was all so easy, so casual, so *good*.

Blake and I hadn't talked much since the revelation about Maggie and me last Sunday evening. The week had been spent in careful avoidance of the subject, as if we both needed time to deal with the shock, though his eyes were filled with unspoken apologies for the way he'd reacted.

I wasn't angry with him. I deserved it. How could I have expected anything different from him or Grace after the way I'd handled things?

I hugged the little girl on my lap. "Thank you for my beautiful cake, Emma."

"You really like it?" she asked with a tiny grin when she tilted her head all the way up to look at me. Ebony eyes blinked up at me for validation. I dropped a kiss on her forehead. "I love it."

CR&SO

"Hey baby, why don't you let me help with the dishes?" Blake folded himself against Grace's back, his hands on her hips and his nose buried in the bob of raven hair.

She leaned back on him. "I've got it...almost finished."

I had to look away. I was struck with a familiar feeling, so much like all those years ago, uncomfortable to witness such intimacy, but happy for my brother and Grace all the same. Not to mention that unavoidable stab of jealousy I'd come to accept was just part of who I was, a reminder of what I was missing.

My mother and father had left a little over an hour before, and the girls were tucked away in bed.

It had been a good day, and with a glance in Blake and Grace's direction, I figured I'd better call it a night.

"Thanks so much for dinner, Grace. Tonight was great."

From the sink, she turned a genuine smile on me. It was obvious she was still feeling guilty, but we were getting close to what we'd once been—friends. "You're welcome, Will. We loved doing it for you."

"Hey, man, don't take off yet. It's your birthday. Why don't we go grab a beer?" Blake said without pulling away from Grace.

I hesitated. "You sure?"

"Yeah, we never get to hang out without the kids. It'll be nice." He pulled at Grace's hips. "Why don't we get a sitter, make a night of it?"

Grace laughed, shaking her head as she turned and hiked herself up on her tiptoes to plant a kiss on Blake's chin. "You two go on and have a good time. I'll stay here with the girls."

Blake pressed her into the counter. "You gonna wait up for me?"

Her eyes were full of playful apologies when she slanted them in my direction, and then she jerked them right back to her husband who hovered above her, demanding her attention. "How about you wake me up?"

"I'm going to hold you to that," Blake mumbled at her jaw and Grace actually giggled.

When Blake moved in to kiss her, I took that as my cue and headed for the back door. "I'll meet you out at the truck." Neither seemed to notice I'd said anything.

I chuckled quietly into the stillness of the backyard. Those two had gotten much worse than I remembered—or maybe better. No longer was their affection filled with anticipation and hope for the future, now it was filled with fulfillment and peace. No questions. Confident in what they had.

Resting my back against Blake's truck, I relished in the starry-night sky. Insects droned. The familiar hum of this place covered me in comfort. Closing my eyes, I saw her face, felt her skin beneath my fingertips.

A breeze stirred, setting the trees in a gentle sway, and I whispered, "Please."

The back door slammed, and I jumped and straightened. An incredulous smile pulled at my mouth at the feigned guilty expression Blake wore as he approached.

"Sorry about that." He smirked and I laughed.

When the locks popped, I opened the door and hopped in. "Sure you are."

A grin took up Blake's entire face when he looked over his shoulder to back out from the driveway. "Nah...you're right. I'm not sorry at all."

I felt Blake sober, scratch his chin. "So, uh, I know we haven't gotten to talk more about it, but have you thought any more about what you're going to do?"

I stared out the windshield, that disturbance I felt every time I'd seen Jonathan bubbling up in my chest.

"It's all I *can* think about." It came out in a flow of helplessness. "I saw him yesterday," I admitted. Even though the attorney had warned me to lay low, after two days, it'd proven too much, and I'd followed them to the park after school. Jonathan had run by me, his feet hesitating in recognition when he'd passed by the bench I sat on. I would never forget the way I felt when I heard his voice.

Jonathan had whispered, "Hi," in return to the broken one I'd given him. His innocent face held so much curiosity, so much kindness, and so much fear.

Maggie's spirit had surged across the space from where she watched us across the play yard, wrapped me up with her watchful eye, alarmed but filled with longing.

"I'm William," I'd said. With an unsure hand, I reached out and ran my fingertips down the boy's cheek. My son's cheek.

He'd grinned and looked to his mother for approval. Six years old, and the child had no idea who his father was.

She'd softly waved him back, holding my gaze as he trotted back to her across the field.

I cut my attention to Blake, hoping he would understand how much it had affected me. "I talked to him for the first time."

Surprise widened Blake's eyes and then sympathy softened them. "Oh man…that's gotta be hard. Where?"

"At that little park over by Mom and Dad's."

Blake frowned as if it were the strangest place for me to have run into the child. He had no idea what that place meant to me. How sad no one really understood how truly important Maggie had been to me or how she'd changed my life. I wanted Blake to know.

In the glow of the dashboard, I distracted myself by picking at the seam of my jeans as I exposed myself in my loss.

"You know...we were supposed to get married." I didn't look up, but just as I always had been able to, I sensed Blake's reaction, the shock that tensed his body as he tightened his hold on the steering wheel, the silent curse from his mouth.

"She was supposed to leave with me that morning," I continued, slowly shaking my head as I lost myself in the memory...how I'd pictured her excitement...how I'd pictured her my wife. "I had some romantic notion of surprising her by going to Las Vegas on the way back to California. I was going to rent the nicest hotel room I could get with my credit card because I knew she'd never experienced anything like that before." Sorrow I'd held in for so long worked its way free. It had always been there, by day, masked in anger, and by night, manifested in my dreams. Now, it flooded me with images of what should have been. "God...I just wanted..." I snorted and stared out the side window. "It was stupid."

At the stoplight, Blake pinned me with a penetrating stare. "You really believe that, Will? That's *love*. It can make us do some crazy shit, but it doesn't make it stupid."

I met the intensity of my brother's face. I nodded in doubtful acceptance. I'd spent too many years hiding it all, blaming my naivety for the pain. I couldn't do it anymore. I set it free in a torrent of remorse. "I was so angry that night. She told me she was staying and I lost it." I swallowed. "I took it out on you and Mom. I was jealous of you and Grace...I wanted what you had...I wanted to be loved back. It was selfish, but I had no idea how else to deal with it. God, Blake...I wish you knew how sorry I really am. I didn't consciously want to hurt you guys, but I did it anyway."

Blake visibly blinked back the hurt flared in my admission then shook his head in understanding. "I get it, Will. Yeah, you hurt me, and you hurt Mom and Dad, but it makes sense now." Blake accelerated through the light, glancing in my direction. "You may have taken off, but you came back when we really needed you. You were there for Mom when Aunt Lara passed. You made my girls fall in love with you. You *stayed*." His brow knitted up in held-back emotion. "None of what happened in between matters, Will. You're still my best friend."

A quiver twitched at my chin. "After everything I've done, I hope you know I always felt the same."

For a moment, Blake's expression tightened as he shook his head. "I just wish I would've noticed sooner. It makes me sick I was so blind to something that was right there all that time."

"We kept it a secret, Blake. You weren't supposed to know."

One eyebrow peaked in objection. "Grace knew." A heavy breath filtered into Blake's truck. "You know, after everything came out, she told me she'd known that whole summer something was going on between you two." Blake raked a hand over his face. "How'd I miss that, with everything that had happened? I feel like I failed you."

Frowning, I regarded my brother. "That's ridiculous, Blake."

Blake shrugged. "Well, I do."

I turned to watch the small town I knew so well pass by, catching faint glimpses of my reflection through the window. "It's crazy that after all this time, nothing has changed—I still want the messed-up girl you warned me to stay away from."

A heaviness filled the cab, Blake's tone regretful. "Did you ever think I might have been wrong?"

Closing my eyes, I thought of how I'd spent the last six years trying to convince myself that my brother had been right. I lifted my face to Blake, wishing someone could understand my torment. I was so close to completely opening up to him about the dreams I'd been having about Jonathan, but it wouldn't form as words in my mouth.

Blake turned right into one of the three bars in town and eased into a spot toward the back of the nearly filled lot. "It'll work out, Will…it has to."

It didn't slide past my attention that Blake didn't sound so certain.

"Two Buds, please." Blake leaned in close to the bartender so she could hear him over the din of the bar.

I rested my back up against the bar with my elbows on top, looking out over the crowded room where I was sure I sorely stuck out. Country music blared from the speakers. Girls who barely appeared to have passed the mark to make them women paraded around in cowboy boots, wearing cut-offs so short they were almost obscene. Men in trucker's caps and Wranglers appreciated them from the stools or from the chairs they'd turned backwards to straddle or flirted with them from across the pool tables.

I took the beer Blake offered. He patted me on the back and lifted his bottle in the air.

"To better times, little brother."

I tipped my bottle Blake's direction. "To better times."

With all of the oppressive questions of the last years put behind us, Blake and I settled into the indulgent atmosphere. We fell back into the easy way we used to be, partook in friendly jeers and unrestrained laughter. Familiar faces stopped by to say hello and joke. Blake filled me in on all the town gossip, telling me who was with who and introducing me to the few who were new to town.

I relaxed into the buzz I felt coming on, welcomed the dulling of the sharp edge that continually cut through my spirit.

Blake laughed, chatting with one of the guys who worked for him, and dodged the attention of a few girls who didn't seem surprised when he balked at their advances.

I sat back, forced myself to relax, to hang tight like Tom had told me to do, until Troy and Kurt walked through the door.

I wasn't even really surprised.

The foul presence seemed expected, as if it were something I could not escape.

Still, hatred slammed into me so hard it sucked all of my air from the room, streaked my vision in reds and blacks. That same hatred raged back through the brown eyes piercing me through when I finally raised my face to meet the contention. It was so thick, I wondered if Troy was really as oblivious to mine and Maggie's relationship as I'd believed him to be. No question, Troy had reasons to hate me, the blow to his pride so severe it was doubtful an asshole like him could ever have recovered.

Defensive intuition told me it went deeper than that. He suspected something, I just didn't know what.

Turning my attention back to our small circle of friends, I battled to ignore the man who claimed Maggie, the man who claimed my son, the one who stole. I had to keep it together. I couldn't risk forever with the slip I was heading for tonight. I squeezed my eyes shut, fighting to keep it at bay. All I saw was the loss that deadened her eyes, heard only the words she had spoken. *I didn't.* Trapped in her sea of pain, I couldn't breathe. I gripped my beer bottle, steadied myself with a hand on the bar.

Blake nudged me with his elbow. I opened my eyes to see him toss me a tensed look, gesturing with his chin toward the door where Troy had just entered.

I tilted my head in silent conversation. *I already know.*

Three beers later, the feeling never faded. It had only wound me in obliterated anger. Dizziness crowded at the edges of my sight, slurring my thoughts and mind. I set my beer on the bar and pressed my fingers to my temples in an attempt to chase it away. I leaned in close to Blake's ear, shouting above the deafening noise.

"Hey, man...I'm going to get some fresh air. I'm not feeling so great."

Concern distorted the relaxed expression on Blake's face. "You okay?"

"Yeah...I just need to get out of here."

Brows drawn, Blake nodded once in understanding. "I'll be right behind you. Let me pay the tab and tell the guys goodbye."

I slithered through the bodies writhing on the makeshift dance floor, desperate for a reprieve. I had to get out of here before I lost all coherency, before I did something so fucking stupid I would ruin every chance I had in getting Maggie and Jonathan back. Face to the ground, I fought the crushing need to take out whatever or whoever had hurt her. Couples jumped out of my way as I cut a direct path through the middle of the bar, their expressions ranging from irritated to frightened by the near derangement I felt tipping me over the edge.

Pushing open the heavy door, I gasped for the cool night air, sucked it in, willing my nerves to subside. Hands fisted in my hair, I inhaled as deeply as I could, filled my lungs, and released it in a whispered, "It will be okay, it will be okay."

The parking lot was oddly quiet, my senses jerked from one extreme to the other. Strains of distant music still thrummed through my veins, while the pulse of the sleeping night seeped into my bones. I squinted into the darkened distance. In the stupor of too many beers and harbored hatred, I tried to focus in on where Blake had parked his truck among the thirty others. I swayed to the left. *Shit.* I ran a hand over my face to orient myself then staggered out into the maze of trucks, wishing I'd not allowed myself this slip of control.

There it is. I eyed the distinct tail of Blake's work truck.

Footsteps quickened over the loose-graveled pavement behind me, faster than I could make sense of them. A blinding crack echoed too close to my ears, then staggering pain tore through my skull and split my vision. Nausea welled and my head spun. I rocked forward, and the ground rushed up to meet my face before I had time to break my fall. Blackness crawled over my consciousness.

Lights flashed, flickers of the softest grays, blacks, and whites. Images played as on a reel, pictures of perfection. Maggie danced, red lips stretched into the freest of smiles. She spun, the sun a bursting halo behind her head. There are my boys, she sang, stopped to stretch out her hand.

Pain seared, shocked through the foggy haze. Oil and dirt clogged my senses as I struggled for a shattered breath, muscles twitching. Blood streamed from the gash on the side of my head and pooled in my ear, cut as a web of scattered trails down my face and neck. They dripped onto the pitted, rocky pavement from my chin. A metal pipe pinged to the ground, tipping back and forth in a slow roll an inch from my face.

He panted near my cheek. Chills skittered across my bloodied flesh and raised the hairs at the back of my neck.

"I'll kill you," came as a low threat near my ear, my words repeated from so long ago.

And just like then, I knew I'd die for her if I could somehow set her free.

Chapter Seventeen

Maggie ~ Present Day

I lay adrift, swimming at the edge of sleep and consciousness. I floated on William's inescapable light. Blackened waters lapped at my skin as I dipped my mind into dreams that were almost a reality. Fingertips ghosted down my cheeks, sent me tripping through desire and stumbling into fear. Heart pounding, anxiety laced its tendrils around me as I found myself on a bluff, standing at the edge where I was left with no choice but to jump.

Snatched back, pain shot through my scalp as I was lifted from sleep by a handful of my hair. Too disoriented, I had no time to block the fist that landed at the right side of my face, just below my cheek. I cried out and crossed both arms over my face to shield the next blow that connected with my forearm. Troy jerked me around to straddle my stomach. He wheezed through frantic breaths. The stench of beer and vileness spread over me in a blanket of derangement. Fists fell in a constant storm. I did my best to protect myself as Troy lost himself in a madness he'd never shown before. His attacks had always been perfectly calculated to exert his control, and I had always done my best to give him the least amount of satisfaction when he enacted it.

But this...this whipped through the room as a violent explosion and rained down in incoherent rage. Gasping, I begged through a sob for him to stop. It was the first time I'd pled with him for any sense of compassion since that night.

My pleas only inflamed him more.

I tried to block it from my mind, to pinch my eyes shut and seal myself in the numbness where I'd survived my entire life, but I couldn't find it. It was too stark a contrast from the adoration I'd experienced in the few short moments I'd allowed myself to indulge in William's touch. The chance he'd offered too fresh and raw. The choice too bright.

I'd allowed Troy to take everything from me, my hope and my son's future.

And I wanted it—God I wanted it—but I had no idea how to break free.

Above me, Troy continued with his assault, belligerence overflowing as he swore again and again that he was going to kill me.

It was in that moment I accepted if I stayed, one day he would.

I glimpsed William in my mind, the need in his words, the tender way he watched my child.

I tucked myself tighter under the protection of my arms. My body yielded in submission to the blows, while inside the lifelong war that had raged was finally won.

I didn't want this.

I never had.

Troy drew in rasping breaths, and his chest heaved as the strength left his body. Exhausted fists landed on my arms and another glanced the side of my head, his anger spent. In one move, he pushed me aside and stood from the bed, wiping the back of his hand across his mouth. Then he turned and left me in a bloodied heap, curled up on my side in the middle of the bed, like the piece of trash he'd always wanted me to believe I was.

Maybe to him, that was what he really believed.

The back door slammed, and Troy was gone.

Hot breaths wheezed from my mouth as palpitations jerked all the way to my core. I sucked in stale, soured air that hung in the room and turned my face into my pillow. I wept from the ache that throbbed over every inch of my body, for the humiliation I could never escape for allowing this to happen, and in distinct relief for the decision I'd made.

Maggie ~ Late November, Six Years Earlier

Huddled in the corner of the bathroom, I rocked myself, staring at the spot where sunlight crawled in through the gap at the bottom of the door. For so long, I'd felt nothing. I'd walked numb through the days and had lain lifeless beneath Troy night after night.

I'd succumbed so easily, giving up on my first chance at joy. The next day, I had been waiting for Troy after he'd stripped the last shred of my dignity, just like he'd warned me to be. I had to protect my sister. She was the last thing in this world that meant anything to me. Troy had taken everything else.

Holed up in his squalid apartment since, I had been nearly comatose. My days were spent on the couch, staring unseeing at the dingy white wall, while my nights were spent lost somewhere in the deepest recesses of my mind while Troy carried on as if we were a normal couple. Part of me knew there were times when he spoke to me, muddled words that things were finally how they were supposed to be, and that he loved me. Part of me knew his hands were on my skin. But the only real thing I had felt was the void, the place inside where William had touched me now a burdened reminder of what I had lost, and the only thing I could really see was the expression on William's face when he'd walked away. That night, he appeared exactly as I felt—destroyed.

Troy had made it so easy to believe I had no choice but to let William go.

Placing my hand on my stomach, I felt a glimmer of something in my deadened heart. A purpose to go on. I should hate it, I knew, despise what Troy had planted in me, but I couldn't.

I didn't know if it'd been an hour or three since I sank to the bathroom floor with the test in my hand. Slowly my mind seeped back to reality. For days, a nagging somewhere in my subconscious had told me what the test showed me now. This morning, I'd walked to the mini-mart up the street with the twenty dollars Troy had given me to buy groceries. While I was there, I swiped a test and stuffed it under my shirt. Even in the daze I'd lived in, I felt the guilt, the bundle of nerves that turned my stomach. Never once had I stolen anything, but I couldn't chance someone seeing me buy that test in this town.

There was only one person I trusted enough to ask for help.

It was unimaginable to think how much it was going to hurt to stand in front of William and tell him what Troy had done. It made me sick to think of him knowing the truth. The night I'd forced him away, I was sure he'd be just as disgusted with me as I was with myself. He'd see I was filthy and unclean.

But I would do anything to save this child.

I waited until Troy was asleep. He panted deeply against the back of my head. His hold was no longer tense, but loose where his arm was draped over my side. Holding my breath, I wound myself out of his hold, keeping my feet silent on the floor.

I'd packed a bag while he was at work. It would have been a whole lot easier to get out of the apartment unnoticed while Troy was at work, but I never would have walked out of town without being discovered.

On my knees, I tugged the bag from underneath the bed. Tiptoeing out into the main room, I slipped on the shoes I'd left by the couch.

I refused to listen to the fear that worked itself through my mind, the fear spurring the anxiety that had my stomach twisted in a solid knot. It screamed, *he will hurt your little sister, he will find you, you will fail.*

I shoved the thoughts back.

There was only one thing that mattered now.

At the front window, I peered outside through a slat in the mini-blinds, searching for any signs of life in the 10-unit complex. Light drizzled down from the yellowed bulbs hanging on the walls beside each door, and a lone streetlight near the office cast flickering shadows across the pavement. The lot was dead, just silenced cars and trash whipped up from a gust of wind.

I bit my lip and squeezed my eyes shut, focusing on making no sound as I slowly turned the dead bolt. In the silence, it rang out like a gunshot. I froze, listening for any movement from behind. When I heard none, I turned the knob and slipped out the door. I quieted my feet on the steps, forcing myself to take them one at a time and fighting against the urge to run. The second I hit the pavement, I gave in. The beat of my heart was almost deafening as I sprinted across the parking lot toward the hole in the chain-link fence at the back.

Before I could comprehend the movement, I was being dragged back by a strong arm across my chest. I struggled to break free from his hold. A knife blade pressed into my cheek, and terror widened my eyes.

Oh God, no.

His breath was hot at the side of my face. "Where are you going, baby?" The rancid words spilled out in a twisted croon and shifted to a menacing tone. "You just don't get it, do you, Maggie? Did you really think I'd let you walk out that door?" He pressed the blade deeper into the flesh of my cheek, eliciting a prick of pain where the knife dented the skin.

Trembling in his hold, horror gripped me, so deep it penetrated to the bone.

With my body limp, he dragged me back up the stairs, my feet banging into the concrete steps as he went. He kicked the door shut behind us and threw me on the bed.

I whimpered as he slid the knife up my shirt. The tip nicked a trail up my torso as he cut it away. With a flick of his wrist, he snipped the front of my bra. Cold, damp air rushed against my skin. I inhaled, a harsh gasp burning down my throat.

Troy laughed and dragged the tip of the knife from my cheek and down my neck, where he dug the tip into the flesh at my shoulder. I cried out as he slowly pulled it through my skin, down along the inside of my arm, all the way to my wrist. The flesh opened up with a searing heat that shocked my mind. Blood gushed, a sticky wetness slipping down my skin and dripping to the bed, my mind fuzzy with fear and pain and loss. Blackness swelled.

Troy smacked me across the face. "Don't even think about passing out on me, Maggie."

He wielded the knife in front of my face, as if he searched for coherency, watched as my eyes flicked back and forth in sync with the movement. He grinned and slashed me from collar bone to beneath the opposite breast. It scorched from the outside in, a slow torment as I came to realize that this was it.

Troy ran the tip of the blade down. I gasped as he grazed it across my stomach, teasing at the flesh. I wept, and, for the first time, I found my voice. "Please...stop."

He laughed in a sickening way and grabbed my chin to force me to look at him. "What are you crying for, Maggie?" The knife was pressed there, just below my belly button. "You scared I might slip?" He pressed it a little deeper. "You think I don't know you're trying to run away with my baby?"

Suddenly the knife was at my hip, burrowing deep in the flesh. His hand flexed on my chin, and he mashed his mouth into the skin next to my lips. "I'll kill you, Maggie." Troy crushed me with his weight, chest to chest, a heavy grunt from his mouth as he tore the knife down the outside of my leg. I cried out in pain and relief when he stumbled back from the bed, still gripping the knife in his hand. He tossed it nonchalantly to the dresser, as if it were his wallet at the end of the day.

He glanced back at me. "We clear?"

Squeezing my eyes shut, tears seeped from the corners and ran into my hair.

I nodded in surrender.

Maggie ~ Present Day

Fear was powerful—crippling. Troy knew just how to manipulate me with what mattered most. He'd forced on me the one thing I'd feared most in my life, then used my sister and son as pawns.

For my son, I had forged on and had lived for him, making the best life for us that I could. In the end, it was a life that was destroying us both.

Lying there in the aftermath Troy had left behind, I thought of William, the secret of my heart. Maybe it was his sudden reappearance that made me brave. He'd always made me feel that way, like a different person—a stronger person.

Or maybe he just made me see who I really was.

Chapter Eighteen

William ~ Present Day

My lids fluttered with the slurred voices shouting next to my head. A white hot spark of light struck at the center of my brain, and sickness pushed up my throat. Spasms twitched my muscles.

Maggie.

"William!"

I sensed the frantic presence beside me. Blake was on his knees, his voice murky. A hollow twang echoed through my ears, swathed across the back of my head like a too-hot blanket I couldn't shake. Feet clamored around my body. The sound of sirens approached in the distance, my senses detached.

"Oh shit...Will."

Blake's panic was palpable, furrowing beneath my skin, cutting and slicing me to the core. Somewhere in the fog I recognized the panic was my own.

Troy knew.

I moaned deep, a gravelly cry that escaped from my spirit.

He knew.

Wrenching forward, I attempted to climb to my hands and knees. I collapsed back down into the blood that had pooled around my head, metallic stinging a path up my nose.

A hand was on my back, an attempt at comfort.

"Don't move, Will." The voice was strained. "Please, man, just hold still."

I lay limp, forcing the air from my too-tight lungs. Dread shackled my limbs and pinned me to the hard ground.

He knew.

A ripple broke apart the crowd when the ambulance pulled into the parking lot. Paramedics prodded, fired questions I could barely discern, and placed me on a backboard as the residual of Troy's hatred seeped into my pores, pricked along my skin—something palpable—wicked and debased.

He knew.

My eyes rolled back, a shuddered groan from my chest. Blake was at my side as they wheeled me to the back of the ambulance. "You're fine, Will. You're going to be fine."

"Blake," a mumbled word from my mouth.

"I know, Will. I know."

⋘⋙

Dense forest suffocated, pressed in, held him back. William panted. A streak of blond raced from behind one tree to the next. Faint laughter drifted through the stifling air, taunted and tickled his ears.

Panic welled.

"Wait," William begged, stretching out a hand. Please.

William pounded through the forest, branches lashing his face.

The child ran, giggling with the game he played.

A surge of protectiveness built and overflowed. William chased him, only feet behind. The boy laughed, a tinkling laugh as he darted up the hill, ducked under trees. "Come and get me." Playful brown eyes looked back at him. William tasted his joy. Wanted more.

The boy mounted the short incline, emerged in a clearing at the summit.

Frantic, William rushed, desperate to hold his son.

Please.

"Please," I whispered as I lay on my side on the ER bed. Fear crawled along my flesh, whispered in my ear.

I no longer knew if it was mine or the child's.

I blinked away the stupor from the painkiller they'd administered when I first arrived. Twelve stitches behind my left ear, and my head was throbbing like it was being drilled by a jackhammer.

The dim room lightened when the door swung open, dimmed again. Blake pushed aside the drape enclosure. "Got your discharge papers."

I sat up. Dizziness hit me and I gripped my head. "Damn it."

"You okay?" Blake's boots filled up my view. "I can call the nurse."

"No, I'm fine. Just give me a second."

When I gathered myself, Blake helped me up by my upper arm. Our footsteps echoed over the linoleum floor, the ER quiet as we exited out the door. Morning teased at the sky, a dull, cloudless gray.

I climbed into the cab of Blake's truck, closed my eyes, and rested my head back.

When Blake headed down his street, he slowed just as soon as he had accelerated. I looked up to see Maggie's van parked in front of her sister's house as we passed by. Blood rushed from my head and weighted my arms. I sat up, whispered, "Maggie," as I strained to see through the rear window.

I knew then that the violence Troy had inflicted on me had spilled over to Maggie. And she had left.

I was out the door before Blake came to a full stop in the driveway, running up the street. I slowed to a walk when I reached their drive. Amber's husband sat on a chair on the porch. Fatigue was evidenced in the weariness of his eyes and untamed bedhead. He jerked upright when he heard my footsteps.

I'd seen him a few times in passing, and his face lit in subtle recognition, though he stood and took on a protective stance. He leaned with one hand on the porch column as if blocking the way, his eyes fixed in warning. "I think you'd better stop right where you are, because I don't see that you have any business coming up this way."

Stopping midstride, my attention went behind him to the door he guarded, and I swallowed, shook. My family was in there. "I need to see Maggie."

Confusion tripped his expression before his face hardened again. "They've had enough trouble without you coming over here trying to stir up more. I don't know what your game is, but I'm telling you right now"—he pointed a finger at me—"as long as they're staying with me, no one is getting through that door."

"I—"

"You need to leave. I don't wanna see you coming around here again."

I wanted to yell at him to look my face, to see what business I had here. Instead I retreated a step. "Just…tell Maggie William was here."

☙

It was unbearable, the waiting, the not knowing. Nearly a week had passed. Each second slipped by in a blur, hours and minutes and days no longer ticking at a steady pace, time suspended, prolonged, stretched out so far I had snapped. When I called Tom yesterday for the fifth time this week, he'd again asked me to give him more time. So far, he'd come up with nothing. He said the statement I'd made to the police after what happened in the parking lot of the bar last week had little bearing as it was purely suspicion and no charges had been pressed. He promised he would continue to dig.

Half-deranged, I'd become an almost permanent fixture in Blake's front yard, watching, waiting. There'd not been one glimpse of Maggie or Jonathan the entire week, although twice I'd seen Troy drive down the street.

The nights, like now, were the worst. I glanced to the small clock that said it was just after midnight.

The wooden floors were cool beneath my feet, a distinct contradiction to my heated skin. Outside the windows, the night felt almost alive. The moon peered down, casting shadows across the floor, branches brushing along the walls. Insects droned. It all added to the anxiety that had every nerve coiled so tight I thought I would implode.

Slowly, I'd fallen, given in. I'd begun to welcome the dreams when Jonathan would barrel into my life and steal my breath. In them, I grasped at my sanity, the boy my reality.

Here, walking the floors, I was sure I'd gone mad.

I succumbed to the exhaustion and collapsed on the unmade bed.

Roused by the quiet knocks at the door, I raised my head and squinted into the shadows of the room. The moon had sunk lower, bled as an alabaster haze across the floorboards. Another tap, an echo that jarred my memory and took me back to the place where she was mine.

Scrambling to tug on a pair of jeans from the floor, I crossed the room in two steps. My pulse was erratic as I was hit with an awareness of what was waiting for me on the other side of the door.

I turned the lock and pulled it wide open.

She was there, standing in the dark, hugging herself. A breeze rustled through the strands of her hair. They fluttered up around the silhouette of her face.

As she slowly came into focus, my gaze traced the lines of her face, the angle of her jaw, the fullness of her lips, finally resting on the softness in her eyes. There were no pretenses there, just distinct vulnerability and a wealth of emotion. No walls, completely exposed.

For the longest moment, we just stared, giving time a minute to catch up to us.

Maggie's eyes fell closed when she spoke. "Make me remember what it feels like to be loved." It raked from her throat as a petition, as if there were any possibility that I could ever turn her away.

I took one step forward and wrapped my arm around her waist, my hand splayed across the small of her back. One touch and I was gone. Fire clipped through my veins, fervent need, this desire buried too deep for too long. I wound my fingers through her silky hair and palmed the back of her neck as I quickly pulled her inside and covered her mouth with mine.

Everything lit in a torrent of need when I tasted what I'd lost.

Her hands trembled as she held my face, and she kissed me back. There was no resistance, but complete surrender to the indestructible bond that had been created between us so long ago. The kiss was filled with a passion and loss that almost brought me to my knees, but her hold against my face spoke of the buried hope we'd always clung to.

"Maggie," I begged as I edged back for a breath, then dove into her again. Maggie.

I loved her. Oh God...I loved her. She was everything, ripped me apart and made me whole.

Maggie whimpered and dug her fingers into my neck in a bid to bring us closer. She kissed me back with every ounce of desperation I felt, our worlds blurring and becoming one.

We collided, body and soul, mouths and hands and whispered pleas.

Stumbling, we knocked into the wall. I was pressing and Maggie was begging. A demanding rumble erupted deep in my chest. Our spirits were frantic, a frenzied thirst as we struggled to reclaim what we'd had.

"Jonathan?" I mumbled at her mouth as my fingers threaded through her hair.

"He's sleeping...at my sister's. I snuck out after everyone was asleep."

Her heated palms caressed up my arms and over my shoulders, and then rushed down to tug at the fly of my jeans. Her eyes flicked up to meet mine as she pulled the buttons free, her expression full of the same hunger that had never been satisfied in me since the last time she'd touched me.

I sucked in a sharp gasp of air, my stomach clenching in hesitation and overwhelming desire as my hands wrapped around her wrists. "Maggie...stop."

We needed to slow down, talk.

She rested her forehead against my chest, shaking her head, before she pulled back just enough to look at me. "Please William...let me feel you. I need to feel you."

At her words, I came undone, unable to stop myself. Sure I didn't want to. "Maggie." My answer was clear in the tone of my voice.

Maggie fumbled through the rest of the buttons and freed me of my jeans and underwear, and she pushed them down my legs, her hands sliding back up my skin. I stepped from them and peeled her t-shirt over her head as I did. Her hair tumbled over her shoulders. My attention went straight to where it brushed along a scar that began as a thick coil at her collarbone and thinned as it angled across her chest.

A lash of fury whipped through my senses and spun my head when I saw another scar ridging the length of the inside of her right arm. My eyes flashed to Maggie's face, and that shattered place in my heart expanded.

"What did he do to you?"

Oh my God. I didn't want to imagine what she'd gone through when he'd inflicted these injuries, how terrified she must have been. And I'd left her.

Tender eyes that had held so much sorrow now bore so much more, shrouded secrets, loss and pain. She ran her fingers down my cheek. "Don't."

She pressed herself to my body as if she could sink inside, as if she could feel the guilt rolling through me.

I frantically covered her with mine, as if I could somehow protect her from what she'd endured.

Each movement became charged, our mouths urgent. Maggie dug her fingers into my shoulders to draw me near. A tiny sting pricked at my flesh where her nails cut into my skin. It felt like heaven—like something real. I wrapped my arm around her back to hold her close, and the other I slid between us to palm her breast over her bra.

She gasped a quiet hiss of pleasure.

I kissed her harder and caressed my hand up her spine to free the clasp. She stepped back and tossed it aside.

Bending my knees, I leaned down to lift her from below the hips. The soft swell of her belly pressed into my chest, and a veil of her hair fell around us. Maggie clung to me, her feet dangling above the floor as I buried my face in her scars.

It all felt like agony, like air.

I captured her breast in my mouth. Maggie's hold tightened. "William...please."

I turned and laid her on the bed, dragging her jeans and panties down in the same motion.

Maggie panted, her face flushed. She arched in silent appeal.

Body quickened with strain, I climbed between her legs. I slid my palms up her sides as I moved higher, and wove them under her shoulders to cradle the back of her head. Her eyes were wide, her lips parted, her heart pounding with the rapid rise and fall of her chest.

I spread my fingers wide and cupped her bruised face in my hands, my thumbs running over her cheeks. The marks had faded, but not the magnitude of what they meant. I trembled in restraint when I settled over her.

"Tell me," I said as I brushed her lips with mine.

Gentle fingers fluttered up to my face, and Maggie traced my jaw. Her eyes filled with understanding, with the same tenderness that had initially caused me to fall in love with her. "I don't know how to stop loving you."

I closed my eyes and let the mirrored words wash over me. Neither time nor circumstance had changed what we'd shared. My smile was soft as I looked down at the same broken girl who'd captured me, both of us so different yet somehow exactly the same.

I shook as I filled her.

"I love you, Maggie."

She gasped and encircled me with her arms. The tremor that rolled through her body became mine. Maggie whispered in my ear. "Every second."

I shifted to my elbows to watch down over the girl who still stole my breath while I stole hers. Her eyes were open and wide, flitting over my face, memorizing, remembering this. Pleasure rippled and danced with the heartbreak. Soft moans and promises neither of us were sure we could keep filled the tiny room.

Everything we'd hidden inside was revealed, six years of pent-up desire and loss poured out between us. Holding her was ecstasy, every touch perfection.

Her delicate hands pressed into my lower back, her mouth hungry for mine.

"William." Maggie strained against me, her back tensed and bowed. "Please."

"Maggie." I rushed, a desperate hand gripping the softness of her hip.

Maggie fell.

Her face filled with the same expression that had haunted me for years, something so free and full of trust. Pink flushed her neck, tinted her cheeks, and my name rolled from her lips.

It was still the most beautiful thing I'd ever seen.

I lost myself in her, in the tiny murmurs that continued to slip from her mouth, in the tremors that shook her body.

I shuddered, hit with the most intense pleasure I'd ever known, need amplified by a flood of devotion. I was determined to never let her go.

Maggie nestled into the pillow of my arm, her head resting on my shoulder. Her heart still thundered against my ribcage, my breaths still short. Fingers intertwined, I held our hands up between us and studied them in the darkened room. Maybe if I stared long enough I would see a visible bond holding us together.

Maggie released a stuttered sigh. "This doesn't feel real," she said.

I dropped my chin to see the wistful smile on her face, her fingertips playing with mine.

I kissed her forehead and whispered against her dampened skin as I tightened my hold, "This is the first time I've felt real in six years."

Her hand dropped to press at my bare stomach when she shifted. Warm brown eyes stared up at me with a tenderness and insecurity I'd almost forgotten. "I love you, William. You always knew, didn't you?"

I swallowed and averted my gaze to the ceiling. Shadows crawled along the surface, like secrets fighting their way out. I played with a strand of her hair, needing something to ground me to the present as I struggled through the past.

"I tried to forget." I glanced at her, and then away. "You broke something in me that night, Maggie. Subconsciously, I knew you were hurting just as badly as I was, but another part of me couldn't handle it. I spent a long time trying to hate you."

Maggie stiffened in my arms, and I looked down to see the pain my admission caused. I caressed the tear from her cheek.

"Maggie...it didn't work. The second I saw you at my mom's...it was like I was standing in front of you in our spot all those years before, and you were telling me to leave again. Nothing had changed. It still hurt just as bad, and I still loved you just as much. And then there was this little boy..." I trailed off. How could I describe what that had felt like?

Lines creased between her brows as she squeezed her eyes shut and seemed to try to block out memories. She rolled to her side and propped herself up on her hand. I reached up to cradle her face in my palm. The six years we'd been apart had wiped out the little innocence she'd had left and added a new darkness I wished I could erase. But beneath it all, I saw she was still the same beautiful girl, the one who'd opened up to me and shared her secret life. The one who, as scared as she'd been of it, had loved me. Tears swam in the depth of her eyes and slid down her face.

"That was the worst night of my life, William. I could barely look at you." She paused. Her bottom lip blanched when she bit it, but her gaze was unwavering. "Troy ruined me that night." She blinked twice and slightly shook her head. "He found me when I was walking back to my parents that evening and dragged me into the forest. He forced me." Maggie pressed her face into my hand as if she needed the support, her tone desperate, "I never would have chosen him over you. Tell me you believe that. I loved you...you were the only thing I ever wanted."

Horror pierced me straight through. That sick bastard had known what would harm her most, where her deepest fears laid, and used it as an easy manipulation. Hatred pumped old rage through my veins.

Blake had been right.

Troy had found a way to make me pay.

I lifted my other hand to her face and tightened my hold.

"God, of course I believe you. Why didn't you just tell me? I would have taken care of you. Gone to the police or...something." I closed my eyes, trying to block out the cruel images. They came at me mercilessly, penetrating to the darkest places of my soul.

He will find a way to make you pay.

"He should be in prison, Maggie." Or dead. Men like that didn't deserve to live.

Regret colored Maggie's face, and she reached out to gently wrap her hand around my wrist. "I was sick with shame. I couldn't stand you knowing what he'd done to me."

"I could never be ashamed of you. No matter what he did, it doesn't change who you are or how I feel about you."

"I understand that now, but you also knew me, William, and you have to know how hard it was for me to believe that then. You were the only one who ever understood how scared and lost I was, and then Troy knocked me lower than anyone ever had. He kept me in that place for years." Maggie ran her fingers over the stubble that coated my jaw, and she inclined her head in emphasis. "I didn't want to be there, but I was helpless to get away."

Wrapping an arm around her waist, I slowly rolled her to her back and climbed back over her. The urge to protect her was too great, the need to make up for what I'd allowed to happen too strong.

I laid low on her body, my arms a cage at her sides. I rested my head below her chest, near the scars that taunted the mistakes I'd made.

"I'm so sorry," I whispered into the warmth of her flesh. "I never should have walked away that night. I did know, Maggie. I knew you were lying to me, to yourself, to us. I didn't know how to handle it. You have no idea how much I wish I could take it back."

Her chest expanded with each panted breath she took. I relished in the sensation, her life beating below me. I ran my hand down her side and over the swell of her hip, wondering how it was possible to love someone this much.

"It's not your fault, William...he did this to us." Her fingers gentled through my hair, scraped over the stitches hidden behind my ear. Maggie froze.

I lifted my head, and her hand moved with the motion to rest on my cheek.

I felt the way her fear made her hand shake against my cheek.

"He knows there's something between us, Maggie. I don't know how much, but he suspects something."

A tremor rolled through her, although she nodded as if she wasn't all that surprised. "He hurt you," she said with a heavy sadness.

"Maggie—"

She cut me off. From her expression, she already knew what I was going to say. "When did it happen?"

"Last weekend. Blake and I were at the bar. I didn't see him, but I know it was him." I left out the warning, the stench of derangement that had seeped from his being.

Reaching out, I traced the marks littering her face, drawing a line back to that night. What scared me most was I didn't know how much he knew or if he suspected Jonathan belonged to me.

"Maggie, we have to—"

She silenced me with two fingers on my lips. "I'm already gone, William. He keeps calling and demanding that I bring Jonathan home, but I'm not going back. He thinks I'm going to, but the second I can sneak away, I'm leaving."

"Where?" I scooted up, holding my weight with my hands.

"I don't know…I'm just…going. Somewhere far. As far away as I can get." Her expression shifted, insecurity lighting in her eyes, her voice soft. "Come with me?"

Maybe she expected me to say no, to give her reasons why it was insane like she'd done to me before. But my answer was easy and given without question.

"Of course." I refused to be anywhere else.

Her expression didn't soften. If anything, it saddened.

"I…I need to know." She searched my face. "If it turns out Jonathan isn't yours, can you still love him?" Words laced with pain, but resolute. She'd put her son's wellbeing before her happiness. I knew that's what she'd been trying to do all along. This time, she was doing it right.

Thoughts of the child charged through my spirit as I immersed myself in the devotion she had for our son. I kissed her, my touch a promise. "Maggie, I already do."

For hours, I held her as we talked through the night like we'd done so many times before. The small house became our refuge, the four walls rising up in protection as we whispered stories of the last six years into its confines. There was no chance I could ever fully grasp what Maggie had been through or the burden of the blame she carried. No chance I could understand how the fear had consumed her every day.

What I did know was I wished I would have ended Troy that night.

"I've made so many mistakes." Maggie's head was back on my shoulder, and she ran lazy circles with her fingertips over my chest. Her tone was full of regret.

I kissed the top of her head, my nose in her hair. "We all have."

Or maybe our circumstances made them for us.

I drew her closer as the first hint of morning lightened the darkness at the window, and I kissed her reverently as I held her cheek in my hand. "Are you ready?"

She leaned into the connection, her eyes closed, and nodded. "Yes."

We dressed in silence, stealing glances at one another, a steady build of anxiety filling the room.

Taking her hand, I led her out into the emerging morning light. Above the trees, the black sky had brightened to a dull grayish blue. There was barely a chill to the air, but Maggie still shivered.

"Are you scared?" I looked her way as we walked hand-in-hand over the graveled driveway.

At the end of the drive, we turned to face each other, our fingers still woven, the air in the six inches of space between us a slowly simmering storm. "Terrified," she admitted.

As much as I wanted to tell her it would all be okay and she had nothing to worry about, I'd never belittle what she'd lived through with Troy. We both knew what he was capable of. Instead I pulled her into my arms and murmured against her head, "I love you, Maggie."

On a sigh, she relaxed into my hold, the warmth of her breath at my neck. "Jonathan's going to be so confused."

My gaze traveled up the street to where our child still slept, unaware the life he knew was soon to be upended. "What will you tell him?"

"The truth, I guess." She tightened her hold, looked up at me from the circle of my arms. "As much as he can understand, anyway."

"Do you think he'll be frightened of me?" Sadness spiked in my chest, grief for the child I felt so close to yet still didn't know.

"I don't know…a little, probably. But he thinks you're good." A pensive smile lifted her mouth. "He'll be okay. He's just going to need some time to get used to you."

I pulled her closer, kissed her softly. "I'll do whatever it takes."

Stepping back, Maggie squeezed my hand between us, and glanced over her shoulder up the street. "I need to get back before Jonathan wakes up. I'll let you know as soon as I'm ready to go."

I nodded. "I'll be waiting."

Her hand dropped away and my heart clenched. Yesterday, I'd been desperate for a resolution, and today, I finally had one. With it came every kind of fear that could ever be found, physical fear for a girl who was the bravest I knew, fear of the intense love I felt for her, fear of becoming a father.

I watched as she moved up the street, her movements slow and filled with contemplation. In front of her sister's, Maggie hesitated, looking back at me. I lifted my hand. My smile was soft, and her expression was knowing.

We were risking it all.

When she disappeared inside, I turned to go back to the guesthouse. I froze when I noticed the figure concealed on the front porch. Blake eased forward and rested a hand above his head on the wood post.

"You leaving?"

I shoved my hands in my pockets and looked up at my brother. "Yeah."

We stared at each other. Blake nodded, and a satisfied smile crept over the shadows of his face.

Chapter Nineteen

William ~ Present Day

Blake followed me into the guesthouse, pausing at the door as he apprised the small room. "You gonna tell me what happened?" He moved to sit at the edge of the chair.

I scratched at the back of my head. "She just showed up in the middle of the night. God, Blake, I can't begin to tell you the things she's been through." My mouth opened on a heavy exhale. "But she's ready to get out, and I'm going with her." I looked over at my brother. "You know I'd stay if I could? This isn't the same as before. I'm not leaving because I'm running."

Blake leaned forward with his forearms on his legs, clasping his hands together. "You think I don't get that, Will? They're your family. You're supposed to take care of them. I'd be disappointed in you if you didn't go with them."

I shouldn't have been surprised that Blake would be one-hundred percent supportive.

"I'll be back. As soon as we figure all this shit out," I promised.

"When are you leaving?"

"Today or tomorrow. This is a huge step for her. I think she's been stalling because she's scared to take it. I wanted to leave first thing this morning, but she said she needed to tell her sister everything first." It killed me Troy still held that dominance over her, the needling of control he'd so precisely woven into her over the years.

"You think she'll go through with it?"

I stilled, thinking of everything Maggie had revealed to me last night. "Yeah, I do."

Grabbing the suitcase from the top shelf of the closet, I began tossing my meager belongings inside, wanting to be prepared for the moment Maggie came for me.

Blake sat up. "What are you going to tell Mom?"

"The truth. I'm going to head over there after I get my stuff packed."

"You know Mom's not going to be happy to learn you had an affair with the girl who cleaned our house."

I recoiled at the assertion, disgusted by the very term. But I had to accept by hiding our relationship the way we had, that's exactly what we'd made it. It wouldn't even make sense to Mom the way it had to Blake. There were no clues for her to snap into place. She had no idea of the way I'd fought for Maggie. I'd not let my mother in, hadn't shown her how my life and heart had been forever changed that summer.

"And she just got you back, and now you're leaving again. This is going to be a lot for her to take in on one day."

"I know, but I don't have a choice. I have to believe she'll understand."

It took me all of ten minutes to pack the few things I had in the guesthouse. I left my suitcase on the floor, ready for Maggie when she was ready for me. Then I followed Blake out.

Neither of us pretended me pulling up the roots that had just been planted wasn't going to hurt. As much as I would miss it here, where I was headed was so much greater.

To Maggie. To Jonathan.

To Life.

Comfort slipped as warmth over my skin, assuaged the fear bubbling under the surface. I now recognized the dreams as a call, a lure for where I was supposed to be.

"All right, man, I have to head to work. Just keep me updated, okay?"

"Sure thing."

Blake leaned in for a shake and pulled me into a hug. "Be safe, Will."

I backed out behind Blake. Accelerating up the road, I traced my thumb over the face plate of my phone and brought it to my ear. I drummed my fingers impatiently on the steering wheel. The phone rang four times then went to voicemail. Silently cursing, I listened through the prompt and waited for the beep. Why I would have expected Tom to answer his work line so early in the morning, I had no idea. It was barely eight my time and much earlier in California.

"Hey, Tom, it's William. Change of plans. I'm getting Maggie and Jonathan out of here." I stirred in anticipation, still trying to wrap my mind around the fact that this was really happening. I swallowed and focused on the road as I drove toward my parents' house, strain evidenced in my tone. "We're heading north, not sure where, maybe New York or Vermont.

Maggie will do whatever it takes to keep Troy away from Jonathan. I don't care what it costs...whoever we have to hire. Just...tell me who to contact and what information you need." I released the air from my lungs in overt gratitude. "You don't know how much I appreciate this, Tom. Thank you."

Pressing end, I dropped the phone to my lap and took the last turn into my parents' neighborhood. Unease curled my fingers around the wheel.

In the driveway, I shifted into park. Dad's truck was gone. He'd have left for work hours ago. The house seemed quiet—no movement from the windows, no sound as I stepped out and rounded the corner to the back of the house.

I climbed the steps, knocking quietly before I let myself in. "Ma?"

"Is that you, William?" she called from upstairs.

"Yeah."

Footsteps echoed down the stairs. Mom smiled in surprised pleasure when she appeared in the entryway, her head cocked to the side in curiosity. "What are you doing here so early?" She walked across the kitchen and topped off her coffee cup. "Would you like some coffee?"

"Sure." I took a seat at the breakfast table, my knee bouncing as I struggled to rein in the discord playing havoc with my heart and mind, smoldering turbulence of hope and joy and outright fear.

And shame.

I should have told my mom, when instead I'd pushed her aside. That in itself made me a coward, a fool who'd rather punish my family than face what had torn me up inside.

When she turned back to me, she had that look on her face, intuition tightening her features, as if in those few seconds with her back to me she'd been stricken with my turmoil. Since

I'd been back, she'd never pushed, although there was an obvious understanding between us that one day I would share whatever secrets I'd kept hidden. It was clear now she knew I was there to finally let her in.

She set the cup down in front of me.

Pulling at the edge of my mouth was a small smile, a minute portion of the joy locked up by the acute anxiety I felt making its way out, though I knew the overriding apprehension was apparent in the way I trembled.

Mom looked away, seemed to take time to ready herself for whatever I said, then settled in a chair across from me with her hands flat on the table.

"You know you can tell me anything, William." Even though she tried to control it, her voice faltered at the end.

I spun words through my mind, searching for the best way to tell her.

I decided to just lay it out.

Looking up, I met the unconcealed worry in her gaze.

"You know Maggie Krieger." It wasn't a question, but a preface, a reference back to that time when Maggie didn't bear Troy's name.

Confusion creased her forehead, and her eyes narrowed as she made sense of the name.

"Well...of course I know her." A tremor of her hands, a twitch of her jaw. I was sure she was sifting through every possible scenario in her head.

Shifting forward, I lowered my voice as if it would lessen the blow. "Mom...Jonathan is my son."

She paled, and her arms dropped to her sides as she shrank back in her chair. Her head shook with a slight movement. Silently she mumbled *no*. "You wouldn't do that," she almost begged, though the tears gathering in her eyes asserted she knew I had. I felt sick when she closed her eyes as if to block the sight of me. "You...you left her?"

I stretched my arm across the table, reaching for the hand that was no longer there. "No, Ma. I would never do that. She ended things with me the night I left. I didn't know about Jonathan."

Her lips pressed into a thin line, still shaking. "But you slept with her?" The legs of her chair screeched across the floor, forcing distance between us, though she didn't rise, just looked blankly at the wall behind me. "The girl I welcomed into this house, to *help* her, you slept with her?" Disgust lined every crevice of her face, her voice cracking with disenchanted anger when her attention snapped back to me. "Where, William?"

I couldn't say anything, just stared at my mother with patent guilt.

"Here? In my house? Oh my God."

"Mom...please...it wasn't like that. I loved her."

"Did you even know why she was here? Did you know anything about her, or did you just look at her like she was one of those little tramps you were so fond of in college?"

"Ma—"

She raised a shaky hand to stop me. "Do you have any idea what happened to her when she was little girl?"

The chair beneath me flew back. A loud crack bounced off the walls as the chair clattered to the tile.

"Stop!" Every doubt I'd ever had slammed into me full force, the worry that I'd pushed Maggie too far, crossed boundaries she hadn't known how to draw. But even if I had, it didn't change anything. "I knew every goddamned thing, and all I wanted to do was help her...save her. I loved her so much I couldn't sleep at night."

I turned away, burying my hands in my hair. I'd not expected *this*. Disappointment, yes. But contempt, no.

Pacing, I worked to gather my thoughts. I looked at the door, forcing back the inclination to run. I refused to walk out like that again. My footsteps were light when I moved back to the table. I pulled out the chair nestled under the table next to my mom and placed it facing her. When I sat, she kept her head bowed, her hands in fists on her lap. Our knees touched when I leaned forward and placed my hand over hers.

"Ma." With my voice soft, I implored with her to just look at me. "Please listen to me, because I don't have much time."

She barely raised her head.

"I came to tell you I'm leaving...with Maggie and Jonathan. They're not safe, and I'm going to do whatever I have to do to change that." My voice wavered, and her hand trembled beneath mine. "I missed so much...Blake's wedding, the girls, the last years of Aunt Lara's life. *You*. I spent so much time running from what I left behind here, and I don't want to miss any more. I have to get them away from here, but I don't want it to be forever. I want to come back. I want you to know them. I'm sorry I disappointed you, but I will never regret loving her. I know what it looks like, and the only thing I can tell you is all I ever did was care about her. We kept it a secret because Maggie wanted it that way. She was scared of...everything." Her father. Troy. Possibilities.

Mom struggled to pull in a breath and lifted her head. Tears streamed freely down her face. "Do you have any idea what it feels like to find out Jonathan is my grandson? After all these years of seeing him from a distance, to know he was right there all this time?"

I squeezed her hand, dipped my head to meet her eyes. "Do you have any idea what it felt like to find out I have a son?"

She stilled as we stared at each other. It was as if I could see it all—experience it with her—the hurt I'd inflicted and she'd harbored through my absence beneath excuses only a mother could make. It was all set free, winding itself through her consciousness, the shock and disillusionment merging, and the underlying faith she had in me covering it all.

She placed her hand on my cheek. "This kills me, William. Why didn't you just tell me?"

"I was hurt...I can't..." Blinking, I waded through the memories and tried to put them into words. "It was easier to be angry, to blame everyone else than to admit how badly Maggie had hurt me."

I chewed at the inside of my lip, then proceeded to tell her everything. What Maggie had done to me, how she'd caused me to trip headfirst into a love that had weakened my knees. I attempted to describe how I'd felt that night, when everything had been torn wide and ripped from me in one moment. What it'd felt like to turn my back and walk away. How I'd hardened myself, feigned indifference. *Hid.* The misery that had come with it and how many mistakes I'd made because of it. The joy I felt now.

"I'm sorry, Mom. Please believe me."

She covered her watery mouth with her hand. "I do. Promise me you'll be careful...and that you'll come back."

Leaning forward, I hugged her, whispered that I would.

Yeah. I was leaving.

But this time it was different.

When my mother and I had said our goodbyes, I drove back to the guesthouse, anxious for the moment when Maggie felt ready. That anxiety compounded when I turned on Blake's street and Maggie's van wasn't sitting in front of Amber's house. It hadn't moved once the entire week.

Hurrying down the street, I jerked to a stop in the drive and grabbed my phone as I hopped from the car. Grace was on the porch, heading my direction. I ran up the steps, and she threw her arms around my neck. Worry clamped my jaw, the words, *what happened,* stuck in my throat.

"I'm so proud of you," Grace whispered near my ear when she hugged me.

Relief slackened my hold, and Grace stepped back.

"Maggie was here and she told me about your plan. She wanted me to give you this." She held out a folded piece of paper.

I opened it, reading Maggie's words.

"She left about twenty minutes ago," Grace continued on, "You'd better hurry."

I reread the message.

I'm ready. I don't want to wait any longer. Meet me in Jackson. I love you.

Beneath it was the address.

We'd already decided we were going to ditch Maggie's van at one of the long-term parking lots near the airport in Jackson. We'd report it once Tom gave us some direction, once I knew who to call and who could help us.

I looked up from the letter.

Grace smiled. "Go."

I grabbed her and hugged her hard. "Thank you."

I hit I-55 on the way to Jackson just before ten. Maggie and Jonathan weren't more than thirty minutes ahead of me, but I couldn't help pushing past the speed limits. Forest rose up on each side as I sped down the open road, weaving around the few cars creeping along in the slow lane. Excitement hammered a staccato at my ribs, crashed with the anxiety that had my stomach in my throat. It left me lightheaded. Every few seconds I glanced at the clock glowing on the dash, every minute bringing me closer to the moment when I got my family back.

I glimpsed the backseat through the rearview mirror. I couldn't imagine what it would be like to look back there and see Jonathan sitting in that spot. Couldn't fathom how much all of our lives were going to change. It was all so sudden, yet somehow felt like a lifetime coming. No, I had no idea how to be a father other than the burning need I had to protect the child, to wrap him up in my arms and never let him out of my sight, to love him as much as I loved his mother.

I figured that was a good start.

As I neared Jackson, the trees cleared and the freeway became more congested, though nothing like the freeways I'd grown accustomed to in L.A. I followed the navigation, a thrill rocketing through my nerves when I exited and took the few turns to the small lot off the road to the right.

I pulled into an open spot near the front of the nearly vacant lot. I craned my head as I searched for her van. An old truck was parked at the far end of the lot, a newer sedan parked in front, and a shuttle idled in the pickup zone just inside the gated lot behind the small building. A handful of cars were parked in the long-term spaces, few enough that I knew Maggie wasn't there.

Maggie's note lay in the passenger seat. I unfolded it, looked over my shoulder to verify the address.

I grabbed my phone and felt a stir of panic when I saw it was void of messages.

Cars flew down the road, traveling both directions. None slowed.

"Damn it, Maggie, where are you?"

Chapter Twenty

Maggie ~ Present Day

Beautiful.

Every part of him.

I had no other way to describe the man who watched me from the bottom of the street. His hand was raised in a goodbye that appeared more like a promise of tomorrow, his mouth turned up in a tender smile of encouragement and devotion.

William would do whatever it took.

I would no longer be the fool who questioned it.

Last night had been something of a dream, a fantasy I'd played through my mind a million times. A connection I'd only shared with one man, our bodies and spirits joined, caught up to a place only the two of us knew existed. Years had not erased it.

Instead it had been amplified in our separation, solidified as a bond that could never be broken.

As a young woman, William had made me see I could be loved.

Now, I finally truly believed it.

I turned from him and headed up my sister's walkway. Disquiet fluttered its wings in my belly, danced and taunted, melding with William's flame that could no longer be contained. The two combined smoldered as a nagging dread.

For so long, I'd survived in surrender, but just existing was no longer an option, even when it meant facing every threat Troy had ever made.

I wanted a future for my son, a chance for him to really live.

And I wanted a chance for myself.

Pressing the key into the lock, I turned the knob. I froze when I saw Amber standing just inside.

"Where were you?"

"Amber..."

"I've been worried sick about you. I woke up two hours ago to check on the kids and you were gone."

I grimaced, hating I'd taken the coward's road once again. But I'd wanted just one night for myself. I'd finally made the decision to take a chance and was going ask William to take that chance with me. I didn't want to explain everything to Amber before I knew for sure myself.

I took a step forward. "I'm sorry, Amber. I didn't mean to worry you."

She sucked her bottom lip in as if trying to bite back the worry I'd caused her. "I know, I just...I was panicking. I almost called the cops. I mean, what if..."

I reached out and took her hand, and Amber stilled. "I need to talk to you."

She frowned, but turned and led me into the den. Darkness still shrouded the room. She eased herself onto the couch, and I sat down facing her.

She remained tense as she anticipated what I would say.

"I was with William."

She sat back, blinking in confusion. "Who? You mean, Blake's brother?"

I nodded and began to relay every detail of the story, beginning with the bonfire that had started it all years before. It was incredibly difficult to tell my sister my secrets. Not the ones about William, but the ones that had kept me here and bound me to this place.

I watched as I broke my sister's heart a little further.

"Oh my God, Maggie. You stayed to protect me?" she asked.

"I didn't tell you so you'd feel guilty, Amber. I told you because I need you to understand why I made the choices I did, and so you'd understand why I'm leaving now."

"Maggie," she choked over my name. I understood everything in it. *It wasn't fair, it shouldn't have happened, I should have just told her.* "You need to call the police. Troy shouldn't be out there."

"I'm going to...I just...have to get out of here first, get Jonathan far away."

She blinked and wiped her nose. "When are you leaving?"

I averted my attention to the floor, pulsing the hand I held in my lap in and out of a fist. "I don't know...soon."

Amber touched my cheek. "What are you waiting for?"

Lifting my head, I met the face of my baby sister. "I don't really know."

She smiled a sad smile. "Maggie, go."

I reached for her hand and squeezed it. It was Amber who pulled me into an embrace.

"Thank you, Amber."

"You have no idea how much I'm going to miss you, but I'm so happy for you. You deserve to be *happy*. I'm so proud of you."

I understood my sister's relief. Worry had plagued her as she'd glimpsed my life repeating our childhood. It had been Amber who'd finally sent our father away. She was the one who'd found the courage to make the call and confirm all the rumors of the town.

For me it had come too late.

Pulling away, I ran my fingers down the side of her face. "Please don't cry." I tried to smile, but tripped over the emotion building in my throat. "I promise it's not forever."

Amber released a soggy laugh and wiped under her eyes. "I know…this is a good day."

Standing, I straightened my shirt. "Okay then." I forced the air through my lips. "I'm going to get Jonathan. I have to somehow explain all of this to him."

Amber nodded and stood.

"I'll give you two some time." She walked from the den and disappeared into the quiet house.

I crept into the children's room. Early morning light glowed behind the drapes. The room was tossed in silhouettes and shadows. Samantha was in the crib, tiny breaths pressed in and out of her open mouth as she slept on her stomach. She looked so big there, no longer an infant. Sadness swelled. I had no idea how long it would be before I'd see my niece again. I ran my hand down her back and murmured that I loved her. She barely stirred.

Christopher was sprawled on his back in his racecar bed, one foot hanging over the side, and his covers on the floor. I kissed his forehead, wishing I didn't have to say goodbye.

But it was time.

I looked to the floor where Jonathan slept on a pallet made of thick blankets.

My precious boy.

Kneeling on the floor, I gently prodded him, my hands a caress as I broke into his slumber. At first, he resisted with a groan, and then he sat up and rubbed his eye with his fist.

"Hi, Mommy," he said, his head cocked to the side with a sleepy grin. His blond bed head was sticking up every which way.

Affection pushed past the boundaries of my heart.

"Good morning, my love," I whispered into the quiet, reaching out to cup his cheek. He leaned into the touch, his face full of trust. "It's time to get up," I said.

Without a word, he climbed to his feet and accepted my hand. Jonathan shuffled his feet restlessly behind me as I led him by the hand back to the den. I stole a glance at him. Those eyes that always saw more than they should were acute with awareness, feeding off the nerves that rocked me now.

"Come here, baby." I lifted him in my arms, breathed in his warmth and light, and allowed myself to finally *believe*. "Mommy needs to tell you something really important."

I settled him on my lap in the rocker angled beneath the window. It felt so similar to the place where we'd clung to each other so many times. A slow calm surrounded me. I rocked us in a peaceful sway as he snuggled against my chest. My fingers ran loosely through his hair. He released a contented sigh, curled up closer, and placed a warm palm at the base of my neck.

I couldn't remember a time in my life when I'd felt more complete, more loved, than now, William's touch alive on my skin, and our son's spirit pulsing, in sync with mine.

How had I ever questioned it?

"Do you remember Mommy's friend...William?"

Jonathan nodded in instant recognition, making the fine hairs on his head tickle my chin.

I deliberated and searched for the best way to explain. "What would you think if we went away with him?"

Jonathan tilted his head up. The tiny dimple above his lip deepened, piqued interest and timid excitement. "Where we gonna go? On a trip? Do we get to stay in a hotel?"

"No, baby. He wants us to move with him...to a new house...to a *good* house." I continued on, painting the picture I had in my mind for my son. I wanted him to see the promise in it all, to understand it was big, and our lives were getting ready to change. "William is going to take care of us...love us."

Confusion stole the excitement.

"Forever?" It was asked in a whispered secret as he struggled to sit up, anxious eyes cast around the dimly lit room.

I *felt* it, recognized his fear. I knew exactly where his thoughts had raced.

"Yes, Jonathan...forever." Hugging him a little closer, I murmured at his head, "William wants to be your daddy now. What would you think of that?"

I had no idea what I would say if he said no, if the fear of the unknown, the fear of Troy, and the small comfort of familiarity would tie him to this place, because today I was taking my son from this life. I just hoped if he thought he were making the choice and was a part of the decision, the sudden upheaval wouldn't be so hard on him.

"I like William," he quietly admitted, as if he were afraid to speak it aloud. Wide brown eyes blinked up at me, silently asking if that was okay.

I ran a hand through his hair, unable to process everything I felt. The joy was too great, the fear too strong. I pushed it aside and focused on the purpose. I knew our journey would be long, and, for a time, confusion would reign, that the three of us would have to learn to be a family. But for now, we just needed to get out.

"Let's get your things."

With the excitement back, Jonathan scrambled from my lap and ran down the hall to the kids' room. By then, his cousins had awoken, and the kitchen was filled with the sounds and smells of breakfast. Amber's voice was soft as she called her children to the table.

I followed Jonathan into the bedroom and knelt beside him as he crammed his few belongings we'd brought here into his backpack, mostly small toys and stuffed animals. A grin was on his face.

"I have to pack my things. I'll be in the guestroom."

"'Kay, Mommy."

Crossing the hall, I entered the small room where I'd been staying. On my knees, I pulled out the suitcase I stored under the bed and began throwing the few belongings I brought with me inside.

With every item, the more this became real.

My heartbeat escalated, pounding a discordant rhythm. Panic beaded up as sweat at the nape of my neck. I fought for some semblance of calm, trying to keep my nerves quiet. With each passing second, that control became harder to maintain. In the bathroom, I swept everything into my overnight bag. The bottles and tubes clattered into a haphazard pile. I shrugged the bag over my shoulder, grabbed the suitcase, and went back across the hall.

"Are you ready, Jonathan?"

"Yep." He zipped his backpack and took my hand.

Terror chained me to the ground when I rounded the corner to the entryway. I stared at the door as if a fire raged behind it. Jonathan kept stealing worried glances my way.

I'd dreamed of this for so long, an imaginary world that had always been unobtainable because I didn't know how to cross the line. I'd never been able to reconcile the true threat holding me prisoner to this place with the knowledge that it was worth taking that risk for a chance at freedom.

Now that chance was right outside the door.

Amber appeared behind me. "Is it time?" she asked.

I nodded, drew in breath, and pushed forward.

With each step, memories warned and scars wept, *I'll kill you* a whispered voice in my ear. And I knew Troy wouldn't hesitate. For Jonathan, for William, for *myself,* I shunned it all, waded through the dread that floated out in front of me like an indeterminable bog.

Daylight blinded me when I swung the door open. I blinked, and my eyes adjusted to the bright light.

This was it.

I looked down at my son. "Are you ready?"

He smiled.

As casually as I could, I led my son to the van, though a fury of nerves pummeled my gut. Spiked and crashed. I couldn't breathe. I dropped the suitcase at my side. Clenched my fist.

I could do this.

Raising the latch, I maneuvered the heavy suitcase up and pushed it inside, glancing behind me to the quiet street. Even though I knew Troy was at work, I couldn't help but fear the invisible hold he had on me. I tossed the little overnight bag from my shoulder into the rear. Jonathan wanted to keep his backpack with him so he could watch over his treasures.

I slammed the tailgate shut.

Jonathan yanked at the sliding door and climbed inside, his backpack clutched to his chest as if a shield. I fumbled with his buckle, forcing a smile as I resituated his bag.

I hated that I was confusing him. My demeanor kept shifting from one extreme to the other, a contention between the girl I'd been forced to be and the woman I chose to be now.

I turned back to Amber who fidgeted in apprehension a few feet away.

"Please be careful, Maggie," she said.

I chewed at my lip and nodded once. "You, too."

We both knew Troy would show up at her door when he found out I was gone. With Amber and Ken, he'd always played it cool, acted the good guy, just another one of the family. I wasn't sure what he'd do when he learned we had run.

"Don't worry about us," she said.

I stretched my fingers out to her.

Amber took them in a light grip, her smile both sad and sweet. "Love you," she almost sang as she swung our hands back and forth in front of us.

"Love you back." I could barely get the words out.

With a tilt of my head and an expression that told Amber how much leaving her hurt, I let her go and climbed in the van.

The old engine stuttered to life. I backed out and headed down the street.

I fought the panic when I saw William's car wasn't in the drive. I knew he would still be at his parents'.

I left the van running while I jumped out, mounted the porch steps, and knocked on the door. Grace answered, not appearing surprised to see me.

"Maggie, hi. William isn't here, but he should be back soon."

"Can I leave him a note?"

"Of course."

Grace left the door open as she went further into the house and was back seconds later. "Here." She smoothed her palms down her shirt as if she was nervous.

I sprawled a note, whispered *thank you*, and ran back to the van before I lost my nerve.

At the end of the street, I turned right. I held my breath as I passed the street to the house where I'd been held prisoner for the last six years. That unassuming house had harbored so many of my nightmares. It had also been the one thing I had ever truly thanked Troy for—a real house to raise my son in. To me, the cracks were visible, the house crooked, slanting to the side, bleeding out a silent cry for help I had always turned away.

On Main Street, I forced myself to stay within the twenty-five miles per hour speed limit as I drove through town. Now that I was free, all I wanted to do was run, to push my van as fast as it would go so I could see William's face again. So I could finally be completely his. So I could watch father and son unite. My heart fluttered and goose bumps popped up on the flesh of my arms.

I passed the street I normally turned down every day. I couldn't face my mom or that past right now. One day I would, when the wounds from today weren't so prominent, when I could see past them to the ones etched so deep. Amber promised to take my place and take care of the woman who'd allowed a man to damage her so badly she could no longer take care of herself.

At the edge of town, I glanced in the rearview mirror. A few cars trailed behind. Instead of taking the freeway, I headed south to loop around the backside of town.

Troy had to work until four, which would put a state between us. I knew when he discovered I was gone, he would search the town, ask everyone the last time they'd seen me, demand answers from my sister and mother, and report me missing. If anyone happened to notice me now, I was headed in the opposite direction of Jackson. Not that it mattered much. By the time he realized I was no longer at Amber's, I would have filed every report I could and pressed every charge they'd let me. I wouldn't be a missing wife, but a fleeing victim.

The town disappeared behind us. We flew by the intermittent houses set back and buried in the shelter of trees. I coaxed the old van near its limit. Jonathan remained quiet in the backseat, watching the trees pass out the side window. Silence hovered between us as knowledge, a conversation unspoken.

The two-lane road stretched ahead, and the random cars dropped behind. I settled into the pace, sped around the curves and twists in the road, and passed the chance car we happened upon. At the junction to Jackson, I turned and wound my way north.

The van lurched and the back window shattered. I screamed. The van fishtailed and screeched as it skidded over the pavement.

I struggled with the steering wheel to regain control. My eyes darted up to the rearview mirror to see Troy's truck barreling down on us again.

This time, I braced myself for impact. Metal ground and tires squealed as our bumpers met.

"Mommy," Jonathan cried out.

"Don't cry, baby," I begged as I fought against the fear that clogged my throat. Every muscle in my body tensed as I pushed the pedal to the floor and silently pled for a way out. Ahead, the road curved to the left. I forced the van as fast as it would go. It rattled as it approached eighty.

Troy slammed us again.

The back wheel caught the shoulder — too fast — too much. Through the rearview mirror, Jonathan's terrified face filled my vision. He screamed. "Mommy!"

And I tried...oh God...I tried, but there was nothing I could do.

Chapter Twenty-One

William ~ Present Day

Ten thirty-five mocked me from the ticking dashboard clock. I kneaded my hands on the steering wheel, my palms damp. The excitement from earlier had thinned to a quickly dissipating mist. In its place, fear had taken hold.

Something was wrong.

I felt it in my gut and sensed it in my spirit.

I tried her cell phone again. Another four rings and another click to voicemail. The sweetness of Maggie's voice sounded too much like an ominous warning.

I scrubbed my palms over my face. *Shit.* Finally I broke down and dialed my brother. Blake answered almost immediately. In the background, men shouted and a hammer pounded. Blake raised his voice. "Hey, you guys on the road?"

I could hardly speak, my tongue tied in dread. "No, Blake...Maggie isn't here, and she's not answering her phone."

I wrenched a trembling hand through my hair again and dug my fingers into the back of my neck as if it could distract me from the growing worry. I couldn't sit still, couldn't control the agitation bouncing my knee.

"What?"

"She left thirty minutes ahead of me. Can you drive around town and see if you can find her?"

"Yeah. Give me a few minutes and I'll give you a call back. I'm sure she's fine, Will," he said, a simple reassurance as his truck rumbled to life, though I couldn't stop the thought that I was sure she was not.

After ten agonizing minutes, my phone finally rang. I jumped to answer it, a small dash of hope infiltrating my heart when I thought it might be Maggie, then swore when I saw it was Blake. "Did you find her?"

Blake hesitated, clearing this throat. "No, I drove by her sister's and her mom's." He hesitated. "Went by her house, too, but there were no cars there. Grace is the last person who saw her."

"Fuck." I pressed the heel of my hand against my forehead.

"Just give her a few minutes, Will. Maybe she had to make a stop," he contended, though he couldn't hide the undercurrent of worry in his words. Blake was clearly trying to waylay my instincts when it was obvious he was thinking the same.

"No, Blake. She would have called." *She would have.* I clenched my jaw. In that instant, panic hit me full force, a full-body blow that stopped my heart. "Oh God," wheezed from my mouth.

"Come on, Will. Calm down."

I shook my head silently against the phone.

Gunning the engine, I backed out and sped from the lot. "I'm coming back to look for her."

The SUV bounced as I hit the road, skidding around the corner as I took the ramp to the freeway. I wove a path back toward home, in and out of cars, driving on intuition alone. In my mind's eye, I recognized nothing, not the cars or road, not the glare the sun splashed across the windshield or the whipping shadows of the trees. All I saw was Maggie—Jonathan—my *family*. Pressure filled my head to the extremes, a pounding ache that stretched taut and pinged in my ears as the miles disappeared below.

Behind every scenario sprinting through my mind, there was Troy.

The trip back from Jackson felt like the longest of my life, even though I made it faster than I ever had. I flew down Main, heading straight for Maggie's house. Troy's house. I skid to a stop in front and jumped from the car. I ran up the walk and pounded on the front door.

"Maggie?" I yelled, my mouth pressed to the peeling wood. I pounded again, the impact radiating up my arm. "Maggie!"

I jerked at the knob. Locked metal rattled back beneath my hand. At the window beside the door, I peered through a slit in the drapes into the darkened house. There was no movement, just the suffocating presence of silence.

Undeterred, I ran around to the back door.

I had to find them.

I had to.

I ignored the quiver in my heart that told me this would all be in vain.

Again the door was locked. I lifted my leg, bracing my hands on the porch supports, and slammed the sole of my shoe against the door near the jam. Aggression lit. I kicked again...and again...a frenzy of movements and need and determination as I fought to break my way in. Sweat gathered in my hairline and ran in rivulets down to catch in the collar of my shirt. I stood back, gathered my strength, and rammed the door with my shoulder. I cried out in pain and relief when the jam finally gave.

The splintered door flew open, exposing the inner desolation of the tiny house. Darkness crawled over its walls, barren, devoid of any good because Maggie had already taken all of it with her.

She hadn't been here.

Still, I couldn't stop myself from screaming her name. The house echoed it back at me.

I turned and ran to my car. The little red light blinked on my phone. A missed call. I fumbled for it, swiping my finger across the faceplate. Blake.

I pressed send, pulling a 180 and spewing rocks as I jerked my car back onto the road.

"Did you hear anything?" flew from my mouth the second Blake answered.

From the reluctance on the other end, I knew he had. I slowed as the foreboding spread. The nausea in my stomach increased with every second of silence that passed. My car came to a standstill in the middle of the road.

"Blake, just tell me." I had to close my eyes to get it out because I was certain I didn't really want to know.

"Will, they...found Maggie's van wrapped around a tree...about fifteen miles out. She was on the back roads. I'm guessing she was looping back around toward Jackson."

My world fell out from under me. Images flashed. The innocent boy with his hands and face pressed to the pizza parlor window. Maggie's expression when she'd stood in front of her sister's house the last time I'd seen her.

"Are…are they okay?" *Tell me they're okay.*

"Will…" Blake stumbled over my name, and the sharp edge inside plunged a little deeper as I braced myself for my brother's news. "They weren't in there."

Silence stretched between us with the confirmation.

My head fell back to the headrest, and my eyes cinched closed, a clash of thoughts behind them. The smallest ripple of relief broke with inundating swells of despair.

How could I be back to this place, to the place where I sat helpless?

The sob that had lain strangled in my throat pushed from my mouth.

I'd seen the sickness Troy was capable of evidenced on Maggie's body, but how far would he go?

"William," Blake said. It sounded like sympathy, a consolation I wasn't sure I would ever find. I had no idea how this would ever end.

All I wanted was for them to be safe. I'd give everything I had in exchange for their joy — my happiness, my desires, my life. I'd always been willing. But I always fell short, every good intention I ever had never good enough.

"How do I stop this?" I didn't expect an answer, and I just received Blake's soundless sadness on the other end.

I sat on the side of the bed in the guesthouse, smoothing my hand over the sheets where I'd held Maggie the night before. If I concentrated hard enough, I could see her there, could smell her sweetness and the intensity of her love, feel the caress of her hand, dip my mind back into the ecstasy we'd shared.

Exhaustion threatened to steal me now, the night I'd spent alive in Maggie and the day of desperation taking its toll. I'd driven the town and roads for hours, searching for…for anything—a trace, a hint, a whisper. In the end, I had let life slip through my fingers again.

I'd gone directly from Maggie's to the police station, begging and pleading—demanding. *It was Troy…It was Troy*, I'd said again and again, a claim that had been met with suspicion. Hushed words had been uttered behind closed doors and an accusation thrown my way, a suggestion at my own blame, that maybe I had somehow been involved, though the officer who'd taken my statement hadn't been fast enough to hide the recognition that flickered in his eyes when I asserted Jonathan was my child. He'd seen it too.

When they let me go, they promised to look into it. My gut told me I hadn't been taken seriously, just like last weekend when I'd made a similar claim, and again I cursed this tiny town. I couldn't help but wonder if they'd protect Troy because they'd rather keep the secrets of this place than have them exposed. I left the small station and drove until I could drive no more, until I traveled the road where they'd found Maggie's van what felt like a million times, until it blurred and bled and I thought I might die, until the sun sagged at the horizon and sank with a gut-wrenching goodbye.

This I couldn't handle. Sickness clawed at my insides, a fear so real it saturated me through. It was as if I could feel their grief, sense whatever torment Troy was putting them through. I both welcomed it and wished I could purge the images that plagued and tore at my soul from my mind. Yet I held onto them because I didn't want them to go through it alone.

I fell to my knees on the hardwood floor. The walls closed in, suffocating…and I felt it, felt them. I cried out, begged her name.

I lay my cheek on the cool floor, nails scraping the slick wood, grasping for something, grasping at nothing.

Consciousness tilted and edged.

Darkness fell.

Laughter floated, an echo, a call. William pushed forward, drawn into the dusky haze. Wind whipped at his feet, stirred up the fallen leaves on the dead winter floor. Each step of his boots was leaden with a burden that simmered somewhere in the periphery of his understanding.

"Bet you can't find me." The innocent voice was distant as it fell upon William's ears, filled with mirth at the game the child played.

Those words rushed as fear through William's veins.

His footsteps pounded in his ears as he followed the trail of the soft voice that lingered on the wind. Among the knotty, sinewy trees, their boughs twisted and twined, William paused to listen.

A branch snapped off to his right — another peal of laughter as the child dashed giggling from behind one tree to another more than a hundred yards away.

"Wait," William called, stretching his hand out in the child's direction. Please.

For a moment, the small boy peeked out from behind a large tree trunk and stared back at him with huge brown eyes.

William's heart lurched with the boy's face, a picture of himself — his son.

The child giggled again, his feet too agile as he took off, his dark blond hair like a flare striking in the moonlight before he disappeared deeper into the darkness.

Panting, William chased the boy, begging him to stop while he stumbled over exposed roots and overgrown earth that seemed almost alive as it worked to hold him back.

The child's laughter drifted along the breeze, brushed across William's face, beckoned him to a place he did not know.

William struggled to find him, to close the distance, but the gap only grew. The laughter faded and shifted. The boy's sudden fear hit him like a knife to the chest. Somewhere in the deepest recesses, far beyond William's reach, he heard the child scream.

I jerked from sleep, body thrumming and my mind keening in awareness.

"Oh God...oh God." I dragged myself to my feet, eyes frantic as I searched the darkened room. I knew. Oh God, I knew. My sight adjusted and I zeroed in on my keys on the bedside table. I grabbed them and raced out the door. The gibbous moon hung low in the sky and sent a flood of muted light slanting across Blake's backyard. A solitary porch light lit the dozing house. It was so peaceful, a dramatic contradiction to the chaos plundering my thoughts.

Doubts filled my consciousness. Not of the certainty of the dream, but for the actions that had been set in motion the second I'd been thrown from sleep. I shoved them back. I had no time for second guesses.

I fumbled with my keys and pushed Blake's house key into the lock, squeezing my eyes shut as if it would somehow hide my presence. But every extra second I had brought me a second closer to Blake being too taken by surprise to stop me.

Inside the house was quiet. So quiet. I could almost hear my apprehension rushing ahead of me, scraping across the floor. I took a step forward and stopped to gather myself when the floor creaked. I just had to go for it.

I managed to slip through the house unnoticed. Blake's bedroom door was open a sliver. A soft snore pulsated from within.

Flinging the door wide open, I flicked the on the light switch and rushed across the room.

Blake shot up in bed, thrashing from the covers. I knew he'd be on the defensive, ready to protect his family. His eyes went wide when they met with mine, filled with a confusion that quickly shifted to worry. Grace grabbed at her covers, pulling them up like a protective shield as she blinked herself from sleep.

I said nothing, just hoped the surprise would keep Blake in bed long enough so I could get in and get out.

At the closet, I raked the clothes aside, exposing the face of the tall safe hidden in the back. I'd lived there long enough to know the safe was there and what Blake kept inside—and I had known Blake long enough to guess what code he'd use.

In an uncontrolled frenzy, I twisted the dial with a shaky hand, counting, counting, praying. It unlatched, swinging open to a shotgun, boxes of shells. A handgun was kept in a separate box on the top shelf. I dug into the box and pulled the handgun out. It felt so foreign in my hand, too heavy, all wrong. Ignoring the thought, I grabbed a box of bullets and dumped a handful into my palm, shoved them in my pocket. I'd do whatever it took.

My breaths came erratic as I closed the safe and spun the dial once. When I turned, Blake sat on the edge of his bed, gripping his head with his hands. "What are you doing?"

I knew well enough he warred with himself, that Blake knew exactly what I was doing—that he both wanted to stop me and wanted me to go.

"I'm getting my family back."

For a moment, Blake blinked in confusion.

"What?" he finally said, pushing to his feet and shaking off the drowsiness. "Did you hear something? You know where they're at?"

"Yeah, I know where they're at," I said. He'd taken them where it all had started. Where Troy had drawn a line and made the connection. Where Troy planned to make me pay.

"Where? What the hell is going on?"

I just shook my head.

I had no time to explain, and even if I did, I didn't think I could. There'd been times when I'd felt tempted, when I'd wanted to share, when I'd wanted someone else to know.

Now, it felt private, something revealed between me and my son when the right to know him had been taken away.

I headed toward the door.

Blake started for me, panic in his footsteps.

"Will, come on, man. Don't do anything stupid."

I looked back at my brother.

Stupid.

I had the urge to laugh, the urge to cry.

"I'll do anything, Blake." It didn't matter if it was stupid or whatever consequences had to be faced, it was worth it. As long as they were safe.

Creases edged Blake's face, a shock of fear, a twist of compassion.

"I have to go." I spun on my heel and headed for the door.

Blake grabbed my arm. "Then I'm coming with you."

I turned on him and pressed my body hard against his chest, my words a fierce whisper. "No, you're not. You're staying here, with your girls. They need you, Blake. I have no idea what's going to happen out there, and I won't let you risk that."

Blake stumbled back as my meaning sunk in, and I took the chance and left my brother staring behind me.

Grace rustled from the bed. "I'm calling the police," she said.

That was fine. I planned on it too, but there was no way I was going to stand aside and leave this in their hands.

I quietly slipped back through the kitchen and out of the house.

Once outside, I ran. Orange lights flashed as I clicked the lock to my SUV. I jumped in, kicking over the ignition and slamming it into gear in almost the same motion. I tore out of the driveway and up the road.

I couldn't bring myself to look in the direction of Maggie's sister's house as I flew by. Grace had spent the afternoon with her while Blake and I had searched. She'd been standing in the middle of her yard when I returned. I'd slowed, locked in the misery of her gaze when I passed. Like me, she was destroyed. I saw it. Felt it. But I hadn't stopped because I had no idea how to share this pain.

Nearing the end of the street, I jammed the brakes and skidded to the side. With my heart pounding, I stretched up to dig the bullets from my pocket. My entire being vibrated as I loaded the gun, the small clink and grate of metal-like little shots of electricity injected in my nerves as I slid each one into the chamber. Unsteadily, I set the gun on the seat next to me.

The town was dead, no traffic or evidence of life.

I flew.

As I left the town behind, I picked up my cellphone and dialed 911. I told the operator where I was going and what I knew I would find. I hung up when I was told not to approach them.

Memories engulfed me, expanded my chest and mind, the anguish and ecstasy of that summer, my hopes, the immense love I'd found in her and the insurmountable heartbreak it'd cost us. As I squinted to find the old dirt road and pulled over to the side, it felt as if it all culminated here, in a moment when I would either win it all or lose my reason to live.

A break in the forest, a barely visible overgrown road.

My spirit stirred.

They were here.

Steeling myself, I took the gun in a sweaty palm and stepped from the car.

Torpid air belted my face, a rush too warm, my skin tacky and moist. Loose rocks crunched under my feet as I inched up the road veiled in branches and bushes, gun braced by two hands and pointed out in front of me.

Curls of aggression snaked around my limbs, muscles tensed as I came up around the bend. Shallow, uncontrolled breaths filled the night.

A roll of hatred tripped my senses when the tail of Troy's truck came into view. My pulse stuttered when I edged around the side.

To the right, Maggie lay in ash and soot with her back propped halfway against a log. Her head lolled, her eyes fluttering as she drifted in and out. Dried blood was caked around a gash on her forehead. Matted, tangled hair stuck to her face. Her lips moved with incoherent sounds and disregarded pleas.

At the far right fringes of the field was Jonathan. He rocked beneath a tree, hugging his knees to his chest. Nearly imperceptible convulsions jerked his shoulders, the child silent as he cried.

And across the long deadened fire, to my left, Troy stood behind a log. One heavy boot was braced near the top and a shotgun was balanced across his thigh.

I emerged into the open field, the gun drawn in front of me.

"Knew you'd come." Troy didn't look my way, just stared across the space at Maggie as he spoke. He shifted in agitation and hiked the barrel higher as he resituated his aim on Maggie. Evil palpitated as a stagnant breeze, rippled and hovered in the air.

In it, I hesitated to even breathe.

Then I heard Maggie moan my name.

I so badly wanted to look at her, to call out that it would be okay. That soon we would be together and I'd never allow Troy to hurt her or Jonathan again. Instead I trained my attention on the sickness in front of me. Troy's face twitched and pinched, a combination of hurt and fury. Derision barked from his mouth, as if he were choking back a sob. He turned his face to me, though the barrel remained steady on Maggie.

"Did you fuck my wife?" Delusional impressions of betrayal clouded his eyes, the sum of insanity, derangement and desperation lurking in the depths. Confusion and anger, as if he hadn't forced Maggie with his vicious hand. I saw it there—the genuine belief that Maggie had been the one who'd hurt him.

I knew the combination made Troy more dangerous than I ever could have imagined.

Swallowing hard, I gripped the gun tighter, my finger firm on the trigger.

"You don't want to do this, Troy. Just...let them go...and you and I...we'll talk about this."

This time an uncontained cry escaped Troy's mouth.

"Talk about this? You *touched* her. I watched her, sneaking out your door...like a *whore*." He tucked his face into the sleeve of his shirt and wiped his eyes, then jerked his attention back to Maggie. "How could you do this to me, Maggie? I loved you."

I inched toward Maggie while facing Troy, desperate to make myself a barrier between them. I slid my feet along the soft dirt, each movement calculated, hoping to distract him without setting him off.

"And Jonathan...oh, God. Look at him. How didn't I see it?"

"Come on, Troy...leave the boy out of it." I hated the way my voice cracked, my fear set on display. I steadied myself, seeking some kind of control, fisting the grip of the gun firmer in my hand. I licked my lips and my heart pounded harder. "This is between you and me."

Scorn lined Troy's forehead. "Leave the boy *out* of it? Leave my family out of it? All these years that I took care of him. Worked every day to provide for him. I should have known."

My family, I wanted to scream. Somehow I reined it in and kept it simmering inside. As much as I wanted to confront him, rush him and make him pay for what he'd done, I knew fighting with Troy was not going to save Maggie and Jonathan. I just had to keep Troy talking and keep the focus on myself. Stalling...praying the police would hurry and get there.

I shuffled an inch closer, but was still off to the side.

"It was me, Troy, you know I wanted her...that I went after her." I edged closer, goading him. *Come on, you piece of shit, look at me, take it out on me.*

In the distance, a siren trilled.

Troy's head jerked with the sound, and the barrel of the shotgun shook as he raised it higher in front of him, tears filling his eyes as he aimed. "Can't believe you made me do this, Maggie. I warned you."

Oh God...no.

I squeezed the trigger.

A shot broke through the night, rang in my ears. Time seemed to slow as the sound echoed and ricocheted in the space. I watched in shock as blood gushed from the small hole in the side of Troy's head and streamed as darkened trails down the side of his face. I shook, the gun trembling out in front of me as I witnessed the shotgun tumble from Troy's hands, the man frozen wide-eyed before he fell to the ground.

How many times had I imagined taking Troy's life? I'd imagined the satisfaction in making him feel some of the pain he'd inflicted on Maggie. I'd thought it would somehow feel like justice, a punishment for every wrong he'd done.

I swallowed down the bile that rose in my throat when I looked down at Troy's lifeless body. There was no pleasure, only overwhelming relief that Maggie was finally free.

The gun slipped from my hand and landed with a soft thud on the ground. I turned slowly, my movements burdened by what had just occurred. I met Maggie's eyes. They were so wide — too wide. She stared back at me as her hand sought her stomach. When she raised her hand in front of her face, blood dripped from her fingertips.

In the moment, I'd been too lost in the horror unfolding in front of me that I'd been unable to recognize an even greater horror was taking place. I'd not even heard another shot.

The girl, the one who'd taken me whole, struggled to take in a breath.

My spirit thrashed.

Crossing the space in five steps, I fell to my knees.

"Nnnn...no...oh God, Maggie, no. Baby, no." My hands flitted inches over her torso. My eyes blurred, and I was powerless to do anything but watch the blood spread from the wound in her belly, soaking the front of her shirt.

Her eyes fluttered as she drifted, and her head bobbed to the side. I grabbed her face with both hands, held her firm as I shook her, kissed her mouth. I pressed my forehead to hers. "Don't leave me, Maggie! Don't you dare leave me!"

She struggled against the tide pulling her away, a sharp breath sucked between her lips.

I held her face firmer, pulled back to search her eyes as I yelled, "Look at me! Do you hear me! Do not close your eyes."

Her mouth lifted at one side, a smile I knew meant so many things. *I love you...thank you...goodbye.* Her eyes pled as she managed to force out our son's name.

"No, no, no...Maggie, no!" I shook her shoulders when her eyes fluttered again. Her head rolled back and snapped forward with no resistance.

I was screaming, begging, I didn't know. Everything tilted and spiraled, the field spinning in my vision.

"Help!" It raked from my throat as I screamed. "Somebody help us!" My cries were drowned out by the helicopter that was suddenly overhead, and a blinding light flooded the field. Trees strained and bowed as they were pushed aside by the fierce gust. Blue and red lights flashed down the road from behind Troy's truck.

Still, I screamed, burying my face in the hair she'd always hidden herself behind. The long strands of auburn were matted, knotted with dirt, but to me they felt soft...so soft...smelled of the girl and the goodness and of my life. If I just got close enough, maybe I could disappear in her. Maybe she'd take my breath and live.

I'd give it all.

I always would have.

"Get back!" The demand was shouted from six feet away, though it barely penetrated my ears.

I clung to her and cried again, "Help her!"

Footsteps quickened and I was dragged back. The Earth seemed to swallow me as I dug my heels into the ground and scooted away. Flurries of ash filled the air, a smothering haze as the chopper stirred the ground. A crushing weight constricted my chest. I felt as if I were being buried alive.

No.

Uniformed men and women swarmed the area, police and EMTs. Paramedics surrounded her, the chopper blades a constant *thwump thwump thwump* overhead.

Need collided with my soul. It was a fear so strong I could taste it.

Jonathan.

I jerked my head to the vacant spot beneath the tree.

Laboring to stand, I could barely make out the woman screaming at me to get back on the ground. I never considered stopping. I pushed forward, drawn into the dusky haze. Wind whipped at my feet and blasts of hot air blew against my face.

"Jonathan!" I screamed as I stumbled into the edge of the forest. The name slipped and rustled through the leaves.

My footsteps pounded in my ears. This time there was no laughter or mirth, no child's voice teasing at my senses. There were no big-brown eyes staring back at me. There was only devastation and pain as I hurtled through the forest. Roots worked to hold me back, branches slapping my face as I flung myself into its depths, frantic as I searched. "Jonathan!" I screamed.

The boy ran just ahead.

I rushed, winding my arms around him as I pulled his back to my chest. His legs flailed, and his fingernails dug into my hands as he fought to get away.

My mouth was at his ear, promising, "I've got you, Jonathan. I've got you. Shh...shh...I've got you," I said again as I shifted him around.

Jonathan crumpled in my hold and pressed his face into my chest. His tears wet my shirt that was stained with Maggie's blood. I held my son as he wept, running my fingers through his hair, hugging him as close as I could. "I've got you."

I would never let him go.

"I've got you."

Our spirits met in a tangle of too many emotions. Trust and love and grief. I knew Jonathan felt the connection we shared. I had witnessed it in his eyes the few times I'd been blessed with his presence. I also knew instinctively it was not the same, and the dreams had been given to me alone.

I'd been called to be here this day.

"I've got you."

I wound us back through the forest, clinging to my son while he clung to me. When we came to the field, I held Jonathan tight, my hand on the back of his head as if I could shield him from what was happening. Officers worked over Troy's body. Measurements were drawn. Evidence gathered. An orange tag was staked in the spot where I had dropped the gun. I didn't take the time to contemplate whether they'd question my motive.

The only thing that mattered was Maggie.

She was strapped to a stretcher, her hair hanging limp over the top. Paramedics worked in a controlled chaos, shouting, moving, prodding. The police chopper had gone, and a MedEvac flew in low overhead to take its place. It hovered and dipped, and then disappeared behind the trees to land on the paved road.

I just stood there, my world falling apart while I tried to hold my son's together. Her smile echoed in my mind, her caress an imprint on my skin. I'd lost her once. I didn't think I would survive it again.

And I prayed, the word silent on my lips.

Please.

Chapter Twenty-Two

William ~ Present Day

I sat in a plastic chair beside the emergency room bed, twisting my fingers through my son's hair. His breaths were uneven, shallow then deep as he slept through the exhaustion and trauma. When the paramedics in the field had first attempted to get him onto the stretcher, Jonathan had fisted his hands in my shirt, begging no. It tore at me and filled me the same, knowing Jonathan needed me. I'd coaxed him, convincing him they just had to make sure he wasn't hurt and promising I wouldn't leave his side. With my hand on his chest, Jonathan had finally conceded. The ambulance ride had been taken in silence, Jonathan's hand in mine the entire time. I'd felt the tremors rolling through him as the shock was finally expelled from his body.

Now he slept in the quiet room, awaiting discharge. He was uninjured—all except for the emotional trauma that I wasn't sure could ever be healed.

I released a tortured breath, and shifted closer to lay my head on the bed next to my son's. So innocent. I traced the back of my hand down the soft roundness of his cheek. When I'd fallen in love with him, I wasn't sure. Maybe it had been the same as it had been with his mother—in that first moment when my spirit had stirred in awareness. It'd been a moment I'd fought to deny with both of them. They both had seemed such an impossibility.

Outside the door, Amber spoke with the staff, stepping in as next of kin when the hospital realized I had no legal rights to speak for Jonathan. Troy was on his birth certificate, and his mother was still in surgery somewhere upstairs.

Inching closer, I touched my forehead to Jonathan's, just needing to feel the connection.

Everything hurt. It was a throbbing that emanated from my soul and reached out to consume my heart and mind, burned beneath my skin. I was stripped bare, left abraded and raw. It destroyed me to imagine what Maggie had been through, what she was going through now. Destroyed me to imagine life without her.

The door cracked open. Light streamed in from behind and cast Amber's face in shadow. She entered slowly, every step tentative as she crossed to the other side of the bed. She and I had said little. When she arrived, she'd appeared almost numb, as if she refused to accept what Troy had done. Now that stupor seemed to have cleared, and her eyes were watery as she stretched out a hand to caress Jonathan's back. I lifted my head to look at her.

"They signed the discharge papers. Jonathan can go," she said. Her lip trembled and the tears broke free. They slid down her face along the edge of her nose, her head inclined as she wove her fingers through Jonathan's hair. She seemed unable to meet my face. "She loves this little boy so much. She'd do anything for him." Sorrow filled her face, and her mouth crested with a mournful smile. "Whatever happens..." Her words broke. She swallowed and finally turned the force of her gaze on me. "You know you saved his life, don't you?"

I flinched. How many times had I heard a news story of a man taking the lives of his family then turning the gun on himself? At times they'd seemed almost unbelievable because I couldn't fathom that kind of insanity. But we all knew that's what this had been. Troy had no intention of any one of us making it out of that field alive.

"Listen..." Fidgeting, Amber diverted her attention to the floor as she seemed to gather herself before she turned back to me. "I need to know what your intentions are...with Jonathan if..." She fisted her hand in front of her.

Neither of us wanted to have this conversation. Neither of us wanted to acknowledge the possibility.

My voice was rough. "He's my son."

More tears came, though she nodded.

"Okay then." She sniffled and gestured toward the door. "We should go."

Picking up Jonathan, I cradled him in my arms. He felt heavier in his sleep, the full burden of his weight placed on me. I brushed a kiss against his forehead.

It was just past three-thirty in the morning when we entered the emergency surgery waiting room. It was empty except for Blake and my mother. They watched me from across the room as I settled into a chair. I shifted Jonathan to rest his head on my shoulder when he stirred.

My mother's expression was anguished when I met her face, longing and sympathy predominant in the way she tilted her head. Her dampened eyes roamed my son, although she stayed where she was. Blake leaned against the wall, motioned at me with his chin. We all knew now was not the time for introductions.

I laid my head back against the wall and closed my eyes, welcoming the reprieve the darkness rendered. Behind the seclusion of my lids, the visions were bright, filled with the only girl I'd ever love. She danced ahead of me with our son's hand in hers. They turned and smiled. Their faces shined, brimming with love and goodness.

I sought out her spirit, refusing to let go of my prayer.
Please.

A nurse came out a few minutes later to give us an update. Maggie was still in surgery and they expected she would be for a while. There was very little information she could give.

The waiting was harrowing. Hours passed, and the window at the far end of the room dawned with light. Anxiety and fatigue contended, twitched at my muscles and tugged at my mind. I slowly rocked, held my child closer.
Please.

At six twenty-four, a man dressed in blue scrubs finally emerged through the door labeled *Emergency Surgery*. He appeared haggard, his shoulders slumped and eyes weary.

"Family of Maggie Clemons?"

Shaking, I stood, unable to feel my legs beneath me. The only sensation I had was my son in my arms and the need in my heart. Amber came to my side, and my mother and brother rallied behind us as the man crossed the room.

"I'm Dr. Braswell." The surgeon glanced between Amber and me. "Maggie pulled through the surgery."

I turned my face to the ceiling, blinking back the tears I could do nothing to stop. Relief flooded as a hurricane, full force, an inundating surge that almost knocked me from my feet. I exhaled the rush of emotion, a choked cry that sang of both praise and torment.

She made it...she made it.

Blake placed his hand on my shoulder in a silent show of support.

I brought my attention back to the doctor whose expression didn't evidence the exquisite relief I felt.

"She has a long way to go." The surgeon's brow creased, and he angled his head as if searching to see that we understood the seriousness of what he was trying to convey. He continued on, speaking softly and slowly. "Her injuries were severe, but she got here within the one-hour window after injury which significantly raises her chances of survival, plus the gunshot came from a distance where the buckshot had begun to spread." He used his hands to demonstrate, spreading them wide across his midsection. "Had the shot come from a closer range, she most likely would not be here right now. She's been transfused for massive blood loss, and lacerations to her intestines have been repaired. Her biggest risk now will be infection. She's, of course, still intubated after the surgery and will be in the recovery room for about an hour before she's transferred to intensive care on the fourth floor. If you want to wait upstairs, they'll let you know when you can see her. Can I answer any questions?"

I had what felt like a million of them tumbling through my mind, all adding up to one thought—*Just tell me she will be okay.*

Instead of voicing it, all I could manage was a small shake of my head and a mumbled, "Thank you."

The man nodded and extended a tired, sympathetic smile that appeared truly genuine. "I promise we're doing everything we can."

Then he turned and walked away.

I pushed open the door. Another hour of waiting had passed, though this one had been filled with a hope that had blossomed and grew to penetrate every nerve, every cell, and every breath.

Subdued light glowed from beneath a cupboard mounted on the wall, illuminating a relatively small room. In the middle, a bed sat higher from the floor than normal, and machines were cluttered around it. I slowly approached. Tubes trailed from bags to fill her veins, others pumped toxins from her body, and more beeped as they monitored for life. Most prominent of all was the ventilator that rhythmically inflated and deflated her chest. But really, I saw none of those things.

I could only see the woman who had haunted my years and now possessed my future.

I swept back the hair that was matted to her forehead and pressed my lips to her clammy skin.

So broken.

The first time I'd seen her, I'd recognized it. Across the flames that had crackled and lit, I'd witnessed it in her eyes, had felt it pierce me somewhere deep. I'd known it in her smile, in her words, and in her touch. I'd seen it when I returned, when I ran her down and unleashed my anger on her in the middle of my parent's street. I'd felt it when I held her in front of her mother's back door.

I also knew she was the bravest person I'd ever met.

She'd been terrorized her entire life.

And still she'd taken the chance.

I took her hand and whispered near her ear, "You can't leave before you get the chance to start."

Epilogue

Sunlight seeped between the trees swaying in the gentle breeze. Yellow and red leaves fell from branches and flitted to the ground, the October air cool and crisp.

As I always had been, I was drawn to her. My eyes swept across the lawn to where she rocked gently on my mother's porch swing next to Grace.

It had been eight months since the night that had nearly destroyed our lives.

Her auburn waves tumbled over one shoulder, and her head was inclined as her mouth lifted in an unrestrained smile as she listened to whatever Grace had to say.

With a look, Maggie still stole my breath.

She glanced up as if she felt my gaze. That unrestrained smile softened and filled with an emotion that she reserved only for me.

The one I returned was full of adoration.

I'd never imagined it could really be this way. For so long, she'd been something forbidden, something I could never fully attain. A dream. A girl I'd been desperate for, but one who had remained so far out of reach.

Now, she was mine, and I was hers, the secrets we'd whispered with our mouths and bodies no longer concealed or hidden away.

Grace continued to speak, and Maggie smiled in a gentle way that promised *later* before she turned back to the conversation they were sharing.

I couldn't help the joy from forming on my face.

"Uncle Will, you're it!" Emma squealed, smacking the back of my leg as she ran by. I laughed and jumped back into the game. Emma dashed ahead, her smile wide when she glanced over her shoulder, black hair flying as she raced across my parents' front yard.

"Come on, Emma!" Blake called his encouragement from where he stood manning the grill. He tossed me a knowing grin. "Don't let him get you!"

"I'm right behind you," I teased as I drew closer, allowing her to stay a foot ahead.

She howled with laughter. "Run, Jonathan!" she screamed and reached a hand out toward him as she flew by. "Or else he's gonna get you!"

Diverting my path, I darted toward Jonathan whose eyes went wide from where he stood frozen before he turned and ran. A giggle started in his belly, a low and subdued rumble before it burst from his mouth. He threw his head back and laughed toward the sky. "No, Daddy! No!"

My chest tightened, so full, so much.

No, I never imagined it could be this way.

It didn't mean our lives weren't filled with hardships, that each day there wasn't a small struggle we had to overcome or a giant obstacle we had to face.

It just meant it was worth it.

Maggie's physical recovery had been long and difficult, but it was the emotional wounds that still plagued our days and haunted our nights. On some level, I knew they always would, though each day seemed to get a little easier than the last.

When Maggie had been released from the hospital, we had moved into my old room in my parents' house for about a month to give Jonathan a safe, neutral place to adjust. A quiet place for Maggie to heal. A place where Jonathan and I could learn each other and reclaim the relationship we'd never had.

An old couch had been shoved against the wall below the window. For a month I'd slept alone on it in the few moments when any of us could actually sleep.

Immediately, Jonathan had been placed with a therapist, someone to help him begin working through the trauma he had witnessed that night. Really, to help him work through the abuse he'd witnessed all of his life. It was then the nightmares had begun. It seemed once he finally felt safe during the day, the fears he'd kept long-repressed had sought release during the night.

For both Maggie and me, they had unleashed the guilt from our mistakes—me for running, Maggie for staying.

I had paced with the child for hours, back and forth over the creaky floor, holding him in the security of my arms while he cried. Then I would hold Maggie in my old bed while she wept after Jonathan had fallen back to sleep. She'd cry that she had done this to her child, while I promised her it wasn't her fault. In her exhaustion, she would finally drift and I would stare sleepless out the darkened window, wondering why in the hell I hadn't done things differently.

Guilt was deceitful that way.

I would often sit in the hall while Jonathan and Maggie were in their sessions, banging my head and wishing I could somehow remove all of their pain.

That had been something I'd had to accept—I couldn't just make it all better or make it go away.

But I could love them and support them, show Jonathan what it was like to have a dad who loved his mother, a dad who treated her with respect and like the treasure she was. A dad who was there for his son and listened when he spoke and paced with him in his arms when he cried.

It had taken Jonathan three months to call me that— *Daddy*. They'd warned me he may have a negative association with the term, and I had been told I should allow it to come naturally. Jonathan knew I was his father, and when he was comfortable, it would come out. When it finally did, it left me without words and with Jonathan in my arms.

I still wasn't sure whether I believed time could heal. Six years apart and the depth of what I felt for Maggie had never dimmed, could never be buried or contained.

But I was sure love could heal.

No. We would never be completely free of the past, and the memories could never be entirely wiped away, but we *were* healing. Jonathan's dreams came further and further apart, their intensity less. Maggie rarely cried herself to sleep anymore, and I no longer stared unseeing out the window, but instead slept wrapped around the girl.

The girl I was going to marry as soon as she was ready. I didn't want to push her. I would wait until just learning how to breathe didn't consume her days.

I ran behind Emma and Jonathan as they rounded the end of the yard and headed back the other direction.

"Grammy is base!" Emma called and the two children ran, their legs sprinting them across the grass. Little Olivia did her best to keep up with the *big kids*, suddenly cutting across the yard midway, completely oblivious to the "rules" Emma had set up for their play.

Jonathan and Emma tumbled into their grandmother who waited with outstretched arms under the tree at the edge of the yard.

"Safe!" she cried as the two tackled her.

My dad whistled from his spot on the porch. "You made it, Emma and Jonathan!"

I laughed and fell to the ground beside them.

"You two are way too fast for me." I panted as I tried to catch my breath. I tugged Jonathan onto my lap and hugged him close. He tucked his head under my chin and grinned up at me. A rush of emotion spread.

Joy.

"Hey, Will, can you give me a hand? These steaks are ready," Blake said while he tried to balance a large metal tray in one hand and tongs and a spatula in the other.

"Sure."

Mom stood from the grass and dusted herself off. She smiled as she took Jonathan and Emma by the hand. "Why don't the big kids help me set the table? Do you think you could do that?"

Her suggestion was met with another squeal from Emma and a shy smile of delight from Jonathan as he glanced back at me.

I caught Maggie's expression, saw it in her eyes, a thankful satisfaction, another small triumph for our son.

He'd come such a long way.

I crossed the yard and clapped Blake on the back. "Smells good."

He handed me the tray and maneuvered the steaks from the grill. He smirked. "Well I made them, didn't I? What'd you expect, little brother?"

"Don't let it go to your head. I was just trying to be nice." I shook my head sadly, my eyes dropping to the pile of steaks then back to my brother. "I mean, look...you ruined them. They're all charred." Laughing, I ducked when Blake tried to smack the back of my head. I wove back and forth as he chased me up the stone path. I tried to shove him back when he gained on me.

We were both laughing by the time we pounded up the porch steps.

"All right, you two, knock it off before your mom has to send you to your rooms," Grace said, grinning up at her husband who swept in to kiss her.

"Mmm...I think I like that idea," he said against her mouth.

Grace pushed him back and patted his cheek. "You only wish." She stood, ignoring her husband who wrapped himself around her back. "Here, Will, let me take those for you."

"Thanks," I said and passed them off.

Blake followed her in, whispering something in her ear. Maggie struggled not to laugh, her face red with my brother's overt display. I just watched them, no longer affected by that anticipated twinge of jealousy.

Instead, I smiled at Maggie and reached down to help her up. I was complete — whole — that place reserved for Maggie no longer aching to be filled. I pulled her close, and splayed my hand across her lower back. Her skin still burned me through her clothes.

"Hungry?" I brushed her bangs from her face, wondered again how it was possible to love someone so much.

"Starving."

"Good, because those steaks smell delicious."

Maggie laughed, and I tightened my hold.

Tenderness filled her eyes as she inclined her head to the side, her fingers fluttering up to caress my jaw.

I moved to run my lips across her fingers. "I love you so much, Maggie."

A soft smile formed on her mouth. "I know."

ಌ⁊

Maggie

I'd never known what home meant.

To me, it'd been a prison, a place I longed to escape. A place where horrors were harbored, concealed behind closed windows and lies.

I looked up at the small house as we pulled into the drive. That flame I'd once kept buried inside burned bright.

Home.

I knew it now — I knew what it meant.

William pulled into the garage. He pressed a warm palm to my cheek before he climbed out of the car. The warmth spread through my consciousness, covered every inch of who I was.

Jonathan had fallen asleep on the way back from his grandparents'. William unbuckled our sleeping child from the backseat. He kissed Jonathan's head when he pulled him into his arms. A contented sigh flowed from Jonathan's mouth as he struggled to sink further into William's chest.

William murmured at his head — loved our little boy.

My spirit soared, the thankfulness I felt overflowing. How many times had I prayed for someone to save us? William had.

I followed them inside and down the hall. We passed by the small office where William did contract work. He wanted to stay close to us during the day in case we needed him, so he'd begun doing the books for a few of the small businesses around town from the house.

I flipped on the nightlight in Jonathan's room so William could tuck him in bed. Jonathan stirred when William set him down, blinking as he took in his surroundings. William knelt down beside him.

"Mommy and Daddy are right across the hall if you need us, okay, buddy?" William said, his words a simple reassurance for our son. *We are here.*

Jonathan nodded. "Okay, Daddy."

Then he closed his eyes and snuggled under the covers when William pulled them to his chin.

I climbed to my knees beside his bed. "I love you, Jonathan."

I placed a kiss on the side of his head and ran my fingers through his hair. I'd spent so much time fearing for him. For his future, for his safety, and for his heart. I'd struggled to supply the needs I didn't have the strength to provide, to give him hope when I had none, to give him joy when I had little to share. All I'd have to give him was my love.

William had shown me that was enough.

William helped me to stand, and a soft smile filtered across his face as he drew me near and wrapped a strong arm around my waist. I flattened myself against his warmth, and he rocked me in the solitude of Jonathan's room.

"Let me get ready for bed," I said.

He kissed me gently below my ear. "Don't be long."

"I won't be."

As if I could stay away from him for long.

He turned his attention back to Jonathan as I headed out the door.

In the bathroom, I tugged my shirt over my head and shrugged out of my jeans. Sometimes my mind still fought to recognize what had happened that night, and other times, the memories would slip over me like the residual of a nightmare. My blood would run cold as I was struck again by what Troy had planned to do.

I still had at least two more surgeries to remove the scars, but even when they were gone, I would never be able to forget.

William had saved us. He had been willing to give it all. He would have given his life to save ours. Instead he'd taken Troy's.

I knew it haunted him more than he'd ever admit.

I'd never known more fear than the day that had been spent in that field. Troy had snapped. The true derangement he'd hidden behind a hardened exterior had finally broken free. I'd begged him to spare Jonathan, telling him I'd do anything if he'd let him go. It'd only incited Troy more.

By nightfall, I'd given up and succumbed to the realization that it was the end. Again, I had failed, and my son would pay the ultimate price for every mistake I had made.

And then William was there.

Shaking off the memories, I washed my face, brushed my teeth, and slipped into the little white nightgown. I paused in the doorway between our bathroom and our bedroom. William was stretched out on our bed. His was propped up on a pillow that rested against the headboard, wearing only pajama bottoms. His body was lean and strong, and his hair flopped over his eye as he angled his head so he could see the book he read in the light from the small lamp on the nightstand.

A thrill shot through my middle. It was a feeling I couldn't quite describe, something that hinted at desire, though it went so much deeper than that. It was unending trust, an overwhelming love, and an intense passion. A consuming need that made me want to bury myself in the man who smiled over at me when he noticed me standing there.

"Hey you," he said as he placed his book on the nightstand and shifted to his side.

There'd been so many things I'd never been able to appreciate before. The way his bare feet looked when he stood on the tile floor, how rumpled he was in the morning, how he squinted when he was absorbed in what he read.

But all this time, I knew him.

I knew the kindness and the goodness.

None of what I felt was a result of my past or anything I'd been through in my life. I wasn't clinging to William as a savior or blinded by the circumstances.

Underneath all the scars that lined my body and lined my soul, William saw me. And he loved me as much as I loved him.

I crossed the room, and the hem of the little white eyelet nightgown I wore brushed over the tops of my thighs. I'd picked it out just for him—just for tonight. I'd been building up to this, searching for the courage to find my voice, for the place inside me that knew it was okay to ask for what I *wanted*.

His expression shifted when I climbed on top of him and straddled his lap. I leaned in and kissed his mouth, grasping his face as I showered this man who'd been willing to sacrifice everything for me and our son with love.

"What are you doing?" he mumbled with a smile against my mouth.

"Kissing you."

He laughed low. It was a sound that originated somewhere deep inside of him, and he grinned and flipped me onto my back.

I gasped when he pounced on me.

"I like this," he said with his mouth at the strap of my nightgown. He nudged it aside with his nose. He kissed my shoulder, the warmth of his mouth traveling over my collarbone and under my jaw. He pulled back to look at me. The emotion in his eyes was so powerful—enough to fill me up and sustain my life. He ran his knuckles down my cheek. "But I love this."

I felt the flush that washed my face and neck, a feeling of innocence that sent butterflies flitting through my belly.

I touched his face and got lost in the man who had always made me feel this way—both special and normal. The man with gentle hands and a pure heart.

He edged the straps lower. His hands ignited a fire where they caressed over my skin.

The night when I stood in his childhood bedroom and he'd first told me he loved me, I'd known it. It was the night he'd made a choice to fight for me, no matter what the consequences. And I knew it now.

I wanted it to be him. In every capacity. In every way.

I ran my hands up his arms and palmed his perfect face. My nerves raced as I searched the eyes of the man I would never stop loving.

"Marry me?" My voice broke when I uttered the words that were filled with hope for a future that for so long I'd never believed I'd have.

William blinked softly, as if he had to take a moment to comprehend my words, and then he pulled my hand from his face and pressed my palm to his mouth. "Do you have any idea how happy that would make me, Maggie? I meant it then and I mean it now. Nothing could make me happier than promising you my life."

But he'd already promised it. He had been willing to give it. For me. For our son.

Finally, I was brave enough to give him mine.

As many as one in three girls and one in seven boys will be sexually abused at some point in their childhood.

Briere, J., Eliot, D.M. Prevalence and Psychological Sequence of Self-Reported Children Physical and Sexual Abuse in General Population: Child Abuse and Neglect, 2003, 27 10. —10/01/2012

If you need help, please call ChildHelp at 1-800-422-4453

One in every four women will experience domestic violence in her lifetime.

An estimated 1.3 million women are victims of physical abuse by an intimate partner each year.

Almost one-third of female homicide victims that are reported in police records are killed by an intimate partner.

-National Coalition Against Domestic Violence —10/01/2012

If you need help, please call The National Domestic Abuse Hotline at 1-800-799-7233

Connect with A.L. Jackson

www.aljacksonauthor.com/

www.facebook.com/aljacksonauthor

The Regret Series by A.L. Jackson

Lost To You (0.5)

People come into our lives. Some stay, and many go. Some build us up, while most tear us down. They become our friends, our enemies, our lovers, our tormentors. Christian Davison came into mine, and I knew I'd never be the same.

Take This Regret (1)

There are some mistakes we make that we will regret for the rest of our lives. For Christian Davison, it was the day he betrayed Elizabeth Ayers.

If Forever Comes (2)

Their love is intense and their passion only grows as they set out to rediscover each other. But life is never easy.

Other books by A.L. Jackson

Pulled

Will the power that drew them together be enough to heal the wounds from their past?

Come To Me Quietly ~ Coming January 7, 2014

From the acclaimed bestselling author of Lost to You and When We Collide comes a new adult novel of one woman's obsession: a man who's as passionate as he is elusive—and as tempting as he is trouble....

37904246R00203